# Blood Wolf

# Blood Wolf

A WEREling NOVEL

## STEVE FEASEY

FEIWEL AND FRIENDS
NEW YORK

A FEIWEL AND FRIENDS BOOK
An Imprint of Macmillan

BLOOD WOLF. Copyright © 2010 by Steve Feasey. All rights reserved.
Printed in the United States of America by R. R. Donnelley & Sons Company,
Harrisonburg, Virginia. For information, address Feiwel and Friends,
175 Fifth Avenue, New York, N.Y. 10010.

A CIP catalogue record for this book is available from the British Library

ISBN: 978-0-312-65352-1

Originally published as *Changeling: Blood Wolf* by Macmillan
Children's Books, a division of Macmillan Publishers Limited

Feiwel and Friends logo designed by Filomena Tuosto

First U.S. Edition: 2011

10 9 8 7 6 5 4 3 2 1

macteenbooks.com

4763 4836   13/11

*For my three big sisters: Netty, Les, and Debs,*
*who locked me in the shoe cupboard,*
*but also gave me so much love.*

*And for Shanders, who simply said,*
*"Go for it."*

# 1

The first time the girl woke had been the worst.

*She crawled out of the foggy darkness of oblivion toward the sounds of the medical equipment to which she was hooked via various tubes and sensors. She'd felt groggy and disoriented, and she had slowly opened her eyes to look around for a drink to ease the soreness in her throat. The vampire had been sitting at her bedside, looking back at her with an expressionless face. He had nodded at her and a sad smile had momentarily flashed across his features before disappearing again. Her breath had caught in her throat and she had frozen, unable to do anything but stare at the abomination sitting at her bedside, staring back at her.*

*That he was a vampire she had no doubt. There were no fangs or talons, and except for the fascinating pools of gold and ocher that were his eyes, there was nothing to distinguish him from any other tall, handsome, middle-aged man. But one look had told her everything that she needed to know about his true nature, as if she were still looking at things through eyes that were not her own, through the eyes of the demon that had lived inside her. She frowned at this last thought, pushing away memories that threatened to pile in on her.*

"How are you, Philippa?" Lucien Charron had asked.

The rising terror that had built up inside her exploded into every cell, consuming her completely. A high, keening sound filled the little room, and she realized that it was the sound of her own scream. The panic-stricken noise went on and on, continuing until all the air in her lungs had gone. She sucked in a great shuddering breath, closing her eyes for a fraction of a second, and when she opened them again the vampire was gone.

She'd stared around her in panic, her eyes skittering about the room to see where the creature might be. She shook her head in disbelief, her breath coming in great gasps as her heart hammered in her chest. There was no sign of him; he'd gone. She looked down at the seat and noted that the slight indentation in the vinyl seat cushion was slowly filling out, returning to a state that would suggest nothing had ever sat there, that nothing had ever been in the room with her. She shook her head again and allowed the tears to fall.

She had gone insane. She knew that she was now quite mad. How else could she explain her belief that she had been possessed by a demon, and that the same demon had used her to get to, and murder, her father in front of her very eyes?

Philippa Tipsbury cried great sobs as memories of the demon that had inhabited her body flooded back to her. A nurse appeared at the door. The middle-aged woman hurried to her side and injected a clear liquid into a tube *hanging out of Philippa's arm. She cooed at the young girl in the bed as she administered the drug, and when she was finished she gently ran her hand across the girl's forehead, hushing her and waiting for the drug to take effect.*

*Philippa felt the coldness creep into her again, and she welcomed the calm that it brought with it. She tried to speak, but the drug was taking effect so quickly that nothing came out but an indistinct mumble before the darkness crowded in again at the edges of her vision and then consumed her completely.*

That was two days ago.

And now they were back.

She tried to open her eyes gradually to the thinnest of slits and peer out at the person sitting in the chair next to her. The room was quite dark, the only light coming in through the glass window set into the door, and it was difficult to make out the features of whoever it was looking down at a book in her lap, but she was sure that it was not the vampire again. It struck her as slightly odd that the person was able to make out any words on the pages with so little light. She opened her eyes fully and took in the girl who was sitting with her legs crossed to support the book, the fingers of her left hand tapping out a tune on the plastic armrest.

"How are you?" the girl asked without looking up.

Philippa instantly shut her eyes.

"We were all so very worried about you that we've been

3

taking it in turns to come and sit by your side. After your last encounter with my father we decided that it might be better if he didn't come anymore. We didn't want to freak you out again."

Philippa knew there was little point in pretending to be asleep any longer. She opened her eyes and studied her visitor.

Alexa Charron closed the book, placing a bookmark— which appeared to be made of brown, coarse hair that had been woven and plaited together—between the pages. She smiled across at Philippa who frowned back as she tried to make out who she was and what she was doing here. The visitor had bright, intelligent eyes set into a face that was extremely attractive. Her black hair was pulled back in a ponytail, and she wore a white T-shirt and jeans. "Hi. I'm Alexa," she said, holding out her hand in greeting.

The girl in the bed ignored the hand, shaking her head as tears welled up in the corner of her eyes. "I've gone insane," she said.

Alexa looked down at the girl in the bed, a sad look on her face. She reached out and gently touched the girl's forearm with the tip of her fingers, letting them rest there.

"No, Philippa. You haven't lost your mind. But what you've been through would be enough to make a lesser person do just that." She smiled a sad smile. "We want to help you get over what happened to you."

"We? Who's we?"

Alexa's eyes stayed locked on those of the girl in the bed. "We have your best interests at heart, Philippa."

"My father's dead, isn't he? That . . . thing crawled inside him, forced itself into him, and he . . ."

"Shh. You mustn't upset yourself again."

Alexa turned toward the small nightstand at the side of the bed. Pouring water from a jug, she helped Philippa to lean forward on her pillows and drink from the glass.

The patient nodded her appreciation, but stared back at the other girl with a look of distrust.

"You look like you want to ask me something," Alexa said.

"You said that that . . . man . . . the one I saw two days ago. You said that he was your father."

Alexa nodded.

"Except he's *not* a man, is he?" Her voice was becoming louder and higher in pitch, and she recognized the hysteria in it. "He's not . . . he's . . ." She sucked in a deep breath, willing herself to say the words. "He's a—"

"A vampire?" Alexa frowned, lips pursed as though considering how best to continue. "Yes, he is." She glanced at the door, as if expecting someone. "You are not insane, Philippa. I know that right now you must believe that you are, but you are not. Lucien is as real as the Necrotroph demon that inhabited your body when you were in the Seychelles with your father." The young sorceress looked at her with pity. "Everything that you remember was real. And yes, I'm afraid your father is dead."

Philippa nodded, unable to speak. Hearing someone else say those words caused a wave of sadness and grief to break inside her. Everything was too much for her: Her father was dead, a vampire had been in this very room with her, and a demon had been living inside her body. She looked away and let the tears soak into the pillow, filling the room with the sound of her muffled sobbing.

Alexa stayed by the girl's side, her hand still resting on Philippa's arm, allowing her to grieve and let out some of the emotions that had built up inside her.

Eventually Philippa looked back at her visitor. "That *thing* was really inside me, wasn't it? I didn't imagine it all."

"No, you didn't imagine it. The Necrotroph left your body and inhabited your father in order to find out what he knew about a mission that some of my colleagues and I were on. The demon used you to get to your dad. Your father leaped from the boat that you were on and drowned himself in an effort to try and kill the creature. It was an incredibly brave thing to do."

Philippa Tipsbury stared down at the white sheets that covered her.

Alexa studied the girl, trying to gauge how much more she should reveal to her, and knowing that it must already be too much for the teenager to take in.

"You still haven't told me who you are," Philippa said in a small voice. "Who you are and what you want."

"Your father worked for my father. He was part of a worldwide organization that seeks to keep creatures like the demon you encountered from entering this realm from the

Netherworld. We're the good guys, Philippa. Your dad was one of the good guys."

She studied the girl's face as fresh rivulets of tears tracked down her cheeks. Philippa continued to stare at the white bedclothes.

"Your encounter with a Necrotroph is quite . . . unique," she said, choosing her words with care. "The demon usually kills the former host upon transfer. Before you, any hosts that were unlucky enough to survive were left completely insane. But you have survived. And as I've said, you are not mad." She nodded at her as if to emphasize this last point.

Philippa remained silent.

"We need your help. We think that the Necrotroph somehow survived your father's attempt to kill it. It—"

"No. It's dead. You said yourself that my father jumped over the side of that boat. He killed it at the bottom of that ocean. It's dead, I know it is."

Alexa continued, trying to ignore the feral, frightened look on the other girl's face. "We don't know how it escaped, but we think that you might be able to help us find it."

Philippa turned her head and stared at Alexa, her features set in a wide-eyed look of disbelief.

"There is a special bond between you and that creature, Philippa. The dark magic that it used to control your mind and body is still a part of you. The Necrotroph left a part of itself behind—in you." She looked back at the girl, their eyes locked and unblinking. "You've felt it, haven't you? You *know* that it's still alive."

"I have no idea what you are talking about," Philippa said, but her eyes wouldn't meet Alexa's.

There was a knock on the door and a nurse put her head around the opening. Upon seeing her patient sitting up in bed, she smiled at Philippa with such warmth that the girl could do little but respond in kind. The hospital worker turned to Alexa. "Your father is here and he wonders if it would be OK for him to come in and talk to you both?"

"Thank you, Greta. Please tell him that I'll be out in a moment."

Alexa waited until the nurse had left the room before turning to look at Philippa again. "It's up to you. You don't have to see him if you don't want to. But you need to know that my father is not the only nether-creature living among us in the human realm—far from it. And unlike my father, the majority of them are dedicated to bringing death and destruction to this world." She paused, pursing her lips before continuing. "I think the Necrotroph has irrevocably changed something in your makeup, Philippa. And I think you already know that." She waited until the girl looked at her. "You can see them, can't you? See the nether-creatures through their disguises? How else would you have known that my father was not what he appears to be?" She let that sink in before adding, "We want to help you, Philippa."

"What does your father want?"

"We think that you may have also acquired a skill that is

unique to the Necrotrophs: the ability to locate their own kind wherever they are. Now, you may not be able to use this ability yet, but given some help we think that you could. The bad news is that if we're right, the demon will also be able to sense you: It will know that you are alive, and that is a situation it will want to do something about." She smiled kindly at the other girl. "You might be our only hope of locating and destroying it."

Philippa closed her eyes, wishing that all of this would simply stop. She wanted nothing more than for the nurse to come in again and inject something into the tube in her arm that would allow her to sink back into unconsciousness—maybe forever.

Alexa waited, knowing that she had to give the girl as much time as she needed.

"What makes you so sure that I have these . . . powers?"

"We're not. Right now it is just a guess. But you *can* see nether-creatures."

"I don't think I can," the girl said, frowning. "At least not in the way that you suggest. It's more a . . . *feeling.*"

Philippa thought back to the moment that she'd woken up with the vampire next to her. Nothing about the creature's outward appearance—except his freaky eyes—would suggest that he was anything but human, but she'd *known*. She concentrated her attention on the wall opposite her, relishing the blandness of it. "And if I *can* locate this . . . Necrotroph for you, your father is going to destroy it?" she said eventually.

"Yes, you have my word on that."

Philippa took a deep, shuddery breath, unable to believe what she was about to say. "OK," she said, nodding. "If you promise to stay with me, I'll talk to your father."

She watched as Alexa left the room and went to fetch the vampire.

# 2

Trey Laporte sat on the edge of his bed, staring around him at the high-tech gadgetry and equipment that furnished his room. Like all of the rooms in the penthouse apartment in Docklands, it was equipped with enough electronic gizmos to leave your average techno-nerd drooling with desire, and he was feeling slightly reluctant to be leaving it all behind him.

A light knock on the door shook him out of his reverie and he called out for whoever it was to enter.

Alexa pushed the door open and stepped inside. She pushed her hair back over her ear and smiled at him in a way that always totally disarmed him. He nodded back at her, feeling his pulse quicken as she came and sat down by his side on the bed.

There was a short silence while each of them considered what to say.

"So you're all packed and ready to go?" Alexa said eventually, staring down at the large bag on the floor.

Trey nodded. "Yep. My flight to Vancouver is at seven o'clock. Tom's kindly offered to drop me off at the airport." Trey turned to his friend and smiled. "No doubt I'll get the full safety lecture from him on the way: the one about not taking unnecessary risks and demanding that I call Lucien at the first sign of any trouble. I've already had it in one form or another from your father on at least three occasions."

"Dad's just worried, Trey. He still hopes that you'll change your mind and agree to let one of us go along with you."

"No, Alexa. Don't *you* start. I'm going on my own. It's something that I feel I have to do—" He held up his hand to stop her from interrupting him. "Please, don't let's go over it all again. I'll be fine."

She nodded, a sad smile playing at her lips. She pointed at something in his luggage. "Is that that disgusting old sweatshirt? I told you to chuck that out; it's awful!" She leaned forward to try to grab it, but Trey caught her arm at the elbow and playfully pulled her back.

"And I told you to mind your own business, Alexa. If I let you have your own way, I'd be changing my entire wardrobe every two months, regardless of whether I'd worn half of the stuff or not."

"Some people have no idea about fashion."

"And some people have no idea about not spending money as if it's a race to see who can max out their credit cards first."

"Nobody would ever guess that you were rich."

"Nobody would ever guess that you were clever."

"Skinflint."

"Spendthrift."

"Scrooge."

"Spoiled-spendaholic-wanting-whining wastrel."

Alexa narrowed her eyes at him, trying to think of a comeback.

She laughed and leaned her head against his shoulder, allowing her body to rest against his. "When did you say you were going, Trey? Because it *really* can't be soon enough."

He laughed back and leaned his own head down, breathing in the vanilla smell of her hair. He felt the familiar rush of emotions he experienced whenever he and Alexa were alone like this, and his face flushed. A part of him wished that she were going with him. Hell, a part of him wished that they were all going with him: Lucien, Alexa, and Tom. But something told him that this was a journey that he must make alone, to try to discover for himself the truth about what he really was. And to do that he would have to leave behind the closest thing to family that he had had in a long time. Except that wasn't quite true anymore. The reason he was making this trip was because he'd discovered that he *did* have a member of his real family who was still alive: an uncle Frank, who was living in Canada.

An uncle. A living relative. A werewolf, like him. He shivered at this last thought, unsure of how he felt about meeting up with another person who had to live with the terrible affliction that had been passed on to Trey from birth. Lucien had told Trey that he was unique, that he was the last of his kind—a revelation that had had more of an impact on the teenager than he could have imagined. Alone: an orphan who'd had to live in a care home after the death of his grandmother, he'd already lost everyone and everything when Lucien had rescued him. Lucien had been nothing but good to Trey, taking him in and treating him like a son. But he had also lied to him, keeping the existence of his uncle from him.

As if reading his thoughts (something that he was sure that she could do if she really wanted), Alexa looked up, searching his eyes with her own. "Try not to get hurt over there," she said in a voice that was little more than a whisper.

"Alexa, I've just told you. Tom and your dad have given me the—"

"I didn't mean like that." She sat up now, her gaze steady and unwavering. "You seem to be placing an awful lot of hope on this trip. I just want you to consider that your uncle might not be everything you want him to be."

Trey held her look, scanning her face for any sign that she might know more than she was telling him. "He's all I've got," he said finally.

"That's not true."

"You know what I mean."

Alexa nodded and stood up. "You take good care of yourself over there, Trey Laporte."

He smiled up at her. "I've been doing that all my life, Alexa Charron."

She grinned then, a mischievous look in her eyes as she leaned forward. She lowered her voice as she spoke. "Tom's organizing a farewell dinner for you tonight. He's got the caterers bringing the food—much to Mrs. Magilton's disgust—and he wants us all to sit around together. It was supposed to be a surprise, but I thought I'd let you know. I know how much you hate surprises."

Trey nodded his thanks. "Lucien already told me."

"Oh, did he now?" She was laughing as she straightened up, shaking her head. "Honestly, this place. You can't have any secrets here." She moved off toward the door.

"Thanks, Alexa," he said, just as she was about to leave.

She stopped at the door and turned back to face him again. "Whatever happens, Trey, just remember that you have a family here now. And we want you back safe." She hovered in the doorway, and Trey knew that he should say something. He wanted to tell her how much they had all come to mean to him. In particular, he wanted to tell her how he felt about her: to tell her how special she was to him. But none of the right words came, so he just nodded, swallowing the lump that had formed in his throat.

"Thanks," he repeated, and watched her turn and walk away.

The meal went well enough. They all sat around the table in the dining room to eat. Tom had arranged for the caterers to prepare all of Trey's favorite food and he now sat back in his seat with a belly full of steak that had been followed up with a banoffee pie that was to die for. Lucien had picked at his food, as he always did, but Trey thought that he seemed more uncomfortable than usual tonight. Lucien kept looking over at Trey's plate, and he thought that he detected a strange look on his guardian's face when he caught sight of the blood that had seeped out of the rare steak.

The conversation around the table had been stilted with everybody skating around the subject of Trey's departure in the morning and struggling to think of alternative things to talk about.

In the end it had been too much for the teenager, who rolled his eyes when Tom started to talk about the weather again. "Oh, for goodness' sake. Will somebody *please* say something—anything—about my trip? You all avoiding the subject isn't going to change anything—I'm still going. Jeez, anyone would think that I was planning a trip to the Netherworld on my own."

"Have you contacted your uncle as I suggested, to let him know that you are intending to visit?" Lucien asked.

"No. I know that you think I should, but I don't want him getting scared and doing a disappearing act on me. He hasn't ever tried to contact me, so I'm guessing that he doesn't really want me in his life. I'm planning on just turning up and seeing what he has to say for himself."

Lucien inclined his head to one side and arched his eyebrows in a way that Trey took as a signal that he thought the teenager's reasoning was flawed. However, the vampire kept any further views he had on the subject to himself.

When Lucien next spoke, it was to Alexa. "Tom and I have arranged for somebody to meet Trey when he arrives in Canada." His voice was like polished mahogany, and Trey smiled as he remembered the fascinating draw the voice had had on him when he had first met the vampire in the care home. The vampire looked as enigmatic as ever: He was handsome, in a dangerous-looking way, and he exuded an aura of confidence that was difficult to resist. It was this certainty and authority that had made Trey trust Lucien that day: The tall, mysterious stranger had taken him away from his dull and sad life, and introduced him to one that was filled with demons and vampires and djinn. It was Lucien who had revealed to Trey the terrible truth about his lycanthropy, and about the legend that the vampire believed the boy was to fulfill: to overthrow the evil vampire Caliban, who was building a powerful army in the Netherworld, and to restore peace between the human and demon realms.

Lucien caught Trey's look, smiling back at his young ward. "After much . . . negotiation, Trey has finally agreed to allow me to have somebody escort him until he manages to make contact with his uncle. Much against my will, our representatives over there will leave Trey to his own devices as soon as that contact is made."

"I still say that it's madness!" Tom said, turning to Trey. "What exactly is your problem with having somebody with you over there to keep an eye out for you?"

"We've been over this again and again, Tom," Trey said with a sigh. "I want to meet up with my uncle alone. I don't want to be followed around the country by a demon acting as a bodyguard, and I certainly don't want you or Lucien clucking around me like a couple of mother hens." He looked over at Lucien and held his gaze. "I'll never get a better chance than this. Since Gwendolin's death, Caliban has been almost powerless. Without his sorceress he can't open portals into this realm from the Netherworld as easily as he used to. You said yourself, Lucien, that he is extremely quiet right now. I want to do this, and this is the best opportunity that I'll have." He realized that his voice had increased in volume, and he shook his head apologetically. "As much as I really appreciate your concern, you are going to have to trust me." He looked back over at Tom. "I'll be careful. I promise. I'll call you and Lucien every day so that you can have a good cluck at me on the phone."

"Madness," Tom said one last time before reaching out for his wineglass.

Lucien smiled over at his friend before returning his attention to Trey. "We have to respect Trey's wishes, Tom. Besides, my understanding is that the area in which Frank Laporte lives is heavily protected from the likes of me and my kind—an arrangement that Trey's uncle struck up with a demon lord some time ago. Once Trey is with his uncle, he should be as safe as if he were here with us." He paused, his stare intensifying. "Safe from vampires, at least." He ran his fingers around the edge of his wineglass, and smiled at the ringing sound it produced. "Trey knows that we can get our people over in Canada to assist him if he should find himself in any trouble. Trey has made up his mind, and we, his friends, have to go along with his request."

They had all finished eating, and as if some silent signal

had been passed to them, Alexa and Tom stood up as if to leave.

Trey looked between the two of them and Lucien, aware that this had been planned beforehand.

"I'd welcome the chance to have a few words with you before you leave us," Lucien said by way of an answer to Trey's quizzical expression.

Tom and Alexa left the room without another word.

"Well," Lucien said once he was sure that they were alone.

"Well," repeated Trey.

"I take it that you have everything packed?"

"Yeah. Anything that I don't have, I'll buy when I'm out there."

"Of course."

An uncomfortable silence filled the room. For the first time, Trey noticed the ticking of the clock on the far wall, as though the device had chosen that particular moment to start its monotonous reckoning.

"Thank you, Lucien," Trey said. "I know how difficult this is for you."

The vampire nodded and picked at a fleck of material on his jacket sleeve.

"I *was* going to tell you." Lucien looked over at Trey, a strange and unreadable expression on his face. "It was never my intention to keep the existence of your uncle from you. I was merely waiting for the right time. It seems that you and I have had precious little time to really talk about the things that matter since that first time we met. That is something that we shall have to put right upon your return."

"You're certain that I will return?" Trey said, and immediately regretted allowing the words to escape him.

Lucien paused, considering the response. "I hope so, Trey. I really do. This is your home—the best place for a boy with your powers to be safe."

Trey listened to the sound of the clock's mechanism, irked by it now that it had come to his attention. "They didn't like each other, did they? My father and his brother."

"And what makes you say that?" Lucien raised a quizzical eyebrow.

"My father's journal," Trey said by way of an explanation. "To be honest, it was a big disappointment to me. I don't know quite what I expected to find in it, but it's all a bit . . . cold. Facts and appointments, mostly. Some references to you and missions that you both went on. Then there's the entry about a visit that he made to my uncle with my mother. Shortly after that there's a single line: "I wish that I'd killed Frank when I had the chance." I'd say that constitutes a pretty strong dislike, wouldn't you?"

Lucien looked over at the boy, weighing up how best to answer him. "It wasn't as simple as that, Trey. They were both werewolves. They were not the only ones. A pack of sorts began to emerge, and in that situation there has to be a leader: an Alpha. There were only two contenders for that position. Somebody was bound to be disappointed. Disappointed and . . . embittered.

"I would tell you more, Trey, but I do not wish to sway the opinion that you will form of your uncle. It would be unfair for me to do that. You will make up your own mind about him, and about what you want to do afterward. People change, Trey, and he is unlikely to be the same person that he was when I knew him well."

"But you have kept tabs on him, Lucien. If not, how else would you have known his whereabouts?"

"I have merely kept myself informed of his movements. Not that there have been any. I have not seen or heard from your uncle in a little over fifteen years."

"That's a long time—about the time that I was born." He studied the vampire for any reaction.

The vampire smiled. "When you have been in existence for as long as I have, it's a mere blink of an eye."

It was Trey's turn to smile and nod. Looking at his guardian, he found it impossible to imagine that he was over two hundred years old.

"Remember, Trey, if you are at all unsure of anything that happens to you while you are in Canada, you should call me immediately. You must promise me that you will not endanger yourself out there."

"I promise, Lucien. I'll be careful. Thank you again."

"I'll be around in the morning, to see you off. You'll excuse me if I don't accompany you and Tom to the airport,

but the early morning sunshine doesn't agree with me."
Lucien stood up and motioned for Trey to join him. "Come
on, let's get back to the others. They will want to spend as
much time with you as they can before you leave." He placed
his arm over the boy's shoulder and gently pulled him toward
him in a gentle embrace. "We are all going to miss you, Trey,"
he said, and escorted the boy out of the room.

# 3

Trey flew first class. Lucien had insisted that he would pay for the flight despite Trey's protests, and when the tickets arrived, he saw that he would be flying in comfort. The ticket was open, so that he could come back whenever he wanted to, and when Trey had asked Lucien how much it had cost, the vampire had merely waved the question away.

He spent a great deal of the flight with his head stuck in books or listening to his MP3 player—anything to distract himself from what lay ahead. Every time he allowed himself to think about meeting up with his uncle Frank, his stomach rolled sickeningly and he was filled with doubt and worry about how the whole thing would go. Better not to think about it, he told himself. Better not to build his hopes up too high.

As he walked out of the arrivals gate, he paused, releasing the handle to brake his luggage trolley and scanning the groups of people at the chrome barrier. Most of them were on tiptoes, straining to see through the crowd and eagerly scanning the face of every person who emerged through the automatic doors. Some held homemade placards with the names of the arrivals that they were waiting for. He

23

spotted his escort immediately. Lucien's choice of chaperone was standing holding a large board with Trey's name on it. The creature was so obviously out of place that he might as well have done away with the human mantle that he wore to disguise himself in this realm and stood there in all his Netherworld glory. Trey guessed that the demon must be almost seven feet tall, and it towered over everybody else around it. It wasn't just tall, it was gaunt with albino white skin stretched tightly across its features. The overall effect was positively alarming—Lucien had sent Lurch from *The Addams Family* to meet him. Trey smiled when he noted that while other people jostled against each other in an effort to find a place near the front of the barrier, the demon stood in a little island, unbothered and untouched by anyone else around it. Trey pushed his trolley through the opening in the barrier and approached the creature.

"Mr. Galroth?" Trey said, using the name that Tom had given him.

The creature visibly flinched at the sound of his voice, and Trey watched as it slowly turned its eyes upon him and scanned him up and down.

"Mr. Laporte?" it said with thinly disguised disdain. It held out a hand, but from the look on its face, Trey guessed that it was hoping he would not accept the appendage.

"Please call me Trey."

"Very well . . . Trey. I must say, having heard of some of your recent exploits, you're not quite what I was expecting." The creature had an impossibly deep voice and when it spoke, it did so very slowly, as if it were always reaching for the next word.

"Sorry," Trey said, "I didn't think it prudent to walk through immigration as a seven-foot-tall werewolf. I wasn't sure what the Canadian authorities' stance was on allowing giant, hideous nether-creatures into their country." He looked up and met the demon's gaze. "I can see I needn't have worried."

The demon frowned, and it occurred to Trey that it was trying to calculate whether he was being serious or not. It finally made up its mind and nodded in the direction of Trey's bags.

"If you'd like to follow me," it said and walked off in the direction of the exit without a second look back.

Trey glanced between the receding back of the nether-creature and the trolley full of bags, and shook his head in disbelief.

"Welcome to Canada," Trey muttered under his breath. He pushed his weight into the trolley, and set off after the creature.

# 4

The Incubus demon made its way along the hospital corridor toward the fan of light that spilled out from the nurses' station into the gloom. The inside of the building was hot, and the temperature exaggerated the smell of sickness and disinfectant that wafted out from the wards. The demon paused, looking across at the window set into the wall opposite. The darkness of the night on the other side of the glass transformed the surface into an ebony mirror in which the demon checked its reflection, straightening the white doctor's coat it was wearing and pushing at a strand of hair that had escaped across its forehead. It adjusted the stethoscope around its neck, and cupped a palm, breathing into it to check its breath. Satisfied, it flashed a white-toothed grin at the human reflection staring back at it.

As an Incubus demon, it had the ability to read its victims' desires and transform its own looks to match. In this instance it had not had the opportunity to meet the person that it was trying to seduce, so it adopted a facade that it knew would appeal to most women: a polished and refined version of Hollywood's current biggest-grossing heartthrob. To the Incubus, the face that stared back at it was, like all humans, utterly repulsive. But it knew that it wouldn't be to the woman it was about to meet.

It took in a deep breath through its nose and nodded at its reflection one last time in the window before continuing along the corridor, finally coming to a stop at the desk where a young female nurse was writing up her paperwork.

"Hi," the demon said, leaning over the high countertop and feigning interest in her notes. "I'm Dr. Cash. I'm the locum tenens SHO for psychiatrics. I'm here to see a Miss . . ." It paused, glancing down at the clipboard that it was carrying. "Tipsbury . . . Miss Philippa Tipsbury."

The young nurse looked down at her notes and frowned. "I'm afraid that I don't seem to have a message to say that you would be coming, Dr.—?"

"Cash. But please, call me David. No, you won't have. I've just finished my shift and I thought that I could pop along and have a quick look at the patient's notes before I leave for the night. I'll be doing the rounds here tomorrow. You wouldn't be a love and get them for me, would you?" The demon looked up at the board on the wall at the rear of the nurses' station and scanned the patient information that had been written in marker. The Tipsbury girl was in room five, just down the hall from where it was standing. The Incubus was keen to get out of this place—it hated hospitals; the smell was terrible. But first it had to get rid of this nurse. On its way up in the elevator it had considered ignoring the instructions of the Necrotroph that had sent it on

27

this job, by simply walking up to the station and killing anyone present. But it would not do to displease the Necrotroph and its master, Caliban, by disobeying orders. The Necrotroph was not to compromise its latest host-body disguise. It had to infiltrate the vampire Lucien's organization again, so the Incubus had been dispatched to do its dirty work for it.

The demon returned its attention to the nurse, catching the look in her eye. It was a look the demon knew well.

"They didn't tell me that the nurses up here were as good-looking as you," it said, leaning its elbows on the counter to bring its face nearer to hers. "I'd have come by before if I'd known." The demon smiled its pearly white teeth at her as she blushed. "Are you new?"

"Quite new. I've only been here for a couple of months," she said.

The demon gave her a roguish smile. "Look, I know this is a bit cheeky, but I've just come off the back of a fourteen-hour shift. I don't suppose that I could ask you for a cup of coffee, could I?" It saw the doubt flash across her features, her eyes cutting to the corridor to their left, and quickly added, "I'll man the desk here and if anyone asks, I'll just tell them that you popped out for a second to do something for me." The demon held her gaze for a moment, and was relieved when the doubt on her face was gradually replaced with a shy smile.

"OK," she said, "but if any of the patients call, you come and get me. How do you like it?"

"I hope you're talking about the coffee," he said, grinning

as she started to turn pink again. "White, four sugars please. I like sweet things."

The Incubus watched as she stood up and exited into the room behind the workstation. It waited for a few seconds to make sure that she wasn't about to pop back, and then quickly snaked along the corridor to the door it had identified previously. It looked through the glass window at the darkened room on the other side, peering in at the single occupied bed that was set against the wall to the left. Satisfied that no staff were attending the sleeping figure buried under the covers, the demon quickly opened the door and slipped inside, letting the heavy fire door silently close behind it. The demon stood motionless for a second, taking in the scene while its eyes became accustomed to the darkness of the room. It took a deep breath and reached inside the white coat to locate the handle of the long, curved knife that it had tucked into the waistband of its trousers. Taking the weapon in its clenched fist, the demon approached the bed and the sleeping figure. It raised the weapon high over its head, the deadly point quivering slightly in the air.

"And what do you think you are going to do with that?"

The voice came from behind the demon and it whirled around to face the tall Irishman who had stepped out of the shadows from behind the door. In doing so, it sealed its fate.

Lucien Charron threw back the covers and was on his feet within an instant. The demon was vaguely aware of the incredibly quick movement behind him and guessed at what kind of creature might be capable of moving at such speed.

It was about to turn and confirm its fears, when the room began to spin and tumble; visual signals still being sent from eyes to brain despite the fact that the demon's head had been permanently separated from the neck that had, up until that moment, done such a good job of supporting it. It saw the floor rushing up to meet it, and then the world went black for the last time.

A volcano-like eruption of black gore spewed up into the air. The Incubus's body remained upright for a second or two before realizing it had no right to do so. It crumpled to the floor, the doctor's coat no longer white as it rapidly became soaked in the black filth that continued to pump from the corpse. Tom and Lucien looked down at the decapitated body as it began to fade from view—the dead demon returning to the world that it had come from. Within a few moments there was nothing to show that Dr. Cash had ever visited the room except for the pile of clothes that contained his name badge. Even the black blood that had soaked the clothes was now beginning to disappear, and Tom bent down to pick them up, catching Lucien's eye as he did so.

"You were right," he said.

"I usually am," the vampire replied with a smile. "Let's go."

They walked out of the room and along to the end of the corridor, stopping at the last door and giving it a quiet tap. Alexa, still wearing the nurse's uniform, peered out at them from behind the glass panel, before pulling the door open and letting them in. They saw the tension drain from her features at the sight of them, and she stood up on tiptoe to hug her father. Breaking away from Lucien, she smiled at Tom, nodding her head at the pile of clothing in his arms.

"It went well then?" she asked.

"As well as we had planned," her father replied. "If it had not been for our people picking up on the movement of the Incubus in this area, we might not have realized what was happening until it was too late.

"Now I think that we need to get Philippa out of here as soon as possible before any other *doctors* come to check on her notes."

Philippa was sitting in a darkened corner of the room. They could see how badly her hands were shaking as she looked back at them from beneath her eyebrows.

"We'll leave now, Philippa," Alexa said. "You'll come and stay with us until we have dealt with the Necrotroph. Afterward, my father will help you do whatever you decide to. We have a spare room and you are welcome to stay as long as you—"

"Will you be there with me?" Philippa asked in a voice that bordered on the hysterical. She would not look at the vampire, keeping her eyes fixed on his daughter instead.

"Yes," Alexa said, nodding in encouragement. "I'll be there with you."

Lucien studied the Tipsbury girl, empathetic to the fear that she was still experiencing and remembering how Trey had reacted when he had first discovered that his world was not entirely what he had always believed it to be. He turned and left the room, not wishing to distress the girl any further with his presence.

"You're safe, Philippa. You have my word on that." Alexa held out a hand to help the girl up.

Philippa stared at the hand for a moment before slowly getting to her feet. She took a deep breath, remembering the reason that she was doing all this: to see the creature that killed her father destroyed. She crossed the room and placed her own hand inside Alexa's. "OK, I'll come."

Alexa began to lead her past Tom and out of the room. The girl halted, frowning down at the pile of clothes, including a doctor's coat that the tall Irishman was holding in his arms. Something about the way that he held them made her certain that she did not want to know who they belonged to, or how he had acquired them. Alexa gently tugged at her hand, and they stepped out into the silent corridor. Philippa noted that there was no sign of the vampire—he seemed to have completely disappeared.

# 5

They transported Philippa to the apartment without a hitch, Alexa speaking to the girl all the way back in the car, her voice light and cheery as if they had known each other for years. The conversation was somewhat one-sided. Philippa had not said a word since leaving the hospital, and when Alexa suggested that they should both share a room that night, she took the other girl's lack of response as a sign that she had no objection to the idea. Alexa described the opulent penthouse apartment to the girl sitting on the backseat with her, detailing the various features on each floor of the building and promising to give Philippa a guided tour once they arrived. She may as well have been talking to herself, but she kept the monologue going, hoping that the sound of her voice might be enough to keep the other girl from thinking too much about what she was getting herself into.

When the car finally stopped in the underground garage beneath Lucien's building, Alexa walked around to the girl's side of the car and coaxed her out, taking her by the elbow and guiding her to the elevator that led up to the apartment as if she were some kind of sleepwalker. The girl didn't react to anything she saw: The huge, luxurious penthouse apartment might as well have not been there as she trudged through it in a trancelike state. It wasn't until Alexa and she were alone just inside the young sorceress's bedroom that the girl seemed to snap out of her stupor, jumping at the sound of the door closing behind her. She turned around, staring about her in consternation, as if completely unaware of what she was doing, or how she had gotten here.

"You're OK, Philippa," Alexa said. "You're in my room. You're safe here. Shall I go and fix you a cup of tea or something? Then we can get you some clothes to change into and—"

"No, don't leave me," Philippa said. "Please, I don't want to be left on my own."

"You can come with me. We'll go out into the kitchen together if you'd prefer."

"Will he be there?"

"My father?"

Philippa nodded again.

Alexa sighed. She sat down on the bed, patting the mattress next to her to indicate that she wanted Philippa to join her.

"You know where you are right now, don't you?" Alexa said.

Philippa nodded.

"This apartment is on the top floor. Below us are other floors that are dedicated to my father's work: namely the protection of humans from the more nefarious elements of the Netherworld. Lucien, and people like him, do everything in

34

their power to protect people like you from creatures like them. He would no more hurt you than I would. But not all of the creatures of the Netherworld are like my father, as you have already found out." She squeezed the girl's hand. "My father will keep out of your way until you're a little happier with yourself and your surroundings. He wants to talk to you, to explain some things and ask you about others. But not yet." She paused, maintaining eye contact with the frightened teenager. "Come on, we'll get something to eat and drink." She stood up, holding her hand out for the other girl to take.

"No. Thank you, but I just want to sleep now. Could you stay in here with me while I do?"

"OK. You get yourself settled down in bed, and I'll stay in the chair here." Alexa smiled at the girl, nodding toward the bed behind her. "You *will* be able to cope with all of this. Sure, it'll take time, but you can do it."

It was only a matter of minutes before Philippa was in a deep sleep. Alexa waited a few more to make absolutely sure that the girl was not going to wake up, then silently rose up from her chair and slipped out of the room. "How is she?" Lucien asked as his daughter met him on the balcony. She came over to him and snaked her arm through his, joining him in contemplating the inky black water of the river Thames as it snaked its way through the city.

"A study in psychosis," Alexa said, with a short, sad snort. "The poor girl probably still thinks that she's insane. And if she doesn't, I bet she wishes she were. On the plus side, she seems to have latched on to me as somebody that she can trust and rely upon."

Lucien nodded.

"She reminds me of Trey when you first brought him here. That horrified look in her eye and the way that she looks at everything and everyone as though they were going to harm her in some way."

"Trey adapted," Lucien said without turning to look at her. "He has come to accept what he is and what that means."

"Has he?"

Her father smiled to himself. He closed his eyes and took in a deep breath of the briny night air.

"Do you miss him?" he asked.

Alexa paused. She turned around so that she leaned back against the balcony rail. "He only left yesterday, Dad."

There was another long silence and Alexa knew that her father was waiting for her to speak again.

"I worry whether he'll come back," she said. "Despite everything that he said, I wonder if his insistence on going alone was a way of telling us that he had no intention of returning."

"You have . . . feelings for Trey, don't you, Alexa?"

It was Alexa's turn to fall silent. The breeze carried the sound of music playing somewhere off to her left.

"Do you think that he will come back?" she asked.

"Yes, I do. And when he does, he is going to need all of our support. I do not believe that Trey is going to find what he is looking for in Canada, and that will be hard for him to take. He thinks that he will find an answer to his loneliness in his uncle, but I'm afraid that might not be the case. That is why I agreed to let him go to Canada alone, despite the obvious dangers. Trey needs to find out for himself the things that are important to him now. The things—and the people—that will help him become what he must."

"What is his uncle like?" Alexa asked.

Lucien blew a short blast of air through his nostrils and gently shook his head. "Trey asked me a similar question before he left, and by way of an answer I told him that I had not seen his uncle in over fifteen years." He stopped and turned to look at his daughter. "I only hope that time has mellowed the man. Because my memories of Frank Laporte were of the most spiteful, hard, uncaring, and ruthless individual it has ever been my misfortune to meet. If he had not been Daniel's brother, I would have killed him long ago and done this world a great favor."

Alexa stared up at her father. It was unusual for him to show any real emotions when he spoke, but the look in his eyes at the moment was nothing short of hatred.

"What did he do?" Alexa asked.

Her father shook his head, unwilling to talk on the matter any further.

"Why on earth didn't you tell Trey this before he went?"

"Would he have believed me?" Lucien replied, his face now as impassive and unreadable as ever. "Trey thought that I had deliberately withheld the existence of his uncle from him. Do you think my telling him that the only living member of his family is a repugnant degenerate would have washed with him?"

Alexa looked back out at the river and sighed.

"Poor Trey."

"Like I said, maybe the man has mellowed with age."

She looked up at her father again and knew that he didn't believe that for one second.

# 6

Trey placed an overnight bag of clothes on the backseat, and walked around to climb into the car that was waiting for him outside the hotel. Mr. Galroth—or Lurch as Trey had begun to internally refer to him—was sitting in the driver's seat, having somehow shoehorned its extraordinarily long body into the vehicle. The car was a large four-by-four, but even so the demon looked hunched and uncomfortable behind the wheel. It turned to look at its young charge in the passenger seat.

"Your eyes," the nether-creature said, with a tip of its head. "You have bags under them. You look terrible."

"Good morning to you too. I'm fine. Just a bit nervous about today. But thanks for your concern, Mr. Galroth."

"Galroth."

"What?"

"Just Galroth, not mister. I have no true sex. I am a non-gendered being."

Trey puffed out his cheeks and waited.

"And where is it that you want to go today?"

Trey sighed. "Look, can we cut the pretense and stop all this I-have-no-idea-what-you-are-doing-here nonsense?"

The demon stared at him for what seemed like an age

until Trey began to squirm in his seat. Eventually the thing next to him blinked and shook its head, causing what little hair it had to brush against the plastic covering that lined the car's roof. "Trey, I really *do* have no idea what you are doing here. Mr. Charron contacted me from his office in London and asked if I would be kind enough to transport you wherever you wanted to go during your visit here in Canada, and to be on hand should you need me for anything. He has not provided me with any information pertaining to your trip or the reason for your visit."

A car horn sounded behind them. The creature shot its eyes toward the rearview mirror to see the driver of the car gesticulating madly at him through the windshield of a bright red sports car. The horn sounded again, and Trey could hear the man shouting. The giant turned its body around in the seat and glared at the other driver. The horn fell silent.

"So, where do you want to go?" the demon asked, turning back to the teenager.

Trey pulled a piece of paper out of his back pocket and handed it to his chaperone. "In a short while I'd like you to take me here. But first I'd like to go to a gift shop to buy a present." The demon looked at the scrap of paper, nodded its head, and put the car into gear.

The house was set way back from the nearest road in a location that Trey guessed would politely be described as *isolated*—although *bleak*, *desolate*, and *godforsaken* were words that also sprang to mind as they approached. The only way to get to the house was down a rutted path that led through high woods on both sides, and had it not been for the GPS in the car, they would never have found it. The track that they bounced along now was little more than two channeled grooves worn into the ground over the years by vehicles that had gone back and forth along it. But the height of the grass growing on the raised central area, and the way that it brushed noisily against the underside of the four-by-four vehicle, suggested that the track was used infrequently. Trey glanced at the map on the GPS, looking for any signs that there might be another road or track that led through the woods, but there didn't appear to be one. He looked out of the window for signs of habitation in this remote, backwoods location, and wondered why his uncle had picked a place like this to live in. And yet there was something about the wooded landscape that stirred the teenager, something that appealed to raw emotions and feelings buried deep down inside of him. He shuddered, dragging his attention away from the forest and focusing on the radio, switching the stations back and forth to try to locate one that was playing rock music.

The bouncing and jostling of the car's uneven progress along the track was beginning to make Trey feel queasy, and after a while he was forced to look up again. The woods were more dense now. Even at this time of day, with the sun high up in the morning sky, the trees' thick overhead blanket denied the light to the leafy carpet that had been laid down over the years, making the woods appear dark and uninviting. It seemed endless; the trees that filled the land on both sides of the track stretched on forever until they merged into a great murky darkness away in the distance.

*It wouldn't do to get lost in there,* Trey thought, imagining wandering around among the tall, dark trees, with no point of reference to find his way out.

"There is something up ahead," Galroth said, pointing with his chin at something he had seen through the windshield. Trey looked up just as the cabin came into view. Even from this distance, it was clear that the place was a ramshackle affair; the land surrounding the squat building was littered with abandoned cars and rusting machinery that the elements had attacked over the years, turning them into ghastly orange-brown effigies. The whole place had a neglected and slightly sinister appearance.

"Looks lovely," Trey said as they pulled up in front of the building. He turned to look at the demon. "Thank you . . . for the lift."

"I will wait until I know that you are safe," the creature said.

"There's no need. I'll just—"

"I will wait until I know that you are safe."

Trey shrugged. "Whatever." He climbed out of the car and grabbed his bag from the backseat. It was colder here. Despite the sun that drilled in low over the building's roof and made Trey screw up his eyes, the temperature was markedly lower this far into the forest. He inhaled deeply, filling his lungs with air infused with the rich, sweet smell of the pine trees off to his left. He could feel Galroth's eyes on his back, so he stepped up onto the wooden porch, the gray stairs giving a short, sharp groan as they took his weight. There was no sign of a doorbell or knocker, and Trey wondered if in fact anyone lived in the place. He balled his hand into a fist and banged on the wooden door, the sound echoing out around the clearing, and causing a murder of crows to take to the air from a nearby tree, their angry cries signaling the group's displeasure at being disturbed.

The knock was answered by the barking of a small dog on the other side, and Trey could hear its paws scratching at the door.

He turned around and nodded at the demon still sitting in the car to his rear. Galroth stared back at him, statue-like. It appeared that the dog was home alone. Trey's heart sank, and he was about to return to the car when he heard the sound of a man's voice.

"Billy, shut your yammering, or so help me, I'll kick you so hard in the rear, you'll be wearing your butt as a new collar."

Trey stepped back a little from the door. Nervous again, his heart beating out an unrelenting staccato rhythm in his chest, he breathed deeply, telling himself to calm down. The sound of numerous locks being turned and released was punctuated by streams of abuse hurled at the dog that, like Trey, seemed to be having a difficult time in controlling its excitement. When the door finally opened, an old man in a shabby bathrobe was revealed. The small terrier was running in tight, excited little circles in and around the old man's slippered feet while looking up at Trey with a stupid grin on its face, its tongue hanging out on one side. Trey smiled up at the old man who seemed to be staring at a spot somewhere over the teenager's left shoulder, his eyes tracking slightly from left to right. The old man appeared to be completely blind.

"Well? Who's there?" the man asked eventually. "Is that you, Jurgen? Because if it is, I am not in the mood for any of your stupid—"

"My name is Trey. I'm looking for a Mr. Frank Laporte."

"What do you want with Frank?" the old man barked. "And who the hell told you that he lived here with me?"

"I got his address from a friend of mine," Trey said, leaning to one side and trying to get a better look inside the house over the man's shoulder.

"You only answered one of my questions, kid. And stop snooping inside at my house."

Trey stepped back and looked into the old man's face again. The eyes were constantly moving; they skimmed back and forth across some invisible horizon, never stopping in their search for whatever it was they sought out in the darkness. The little dog had calmed down now and gingerly stepped out onto the porch to take a sniff at Trey's sneakers.

"I'm from England. My name is—"

"I didn't ask you where the hell you came from and I don't remember asking you for your life story. Now, if you don't mind, I was in the middle of my afternoon nap. So if you'd be so kind as to leave my property, I'll be sure to let

44

Frank know that someone was looking for him when he gets back." The old man began to shut the door.

"When are you expecting him back?"

"What are you, the goddamn police? Go on, get lost." The old man waved one hand in Trey's direction, continuing to close the door with the other.

"I'm his nephew," Trey said quickly before the opening could be shut completely.

The old man stopped. Tight lines formed on his forehead as he took in this last piece of information. His lips moved, mouthing words that Trey could not catch, and when he turned in Trey's direction again, his features were tight and drawn. He shook his head a little, as if unsure that he had heard correctly.

"You're Daniel and Elisabeth's son?"

The old man seemed to stare straight at him, his eyes stopping their erratic movements for a moment. After what seemed an age, he inclined his head to one side and closed his eyes. "What did you say your name was again?"

"Trey . . . Trey Laporte."

The old man nodded at this. He stepped back a little, pushing the door fully open with one hand before holding the other out toward the teenager.

"Nice to meet you, Trey Laporte. I'm your uncle Frank. I guess you'd better get your stuff out of that car and come in."

# 7

Trey watched the old man shuffle away down the hallway. He turned and walked back to the car and Galroth, fishing his cell phone from his pocket on the way. He frowned at the complete lack of bars on the signal-strength indicator. He shouldn't have been surprised; he was in the wilderness and he had the feeling that the nearest cell phone tower could be a very long way away. In addition, his cursory glance at the inside of his uncle's house suggested that he'd be lucky to find running water in the place, let alone a telephone. He put the phone back in his pocket and walked over to the car.

"So that is your uncle," Galroth said with a nod toward the house.

Trey nodded. "You can go now. Thank you for bringing me." He glanced back at the house, unable to believe that a blind man could live in such a place. "I think I'll be staying here for a few days. My phone doesn't work out here, so I need you to tell Lucien that I arrived safely and found my uncle."

The demon stared back at him. "You are certain that you do not want me to stay? My instructions were to—"

"I'm giving you *new* instructions," Trey said with a firmness that he had not intended. He sighed and smiled back at the demon. "Thank you, Galroth. Really. I know you have my best interests at heart, and that you are only obeying Lucien's orders, but I'm fine.

"Lucien and Tom will both be scratchy about you leaving me here, and Tom'll no doubt bawl you out and tell you to come straight back. But I don't want you to do that. I want you to tell Lucien that I am fine and remind him that he said that he would not interfere with my visit here. I'll try and call him soon, but right now I want to spend some time with my family."

Trey looked back at the house. "I don't know when I might be able to get to a phone, but I'm guessing that it'll be in the next day or so."

The demon sighed. It fished inside its jacket pocket, took out a small box, and opened the lid to reveal a number of small stones of a type that Trey had never seen before—each about the size of a man's thumb. They were bright red and slightly translucent, and as Trey peered down at them he could see that the insides swirled and eddied, as if a living, gelatinous substance formed the inside of the crystals. Galroth took one of the stones between its thumb and forefinger, holding it up to the light and examining it for a second. Happy with whatever it saw, the nether-creature deftly took one end of the stone between its thumb and forefinger and wedged it firmly into the entrance to its ear. The creature gave a little push with the tip of its finger, paused, and then began to jam the rest of it deep into the auditory cavity.

Trey watched in horror. "I don't think that's a particularly wise thing to—"

He stopped when he saw that the stone was now fully inside the creature's ear. He was about to make some wisecrack remark when the demon took a deep, sharp breath in through its nostrils, holding it in its lungs. The creature then pushed hard at the stone, forcing the finger impossibly deep into the ear and ramming the stone deeper and deeper inside its skull. Trey gawked when he noticed that the demon's long, bony digit was jammed in all the way up to the hilt, and guessed that the stone must be wedged smack bang in the center of the creature's head.

Galroth finally released the breath it had been holding and removed its finger. The demon waggled its jaw from side to side, opening and closing its mouth a couple of times as it did so. Then it turned to look at Trey and handed him the other stone.

"This one is for you," it said.

Trey stared down at the stone before looking back at Galroth in horror. "If you think that I'm shoving this thing into my—"

"No. You need not insert the stone." The demon's eyes took in the teenager before him. "Besides I doubt your human body would be capable of such a thing. But if you need me to come to you," the creature went on in a solemn voice, "you must hold this stone to your forehead and intone my name. I will hear you and be here as soon as I can. Try not to use this unless it is absolutely necessary. The energy that I would need to use to get here will be huge and I doubt that I could do it more than once. I will tell Lucien what is happening and that I have left you with this insurance should you need to use it."

Trey looked from the stone to the demon again, before curling his fingers around the gem and putting it in his jeans pocket. "Thank you, Galroth," he said. "Please tell Lucien that I'm . . ." He paused, then added, "Tell him that I am thinking of him—him and the others. Please give them my love."

The demon blinked at him. Trey was about to say something else, but the nether-creature simply turned its head to look out of the front windshield, closing the window on him. The car's engine started and Galroth drove off.

The teenager walked through the hallway, noting the faded prints on the walls, and how old the furniture looked. Trey guessed that the place hadn't been decorated in some time, and the house had a musty, mildew smell.

The open door at the end of the hallway led into the living room and he stepped inside. There were empty bottles everywhere. They were arranged in little clusters here and there, the majority of them surrounding the battered old armchair on the other side of the room from the doorway. A solitary bottle stood in the center of a small table next to the chair, half full of a golden liquid, no doubt waiting to join its comrades on the floor as soon as it had been emptied.

He heard his uncle moving in another room somewhere behind him, and he stepped farther into the room to wait for him. Everything appeared to have been left where it had been dropped and it was clear that his uncle received little, if any, domestic help despite his disability. There were signs that somebody had tried to tidy up recently—some dusting and vacuuming had been done and the trash can next to his uncle's chair had been emptied and a fresh liner inserted, but it appeared that Frank preferred to use the floor as the receptacle for his garbage.

It was the smell that bothered Trey. That mildew smell of neglect was everywhere and it was laced with a healthy tinge of dog and stale booze. There was another smell woven in among these that Trey couldn't quite put his finger on—an earthy smell that caused a strange string of unidentifiable emotions to stir inside Trey as he breathed it in.

He moved toward the sofa, shoving a pile of dirty clothing out of the way to create a space to sit down in. On the wall opposite was an old stain that suggested that food or drink may have been thrown against it at some point. Either that or Uncle Frank's interior designer had a taste for the avant-garde.

Trey idly wondered how anyone without the benefit of sight could live in a place like this. It was a death trap. He'd always understood that blind people needed to live in a structured and ordered environment, to enable them to navigate their way around and locate the things that they needed. But this place was about as far away from that as could be imagined. He was deep in thought when the little terrier, Billy, hopped up onto his lap, startling him. The dog nuzzled its head beneath Trey's hand, giving the teenager little option but to stroke it. When he looked down at the scruffy little creature he was rewarded with a frank and open stare, and that same doggy grin that he'd been greeted with at the door.

"You want something to drink?" his uncle shouted from a room somewhere deep inside the house.

Trey looked at the state of the abandoned cutlery and crockery that had been left at various points about the room and decided he wouldn't risk it. "No thanks, I'm fine," he shouted back. He scratched the dog behind the ears and smiled as the little creature wagged a sorry stump of a tail.

Frank shuffled into the room, his slippered feet hardly lifting from the floor as he plowed them through the detritus in his way. He carried a cup of something hot in one hand, the other stretched out ahead of him. He stopped and turned at the beaten-up old chair and sank down into it. No sooner was the old man seated than Billy leaped down from Trey's lap and secured a spot on Frank's.

"So," the old man said, letting the word hang in the air between them. He reached forward with his hand, seeking out the bottle on the table. He unscrewed the lid and poured a large measure of the clear, golden liquid into his cup. Trey watched, waiting for his uncle to continue, but once it became clear that that single utterance was as much as he was going to get right now, he tried to break the ice himself.

"I brought you a present, but . . ."

"Whatisit?"

"I didn't realize that you were—"

"Whatisit?"

Trey dug into the bag by his side and brought out the silver frame. He'd had the picture of his parents with his uncle enlarged and put into a frame. He looked at it now, unable to believe that the haggard thing opposite him was the same person who grinned back at him from the photograph.

"It's a picture. In a frame," he said in a small voice.

"Great. Just what I need," the old man said. He motioned with a hand toward the fireplace. "Put it over there somewhere."

There was another uncomfortable silence in which Trey tried desperately to think of something to say.

"It's a nice place," he said, and regretted it the moment he did.

"It's a crap hole. What's nice about it?"

"I meant the area. It's nice around here. A bit out of the way, but nice."

"S'OK. It's mine. I own it, so I ain't beholden to anyone."

"When you say it's yours . . ."

"All of it. The forest, the land, and everything that you can see for miles around. It's mine," he said as if expecting an argument. "Bought it years ago."

"And you manage OK?" Trey asked. "It must be difficult living way out here if you can't see to get around."

His uncle shrugged and continued to rub the dog's belly. "So what do you want?"

Trey was taken aback. His uncle's choice of words and

the tone that he used shocked the teenager. He hadn't known what to expect from this meeting. He'd looked forward to it—nervous and excited at the same time at the prospect of meeting a living relative. Not just that, he was excited about meeting someone else like him . . . someone who knew what it was to be a lycanthrope. He puffed out his cheeks and shook his head, thinking that the man might at least have pretended to be glad to meet him.

"Cat got your tongue?" Frank said into the silence.

"I don't want anything," Trey said finally. "I just wanted to meet you."

"Everybody *wants* something, kid." His uncle pushed the small dog off his lap and onto the floor. "How old are you?"

"Fifteen," Trey answered and watched as the old man's face changed at his response, breaking into a half smile, half sneer.

"So you've had your Change?" The man nodded to himself as if answering his own question. "You've probably had quite a few of them by now—that is, unless you're a late starter like your father was."

Trey sat quietly and waited. He didn't like the way that his uncle was "looking" at him across the room. And he didn't like the tone he'd adopted when he'd referred to his father.

"How'd you find me?"

"A friend of mine gave me the address."

"So you said, so you said. Am I allowed to know the name of this . . . friend?" The blind man turned his head and stared straight out in front of him. He nodded his head up and down in the air, moving it only a fraction in each direction, as though he had already guessed the answer to the question.

"His name is Lucien Charron," Trey said. "He was a friend of my father's. He's been very good to me. He—"

"I know who and *what* he is," his uncle said. He was completely still now and Trey watched as the man's face went through a series of expressions as though he were playing out different scenarios in his head. Eventually, the scowl that he had worn from the moment Trey had first laid eyes on him returned to his features. "Come over here, kid. Let me get a look at you."

Trey walked over to the chair, standing in front of it. The old man levered himself out of the seat and stood up to face him. He reached out with his hands, placing his fingers on Trey's face; first tracing the contours of the boy's features and then running his hands across his hair. He let his hands drop to Trey's shoulders and then slid them around to his arms, giving the biceps a less-than-gentle squeeze. He nodded, his bottom lip protruding as though he were a man satisfied with the inspection of the horse that he planned to buy at market. His hands moved back up to Trey's neck and paused as they felt the chain that hung around his neck. Trey could sense the change in the old man as his fingers brushed against the metal links. A small gasp escaped Frank's lips. His fingers hungrily traced the outline of the chain, seeking out the silver amulet that hung at the bottom of the long loop of metal links. His breathing had got louder and faster, and his face had taken on an ugly, needy look, lips peeled back over crooked and discolored teeth while the sightless eyes rolled crazily in their sockets.

Trey's heart was hammering in his chest. He didn't like the look on the man's face. He firmly grabbed his uncle's wrists, stepped back at arm's length away from him, and watched Frank waver on the spot, caught off balance by the sudden movement. When he was sure that the old man was no longer in any danger of falling over, he let go of his uncle's arms and took another step backward.

Frank lifted his chin up into the air, the grotesque mask slipping from his features. He nodded—a brief downward jerk of the head. Trey thought that he was about to say something, but instead his uncle shakily reached out behind him for the arms of the chair and sat back down, fluttering his fingers in the air in a dismissive gesture that Trey took to mean that he too was expected to return to his seat.

The old man was shaken. He reached out with his fingers exploring the table's surface until they alighted on the edge of his cup, which he raised to his lips and greedily drank from. He appeared to have visibly shrunk in the last few seconds as if what had happened had knocked the stuffing out of him. He stared sightlessly down into his lap, silently mouthing words. Eventually he stopped and sat quite still again, his eyes fixed on some invisible point between his knees. "Did you get it before your first Change?" he asked.

"Not quite," Trey said, fingering the amulet through his shirt. Lucien had given him the chain when they had first met, telling him that it had been his father's. The amulet allowed Trey to control his transformation. It stopped him turning into the Wolfan—the malevolent werewolf that was under the control of the full moon and that would mercilessly kill and murder during the Change. Legend had it that there were once a number of the amulets in existence, but now Trey's was the only one left.

The amulet was a blessing and a curse.

Because of it, Trey did not turn into a bloodthirsty killing beast each and every full moon. Instead, he became the more powerful, feared, intelligent, and restrained bimorph werewolf. But also because of the amulet—and because he was a full-blood werewolf born of two lycanthrope parents— he had already lost so much. Friends had died, his life had been turned upside down, and he had been forced to kill while defending himself against evil. Because of the amulet the vampire Caliban believed that Trey was the legendary Son of Theiss—heir to an ancient prophecy foretelling that a werewolf would stop an all-powerful vampire's rise to power in the Netherworld. And the vampire had dedicated himself to Trey's destruction.

There was no doubt: The amulet was a source of both powerful protection and terrible danger.

"I thought that it was lost forever," Frank said.

"No."

His uncle nodded. "Daniel, your father, was given the amulet by your grandfather." He paused, waiting for a response. When none came, he went on. "It should have been mine. I was the first son and it should have been mine." A snort of derision escaped the old man's nostrils and his face twisted with jealousy and anger. "Our father decided that I wasn't *responsible* enough to have it. How d'ya like that—not responsible enough. I was just a kid, and my old man thought he could see what kind of man I'd turn into—he thought I was a bad apple." He shook his head, remembering.

"I was *fourteen* when I had my first Change. Daniel was only five years old at the time, and even though he wouldn't need it for another ten years, our father wouldn't give me that amulet. Not even temporarily. 'It's Daniel's,' was all he would say. 'He will be the one to take up where I leave off.' "

Frank's milky eyes had filled with tears that clung to his lashes, threatening to fall, until he sniffed and wiped them away with the back of his sleeve. "I hated him for that. I hated my father for favoring Daniel over me, and I hated my brother for denying me the chance to escape the curse that had been passed on to me by our father."

"It doesn't sound as though my dad had any say in it," Trey said in a small voice.

"Maybe not. But he was given a chance that I never was. I had, and still have to, become that *thing* every month, while he was given the control that you now have. If I'd been given what was rightfully mine, things might have turned out differently for me. I might not have . . ."

A silence followed, broken only by the old man slurping noisily from his cup again.

"So, I ask you again, what do you want?"

Trey looked around him, making his mind up. "I'd like to stay," he said. "If it's OK with you. For a while at least. I have things that I need to ask you, things about myself and what I am." He paused. "And I'd like a chance to get to know you some more."

The old man shook his head and took a deep breath of the stale air. "I'm not good company," he said. "Especially in the . . . lead up. In two days I'll have the Change. Full moon." He frowned and swiveled his head in Trey's direction. "Does the moon still get to you? I know the amulet gives you control, but does it still get to you?"

Trey shook his head and then realized that the man could not see this response. "It does, but I don't have to change during the full moon. I can . . . make it not happen. But it's bad if I do that—I feel like my insides are being torn out and my brain is on fire. If I fight the moon, I can feel sick for days. I tried to at the start, but it got so bad that now it's just easier for me to find somewhere away from everyone and let it happen. I don't have to stay changed for long—just get it done, and then I can go back to being . . . normal."

"Normal, huh?" Frank nodded slowly and began to stand up. "Back to normal." He walked around the chair until he was standing in front of Trey. "Follow me, I want you to see something." He turned his back on the youngster and walked across the room, his fingers outstretched before him to guide him to the rear wall. He stopped in front of a door set into it, reached out, and pulled the handle down to open it.

"Go in, go in," he said, nodding his head toward the door.

Trey stepped through the doorway and his uncle followed.

The back room was a cell. It was a stark, cold space of about twenty square feet. In the center of the room was a large cage. Its steel bars were at least an inch thick, and the entire thing was bolted down into the concrete floor. Inside the cage a small mattress was laid directly onto the floor, blankets piled up at one end. Beyond that, there was nothing in the room.

Trey looked over at his uncle, who seemed to sense the boy's stare.

"Come in and have a proper look," he said, motioning with his head and stepping farther into the room. He walked up to the cage, his arms stretched out in front of him. "Home sweet home," he said when his fingers made contact with the cold metal bars. "Well, it will be in a couple of days."

"You lock yourself in that?" Trey said.

"Yep. The door's got a timer lock on it. As soon as I step inside and slam it shut, it can't be opened for another fourteen hours. It's either that or waking up in the middle of nowhere, not being able to remember if I've torn somebody's throat out."

Trey looked at the cage and then at the man next to it. "But you can't see. How could you be a danger to anyone when you can't see?"

His uncle laughed bitterly and shook his head. "That's the real son of a bitch. That's the thing that makes this curse even sicker than it already was. Because for one day every month, I *can* see! And guess when that is, hmm? The only time that I get to crawl out of this darkness that I live in is when I'm a psychopathic werewolf intent on killing anything and everything in my path."

Trey looked at the man in horror.

"Oh, I can't see great. But one eye can make out enough for me to be able to get around . . . get around and . . . hunt." He snorted again, his face set in a sick grimace. "So I lock myself up. Like all good little Wolfan boys should during the Change. I lock myself up in this room when I could be looking at the world again. How'd you like that, huh?"

Trey didn't say anything for a long time. He stared at the cage and tried to imagine what it must be like to be locked up inside it. "I'll be here this time," Trey said. "I'd like to be with you."

"Like I said, I'm not good company at the best of times." Frank ran his fingers through his thin hair, letting out a long sigh. "But if you want to stay, you can. You've come a long way to be here, so it's the least I can do." The old man turned as if to leave, but stopped, adding, "We might get visitors. I don't live entirely alone here on this land."

# 8

Lucien met the courier outside the elevator in the underground garage at the bottom of the building. The man was dressed from head to toe in black motorcycle leathers, his face obscured by the tinted black visor of the helmet he wore. The man handed the package to Lucien, nodding in the vampire's direction before turning on his heel and walking back to the motorbike that he had arrived on moments before.

When the doors of the elevator opened up into the apartment the vampire hesitated, as he always did at this point, checking to see if he was alone. The apartment was in complete darkness, but Lucien's eyes took in every detail as he scanned the room. Happy that there was nobody else around at this late hour, he approached the door that led through to his office. Once inside, he leaned back against the door, closing his eyes and steeling himself for what lay ahead. Still carrying the large package, he crossed the room to the desk, using the side of the box to clear a space on which it could rest. The delivery resembled one of those small cool boxes used for transporting cold food to picnics or the beach, and his fingers trembled a little as he slid the zip all the way around and opened the semi-rigid top.

Inside were two bags of blood. Both full, their contents distended the thick, plastic containers so that they looked like giant, rectangular berries—full to the brim with a crimson cargo. Lucien reached forward and picked one up. He circled the desk and sat down in the large leather chair. Looking down at the blood bag, he hefted it in his hand, enjoying the weight and feel of it and the flutter of anticipation that it set off inside him.

He opened the drawer at the side of his desk and looked down at the medical equipment that he kept there. He had everything he needed to insert a cannula and administer the blood intravenously—he'd done it countless times since turning his back on his former vampiric existence. He still needed the blood to survive, but he no longer chose to acquire and imbibe it in the way that his kind had throughout the centuries. One of Lucien's many businesses was a blood laboratory, and his daily dose of the life-sustaining liquid was delivered to him at the same time every day.

He reached down and started to pull the equipment from the drawer, his fingers pausing as they brushed against the plastic packaging that housed the needles. He glanced at the blood bag again, and thought about how long it had been since he'd tasted the sweet sticky liquid it contained.

What did it matter how he took the blood into him? What difference would it make if he chose, just this once, to drink it rather than push it into his body through a tube?

He shook his head as if trying to rattle loose these rogue thoughts, a deep frown lining his forehead. He was being foolish. This was not the first time that he had had to fight the animalistic urges that defined his type. But recently he had felt desires and old urges that he had thought were gone forever. However hard he tried to dispute the fact, he had the uncomfortable feeling that something—something long held at bay—had been reawakened in him.

He leaned his head back, a long sigh escaping his lips. Unconsciously, he raised a hand, his fingers tracing the area of his shoulder that had been wounded recently when his brother, Caliban, had sunk his teeth deep into him. Becoming aware of what he was doing, he sat up, lifted his head, and looked down at the area beneath his fingers. He wondered if something more than just the scar tissue might have been left behind as a memento of their last battle—if somehow the infection that had almost killed him might have changed him at a deeper and more primitive level.

He looked at the bag in his hand again, and his pulse quickened. It really *didn't* matter how the blood got into him. As long as nobody was hurt, it was of no consequence. And this blood had been given voluntarily.

He shook his head again, unable to believe what he was about to do.

He opened another drawer, and this time he took out a small knife that he always used as a letter opener. He held the sharp tip against the thick plastic housing, telling himself that this was foolish and yet still pushing gently on the handle. He would just take a small mouthful. Just enough to prove to himself that it was of no consequence and that this had everything to do with the stresses that he was under at the moment, and nothing to do with any physiological change that was happening to him. He would taste the blood, prove to himself that it had no effect on him, and then administer the rest through a vein.

The crimson liquid burst free of the puncture, and Lucien quickly pulled the bag up to his face, closing his lips around the hole and sucking greedily at the blood. He sank back into the chair, tilting his head back and closing his eyes as the cold liquid filled his mouth. A small muffled groan escaped him as he swallowed.

It was too cold. But even so he relished the harsh metallic taste in his mouth. It was a taste that brought with it a flood of memories and emotions. Long-forgotten scenes swam into life behind his eyelids, and he sucked all the harder on the plastic bag.

He would warm the next bag, warm it to the right temperature so that it would feel like it had just come from . . .

He opened his eyes. Sitting up quickly, he threw the bag away from him onto the floor, ignoring the terrible scarlet mess that it made on the carpet. He stood up and rushed to the bathroom, lifting the seat to the toilet just in time as his stomach contracted and ejected a hot spew of bloody vomit into the bowl. He straightened up, wiping at his mouth with the back of his hand.

What had he been thinking? What on earth was happening to him?

He closed the door behind him, trying hard not to look at the growing pool of blood that was now soaking into the floor in front of his desk. He walked out of the office and left the apartment. He needed to walk. Walk and think. He was in trouble and he needed a solution, fast.

# 9

The dull, overcast morning had transformed into a hot and sunny afternoon, and the park was filled with office workers looking for somewhere away from their fluorescent-lit workplaces to eat their sandwiches. Alexa walked among them, enjoying the warmth of the sun on her face and the soft give of the grass underfoot. The bench was set back a little from the path, and she stood in front of it looking down at the prostrate figure that took up the entire expanse of the wooden seat. The bench's occupant let out a loud snore and shifted around to move its face back into shadow again. Alexa waited patiently, smiling ruefully down at the figure she had been sent here to find.

"I know that you're awake," she said eventually, "so why don't you stop pretending and be nice?"

"Sod off," came the gruff reply.

"You were very difficult to track down. My father would have come to visit you himself, but you know how he hates daylight meetings. He said that if you weren't agreeable . . . if you were rude, he'd be happy to pay you a visit in person . . . at night . . . alone."

The Ashnon slowly sat up, sucking its teeth and squinting

up at the girl. It rubbed a hand through its grimy hair. "What does he want this time?"

"A favor."

"I don't do favors. Not even for the likes of Lucien Charron. He knows that. And you might want to remind him that the last time I worked for him, it nearly cost me my life. 'It's a simple job,' he told me. 'You'll only need to be the prime minister for one day, no more.'" The Ashnon reached down beside the bench and grabbed a brown paper bag containing a bottle of something. Twisting the lid off, it swigged greedily before setting it back on the ground. "He knew damn well that that lunatic was going to take a shot at the PM that day. The bullet missed me by inches!"

"It was a human bullet, fired by a human hand. You wouldn't have died."

"That's easy for you to say, but walking around with a five-inch exit wound in your face for a week or so is no picnic, I can tell you."

"My father says that you'll like this job. He says that the reward at the end of it will make you glad to take it."

The Ashnon studied her. They were among the rarest demons of the Netherworld, and this was the first time that she had met one. At least she assumed it was. The Ashnon were unique among nether-creatures for being able to perfectly replicate any human being. They did this without harming the human and, having assumed the human disguise, became invisible to other nether-creatures. Because of this unique ability they were able to charge immense fees to double for heads of state, royalty, and VIPs that might be in danger of assassination or kidnapping. And it was the reason that Alexa had been sent here today.

"You said something about a reward?"

"Where is he?" Alexa asked, making the demon wait.

"Who?"

"The homeless person whom you're pretending to be. Where is he?"

"At a place that I've set up in the Netherworld. As far as he's concerned, he's staying at the Waldorf-Astoria hotel in New York as my guest. All expenses paid. He'll look out the window of the penthouse apartment and see the New York skyline—taxis, skyscrapers, American delis selling hot corned beef—the whole shooting match. All he's got to do is stick to his side of the bargain, not leave the building for a week, and he gets the holiday of a lifetime. Every kind of food and drink he could imagine brought to him by room service, movies on demand, a personal shopper that visits him and then arranges for the clothes to be delivered, a personal trainer to help him out at the gym. Whatever he wants."

Alexa frowned, considering what the demon had just said. "But none of it is real."

"Reality's subjective. When the guy is sitting on this bench drunk out of his brain and seeing pink elephants, believe me, to him, they're real."

Alexa turned her head to look around at the people lying on the grass enjoying one of the rare sunny days this summer.

She turned back to study the figure in front of her, telling herself to remember that it was indeed a demon, but her brain was having difficulty in ratifying the optical signals being sent to it—so perfect was the disguise. She was used to seeing through the human mantle that demons living in the human realm wore, and seeing the true creature beneath. But the thing in front of her just looked . . . human. "And what do you get out of this deal?" she asked.

"Are you kidding?" The creature looked up at her, screwing up its eyes and grinning. It looked down at its body. "I get all this. Unlimited use of a body. I get to experience what it is to be alive."

Alexa shook her head in confusion. "I thought you said—"

"In my demon form, I don't get to experience anything. We Ashnon are . . . inert. We're not physical beings—we're more a . . . coalescence of energy. We've no sense of taste or smell. We don't feel the cold or the heat. We don't experience illness or disease or pain. We don't really experience happiness or sadness. We are nonentities. Lifeless. Dull as dishwater." The face that looked back at her now was a parody of sadness. "In this body I get everything. The homeless are ideal for us, nobody cares what they do—as long as they leave them alone. In this body I can sing, dance, shout, howl like a loon. And nobody bats an eye. I can appear to be drunk out of my mind, laugh like a maniac, or cry myself senseless, and the people will walk on past me as if I didn't exist. Perfect."

"If your demon form isn't physical, how do you make contact with future . . . customers?"

The demon studied her. Climbing up off the bench, he approached her on unsteady legs. "We use intermediaries—people in our employ here in the human realm. Sometimes we might cook up a spiritual visitation—an angel or something like that. You know, a moment of epiphany. That worked for this guy," he said, gesturing down toward the body it was currently inhabiting. Noticing her look of disapproval, the Ashnon put his hands up, his face taking on a serious look. "We're not allowed to harm our hosts in any way, and we're not allowed to outstay our welcome. The body that we reproduce is the one they get back, not the mangled old wreck that they left this realm in. It's like taking your old, battered car into a dealer, waiting a week or so, and receiving a brand-new, shiny one in return. They're free of any disease that they may have had—and let me tell you in this guy's case, there was a whole lot of bad stuff. That's the deal. They give up their place here in the human realm for an agreed length of time, and when they come back it's in a new, pristine, perfect body."

"But you're drinking. You're—"

"It's water." The Ashnon nodded toward the bottle contained in the brown paper bag by the bench. "You can check it if you like. It's just an act. People expect drunks to act out of turn, so I can do whatever my heart desires. Philip Warton—that's my, sorry, *his* name—is residing in a place that I have created for him in the Netherworld. Perfectly safe. Like I say, as far as he's concerned, he's living a life of luxury. I get to be him for a week. When the time is up, he comes back to a fresh start. No liver disease, no cancer, no irritable bowel syndrome, and no halitosis. It seems like a great deal to me."

A thought occurred to Alexa. "What happens to the old body?" she asked.

"That gets left behind in the Netherworld."

"That's it?"

The Ashnon shuffled its feet uncomfortably. "Best not to ask. Let's just say that the old body is . . . recycled."

Alexa raised an eyebrow and waited.

The demon held two hands up in a defensive gesture. "Hey, I have to employ staff. They want to be rewarded for the work they do." It puffed out its cheeks and shook its head. "Like I said, it's best not to ask."

"What happens if *he*"—she nodded toward the human body in front of her—"leaves the hotel?"

"Then he's screwed. Eternal damnation and all that jazz." The demon batted the question away.

"What happens if you don't want to give the body back? If you decide that you're having too good a time."

The demon squinted at her and the smile dropped from its face. "Something a whole lot worse than eternal damnation for me. Like I said, it's a deal—a binding agreement that must be kept by both parties. There's no wiggle room, no cheap tricks. It's a cast-iron, no-strings-attached contract."

71

"It's a hell of a risk—on his behalf."

"So's pumping cheap booze into your liver for years and expecting to see forty-one."

"Amazing," Alexa said under her breath.

"Yes, I am."

Alexa smiled and ruefully shook her head.

"So what's this reward?" the Ashnon asked, scratching at its rear.

"Huh?"

The demon looked at her as if she were an imbecile. "The reward that your father believes will make me jump at this *job*?"

"Oh, he said to tell you that we have a Necrotroph on the loose, and it's yours if you want it." She let the revelation go casually, the way that her father had told her to.

The down-and-out stared at her with an intensity and clarity that took her by surprise, and for the first time Alexa thought that she could detect, hidden deep within those eyes, the slightest hint of the thing that was really inside the human body in front of her.

"A Necro?" it said slowly, the hatred in its voice clear. "It's been a long, long time since I've come across one of those. Perhaps a hundred years or so." It nodded and looked at the ground between its feet. When it spoke again, it was in a voice so low that Alexa had to strain to hear. "Scum. Vile scum. They give Deeps a bad name—a very bad name."

Alexa knew that demons came in two main forms: Indies and Deeps. The Indies were capable of visiting the human realm in disguise, by adopting a human mantle that hid their true form. Deeps, like the Ashnon and Necrotrophs, could only exist in this realm via the acquisition of a human host.

The demon spat on the ground. "We Ashnon are sworn to kill each and every Necrotroph that we discover, your father knows that. He also knows that we are the only way to kill one without the loss of more human life." He looked at her, a sinister smile forming on its lips. "Lucien Charron always did know how to put together a good deal—he should have been an Ashnon." The demon straightened up then, abandoning the hunched and stooped posture that it had maintained throughout their meeting. It moved its head from side to side, loosening the knots that had formed. It was clear that the creature had made up its mind. "Tell your father that I'm in. I'll need his help to find a new body to use—something that I can slip into for a while—this one's time is nearly up."

Alexa nodded.

"Oh, and when you see him, tell him I said thanks." He looked down at the bench, sighed, and, turning away from her, started to rearrange the papers and cardboard on the wooden surface. She couldn't catch what he was mumbling to himself, but she distinctly caught the words *Necrotroph* and *death* in there somewhere.

# 10

Philippa woke up screaming. She sat up in bed and stared around her at the gloom, unsure of her surroundings. Alexa was up and across the room in an instant, kneeling beside her, holding her hand, and talking to her in a soft voice that assured her that she was in no danger.

There was a soft knock on the door. "It's all right," Alexa called out to whoever was on the other side. "We're fine. Just a nightmare."

She returned her attention to Philippa, talking to her in hushed tones until her breathing had returned to normal.

It seemed to Philippa that the other girl's voice was directly inside her mind, pushing back at the panic that had threatened to overcome her so completely. She was certain that this was some kind of magic, and while this should have unsettled her, she welcomed the calm that it afforded her in those first few waking moments.

Slowly, satisfied that Philippa was over the worst of her nightmare, Alexa leaned forward and switched on the bedside lamp, flooding the room with its soft, yellow light. She sat on the bed and looked down at her, waiting.

"I saw it," Philippa said eventually, her eyes widening at

the memory. "I saw the demon that was inside me. The one that was inside my father . . . I saw it."

"When you say you saw it . . ."

"It's transferred. Moved from one host to another. I felt it move between the people." She looked at Alexa, her face full of confusion and doubt.

"Do you know who the new host is?"

"No," Philippa said, shaking her head in the other girl's direction. "It's difficult to describe, but I've felt this before . . . when I was in the hospital. I woke up screaming. I tried to explain to the nurses what had happened. They just looked at me as if I was mad."

"You're not mad. You have to try and be strong, Philippa. You can get through this." Alexa stood up and moved toward the door.

"Where are you going?"

"I thought that I'd go and speak to my father. Let him know what has happened, and that you're OK."

"Don't go."

"He'll want to know."

"It's awfully late. Shouldn't you wait until the morning?"

"I think you'll find that Lucien is up, and not just because of your scream. The nighttime is the one time you can be certain that he'll be around. It's the rest of the time that he's harder to find."

Philippa nodded, trying to return the other girl's smile.

Despite what she had just said, Alexa was far from certain

of being able to find her father in the apartment. Unbeknownst to any of them, he had left the previous night. And when she had gone into his office this morning she had been greeted by a huge bloodstain on the carpet. She had shouted out for Tom, the panic rising in her at the sight of the orange-brown circle of dried blood. As Tom arrived, she spotted the note that her father had left on the desktop:

*Please excuse the unsightly mess. I had to leave in a hurry, but I am in no danger.*
*I will be back shortly. L.*

Alexa looked back at Philippa. Taking her hand off the door handle, she crossed the room and went to sit on the bed again. The terror that Philippa had experienced moments ago was writ large on her features, and Alexa had to remind herself what the girl had already gone through. "I'll stay here with you for a while longer if you like, so that you can get back to sleep."

Philippa shook her head and issued a short snort through her nostrils. "Sleep? I don't think I'll be able to sleep again tonight."

"Would you like to talk about it? It might help," Alexa said.

Philippa closed her eyes. "It's terrible," she said. "I start to feel it as it prepares to move from one person to the next. It's as if it's me that is going to possess someone. I can sense the demon's feelings, its anxiety as to how the transfer will go—it's much warier now, and feels it must stay in the host's body longer than it would like to before shifting to a new one. It doesn't want to make the same mistake that it did with my father."

"Can you feel it now?"

"No," she said and, noticing the disappointment on the other girl's face, added, "I'm sorry."

Alexa shook her head. She stared at Philippa, scanning her features, the seed of a plan beginning to take shape. "And you say that you have no idea who the new host is?"

"No."

There was a long pause. "Philippa, do you trust me?"

It was a big question. Alexa sat perfectly still, hoping that the friendship that had started to form between the two of them was sufficiently strong for Philippa to believe that Alexa posed no threat to her safety in any way. Eventually the girl nodded. "Yes, Alexa, I think I do."

"Thank you," Alexa said. She reached over and took the other girl's hand. "I'd like to try something. It involves magic, but I need your permission to try it." She smiled, hoping to mask the doubt and fear that she really felt about what she was proposing to try to do. She knew that she ought to consult with her father before trying out a spell as big as this, and a part of her wished that Trey were here. Trey with his can-do attitude would simply shrug and tell her to go for it—to believe in herself. Because deep inside, she *knew* that she could do this. True, she'd never tried anything like this before, but her powers—along with her confidence in them—were growing, and the moment *felt right*.

"Will this thing that you want to try help us find my father's killer?" Philippa asked, an edge in her voice now. The two girls were of the same age, and she hated to think of how weak and pathetic she must seem to Alexa. She took a breath and nodded. "If so, I think we should try it."

Alexa's expression became serious and intense. A small frown worried her brow, and she turned her attention to the floor between her feet, her lips moving, whispering words in a strange language that Philippa could not make out.

Philippa felt an odd, rolling sensation, like a boat yawing into a particularly high wave. She closed her eyes momentarily, swallowing to stave off the nausea that the sensation had caused in her. When she opened them again she was standing in the center of a large room. It was empty except for a small, white table in front of her. Everything in the room was brilliant white. There were no windows, but the walls and ceiling seemed to give off their own light that washed over her and made her feel safer than she had in a long time. She looked down to see that she too was dressed from head to toe in white, and when she raised her head again she was not surprised to see Alexa standing on the other side of the table from her. The white suit and shirt that the other girl was wearing also gave off that same strange glow and it occurred to Philippa that she looked like some kind of angel.

Alexa looked toward the table and motioned with her head at something on its surface. Philippa glanced down and saw a red hand mirror. It was facedown on the table, the bright color of it at complete odds with the monochrome surroundings. *Blood in the snow*, she thought. A cold shudder ran right through her, and she quickly turned her head away, not wanting to look at the thing.

When she looked back again, Alexa was holding the thing, her arm fully extended toward her. She wanted to ask her about what was happening, but she somehow knew that both she and Alexa were incapable of speech in this place. Alexa nodded again, as if urging her to take the thing from her.

She slowly reached out for it. The mirror seemed impossibly heavy, and Philippa struggled to hold it up with one hand. Her eyes cut to Alexa, and she was relieved to see the other girl's calm and encouraging smile.

Philippa slowly turned the looking glass in her hand so the mirrored surface faced her. Her arm began to shake with the effort, and her heart thumped noisily, quickening her breath. She did not want to look into the mirror—her eyes danced around the edges of the frame instead. But eventually she forced them to rest on the reflective surface and take in what she saw.

There was a face staring back at her. It was a face that she had never seen before, but behind the eyes of the middle-aged man she could sense the real creature that controlled them now—the Necrotroph demon that had inhabited her body and so nearly killed her.

She brought the hand mirror down onto the tabletop, smashing the glass and sending tiny flashing splinters flying into the air.

Philippa opened her eyes and was sitting up in the bed again, Alexa holding her hand.

"Ronald Given," Philippa said, blinking and allowing the tears to snake their way down her cheeks. "It's in a man called Ronald Given. He works for Lucien—he's a mechanic that looks after your father's cars."

Alexa leaned over and hugged her. "Thank you, Philippa," she said.

"Could it see me? Could that thing see me back through that mirror?"

"No," Alexa said. "If there had been any danger of that, I would not have tried what we did." She held the girl at arm's length and looked deep into her eyes. "We will not allow you to come into any further danger, Philippa. You have my promise on that. You need to sleep now. You are perfectly safe here. I need to go and tell someone about this. As soon as I have, I'll come straight back."

She gave the other girl's shoulder one last squeeze, stood up, and exited the room, leaving Philippa alone.

# 11

Trey was truly thankful for the rubber gloves that he'd found under the sink in the kitchen—he hadn't fancied trying to tackle the grime that had been allowed to build up in the house without something on his hands. He'd started in the kitchen, washing everything down with bleach and disinfectant until his eyes smarted from the fumes. He opened all of the windows and the back door, ignoring the shouts from his uncle complaining about the cold drafts. Billy could come and go as he liked via a small flap in the outside door, but Trey had discovered a small key that you could turn to close the little flap. It was shut and locked now, keeping the animal outside while he waited for the floor to dry.

His uncle had issued a small, derisive laugh when Trey had asked if he'd have a problem with him cleaning the place up a bit. "Knock yourself out, kid. You wanna do some spring cleaning around here, go ahead, but don't move any of the furniture around too much. I won't know where the hell I am if you do that."

Frank had then proceeded to get drunk. He'd anchored himself in the chair in the living room, polishing off the remaining whiskey in the half-filled bottle before falling into a deep, and noisy, sleep—his snores filling the house. The sound carried out to the kitchen, a deep and low rumble, like thunder warning of an impending storm.

Trey welcomed the opportunity to do something to get him out of the dingy back room, something that he could do on autopilot and allow him to consider everything that his uncle had already told him. Despite the man's gruff and hostile demeanor, Trey felt a measure of pity for him. He seemed to have been given a tough time of it by Trey's grandfather, and it was little wonder that he had resented his younger brother as a result of being, as no doubt Frank saw it, passed over for the younger son. There was nothing that Trey could do to put that right, but he hoped that he might be able to get to know his uncle a bit more and uncover another side to him.

The floor was almost dry now, and Trey couldn't ignore the scratching sounds at the door any longer. He turned the key on the dog door, and Billy came crashing in through the opening, jumping up at Trey and yapping in delight at having been let in. Trey looked down at the terrier, his eyes met with a head-cocked look of expectancy.

"What is it?" Trey asked. The little dog ran away for two or three steps, before returning to Trey's ankles to assume the quizzical look again. "Hungry?"

A little yap was accompanied by the dog performing a neat little pirouette, its back legs anchored to the floor while the front ones bounced around to describe a tight little circle.

"OK, let's see what we can find for you."

A walk-in pantry was positioned next to the back door, and Trey entered the cool and musty-smelling cupboard, nosing along the shelves for any sign of dog food. Stacked against one wall were four boxes full of bottles of the whiskey that his uncle had been drinking all morning. He moved toward the rear, the gloom at the back of the room making him squint at the writing on the cans that lined the shelves. Like Old Mother Hubbard, it looked as if Frank had neglected to get in any provisions for his four-legged housemate.

He heard a key rattle in the back door and someone entered the house. The outside door slammed into the open pantry one, closing it and plunging Trey into complete darkness.

Billy was barking an excited welcome at whoever it was that had come in, and Trey could just make out the murmured cooing of the visitor greeting the dog back.

The girl had her back to him as he stepped out from the pantry. At the sound of the door opening behind her, she twisted on her heel, raising the large can of dog food over her head to smash it into his. She stopped when she saw him, her eyes taking him in for a second and flicking between him and the back door.

"Who are you?" she asked.

"I was about to ask you the same question," Trey said, studying her.

She was very attractive. Her long blond hair was braided down her back and ice blue eyes stared out at him from a flawless face. She was tall, perhaps an inch or so taller than Trey, and dressed in a white blouse with jeans that showed off her legs. He thought that she must be about seventeen or eighteen years old.

"My name's Trey," he said, extending his hand in greeting.

She was still holding the heavy metal can over her head, and she made no effort to lower it and take up his proffered handshake.

"And what the hell are you doing in here?" she asked. She had a slight accent. Trey couldn't quite work out what it was, but it sounded vaguely Scandinavian. He idly wondered if he just assumed this because it fit with her appearance. Standing there defiantly waving a heavy can of food as a weapon, she certainly looked as though she could be from Viking stock.

"I'm Frank's nephew. I turned up this morning. I've come over from England to visit him."

"Frank's never said anything to me about having any kin. How do I know you are who you say you are? You could be a burglar for all I know."

"A burglar in the pantry?" Trey said, raising an eyebrow.

"It's all right, Ella." Frank's voice came from the doorway behind her. Neither Trey nor the girl had heard him creep up to the kitchen. "He's my brother's son."

She slowly lowered the makeshift bludgeon, but her face

maintained the cold, hard look that she had worn throughout the encounter. She nodded toward Trey by way of a greeting.

"Nice to meet you too," Trey said.

"If you two want to get acquainted, keep the noise down, I'm trying to get some sleep in here," his uncle said, turning his back on them and shuffling away noisily. "And one of you can fetch me a bottle of Scotch from the pantry there. Someone's drunk all mine."

They sat down at the kitchen table together, two cups of coffee resting on the gaudy light blue Formica top between them. A lance of light coming in from the window illuminated dust particles that danced lazily in the air. Ella sat in the chair opposite Trey who, try as he might, couldn't help but stare at the puckered pink scar that dominated her right forearm. She made no effort to conceal the wound with clothing, and when she lifted her cup to her lips, the snaking scar was shown off to its best effect.

"How'd you get it?" Trey said, knowing there was little point in pretending he had not been looking at it. "The scar, I mean. It looks nasty."

Ella's eyes held his for an uncomfortable moment. "Yes, it is—was—nasty. Are you always so rude when you meet someone for the first time, or have you been picking up tips from your uncle?"

"I'm sorry, I didn't mean to—"

"It's OK. It *is* quite some scar." She gazed down at it, a sad smile forming on her lips.

"It looks like some kind of animal bite," Trey said, looking at her carefully over the rim of his cup.

The girl did not respond; instead she turned her head and smiled at Billy, who was wolfing down the food that she had placed in his bowl.

Trey took the opportunity to study her face more closely and discovered that she was even prettier than he had first thought. Her eyes were so blue that he was almost convinced that the color could not be natural, but there was no evidence of the contact lenses he had suspected. She had a strong jaw line, but this was softened by full, luscious lips that lent her a permanent pouty look that he knew Hollywood film stars paid a fortune to achieve with collagen injections.

She became aware of his attention and returned his stare, a hint of a smile forming on her mouth when she noticed his embarrassment.

"How do you know my uncle?" Trey asked.

"I live on his land," she answered. "In a cabin, next to a lake a little to the west of here." She stopped, looking directly at him as if trying to calculate how much he already knew. "A number of us live there. I'm guessing that's why you came here?"

It was Trey's turn to avoid eye contact now, and he used the surface of the hot drink as a means to that end. "You said a number of you live here. How many?"

"There are six of us. The new LG78."

"LG78," Trey said, more to himself than to her. "I've

heard of you. You're all Wolfan, aren't you? Werewolves."
He looked up, frowning at her. "But I thought that the LG78
had disbanded, that it had been split up."

"You say Wolfan like it's a dirty word, Trey. As if you
did not carry the same blood in your veins as your uncle.
Why is that?"

"I didn't mean—"

"Yes, you did. But that's OK. Everyone finds it hard at
first. Even our own kind."

There was a silence, punctuated only by the sounds of
the dog snaffling its food out of its bowl.

"You're a girl," Trey said.

"Well done. I see that your grasp of anatomy is as finely
honed as your manners and conversational skills." She looked
over and smiled at him for the first time. It was a full and
genuine smile, and it utterly disarmed him.

"I just meant—"

"I'm a *Bitten*. A bite survivor. That's how I came to have
this lovely-looking trophy on my arm. But I sense that you'd
already figured that out for yourself. I'm the only female
werewolf alive anywhere in the world. How do you like that?
I'm unique—imagine that."

Trey didn't have to imagine anything. As the last full-
blood hereditary werewolf he knew exactly how she felt.

She stood up, the chair scraping against the floor tiles
behind her. "Jurgen will want to meet you," she said.

"Who's Jurgen?"

The smile slipped away from her face and she cut her eyes toward the door, as if expecting Frank to be standing there again. "How much has your uncle told you?" she asked with a coldness in her voice that he had not heard before.

"Who's Jurgen?" he repeated.

"Jurgen's the pack leader," she said. "He's the Alpha male."

# 12

Trey stepped through the front door, and the usual oppressive silence of his uncle's house greeted him until Billy came up to welcome him back with a little bark. He reached down and gave the dog's ears a playful rub and was rewarded with a lick on the hand.

He took off his coat and hung it over the bottom of the banister. He'd been for a walk to think about things and prepare himself for the evening ahead when he would witness his uncle Change with the full moon while locked inside that metal cage. He walked up the hallway and looked in at the reclining figure of Frank, who had drunk himself into another blind stupor. If Trey hadn't seen him do the exact same thing for the last two days, he might have assumed that Frank only did this on the day of the full moon— Dutch courage in preparation for the ordeal of having to lock himself away in that enclosure. But that clearly wasn't the case. Frank was a chronic alcoholic. The drink made him even more scratchy and insufferable than he was when sober, a fact that Trey would not have believed possible had he not witnessed it firsthand over the short time that he had spent here in the house.

"What are you lookin' at?" his uncle shouted across the

room at him. Trey had thought his uncle was asleep, and the sudden outburst made him jump in alarm. The man had an eerie ability of knowing when he was being watched. "Don't think you can stand there gawking at me as if I'm some exhibit at the damn zoo. I might be blind, but I know what you're thinking. I won't be judged by you, you understand?" His uncle reached out for his glass again.

"I didn't ask you to come here, did I?" Frank's voice was slurred as if his tongue were too big and thick for his mouth. "I didn't invite you. If you don't like what I am and what I do, you can go back to England. Go back to your vampire friend, Lucien Charron." His uncle spat those last words, staring ahead of him, waiting for a response that never came.

Trey let the silence draw out for a moment or two. Out of the corner of his eye he saw the terrier, Billy, making his escape into the kitchen. The dog clearly knew when it was best not to be around its owner.

Trey wasn't so easily perturbed. He stepped into the room and took up a seat on the settee facing his uncle. He heard the dog flap in the back door swing open and shut. *Coward,* he thought.

"Do you get scared?" Trey asked when it was clear that the old man had calmed down a little.

"Scared?"

"Of the Change. I don't know what it feels like for you. I know that the talisman means that I can change to and from my particular werewolf form without too much pain, but I remember the first time that I almost changed involuntarily and the pain was—"

"It's like being ripped apart from the inside," his uncle interrupted. "Like something reaches up your arse, grabs hold of a big handful of you, and then turns you inside out like a pair of jeans. You feel like you're going to die. And the pain doesn't stop. It just keeps going, more and more of it piling in on top of itself until all you are *is* pain. You want to die it's so bad. You want to smash your skull into the nearest wall and let your brains fall to the floor so you can stamp on them and stop the pain."

Frank turned his head to look at Trey through blind eyes. "Is it anything like that for you?" he asked with a sneer.

"No."

"Didn't think so," Frank said and lifted his glass to his lips.

"Tell me about the LG78," Trey said after another long silence.

"What do you want to know?"

"Uncle Frank . . . please."

The old man sighed and closed his eyes. "LG stands for Loup Garou: the French word for *werewolf.* I always thought it sounded much more elegant—more refined, you know? The first time a bunch of us got together in 1978, we called ourselves the LG78. We formed a pack—a pack of were-wolves. It took quite a while, but I finally bought this land and then got some demon lord to place some Netherworld hoodoo-voodoo on the place to protect us from your friend Lucien's brother, who at that point was intent on killing anything and everything that even smelled wolfish. I paid a heavy price for that protection, but it was worth it because we knew we could be safe here, we could exist together."

"We?"

"Me and a bunch of other lycos." He turned his head to face Trey, his eyes dancing backward and forward in their sockets. The spite and anger that had been in his tone moments before had dissipated now, and he continued. "There are advantages to being in a pack, Trey. That feeling of running through a forest with the other members of your group, the feeling of unity and trust and . . . love that you have for your pack members. It's exhilarating. Truly, there is nothing like it. It's the best feeling in the world."

Trey frowned, trying to assimilate what his uncle had just said. Finally, he voiced his concerns to the old man, who was still looking over in his direction, a smile forming on his lips as if he could read the boy's thoughts.

"You told me that you don't remember what happens to you during the Change. You told me that you'd wake up in the middle of nowhere not knowing how you got there . . . or what you had done." Trey thought back to the morning after he had experienced his first-ever Change and the amnesic void that he'd felt—his·room and possessions all destroyed without any clue as to who, or what, might have done it.

"That's right."

"Then how—"

"You're talking about a moon-induced Change, like the delightful little episode that I shall be experiencing tonight, or indeed an accidental Change that can occur if a lyco completely loses control of his emotions—unabated anger can bring that Change about. And yes, an unfortunate—or fortunate, depending on how you look at it—result of that is an almost complete memory loss for the lycanthrope. Once the transformation is complete, there's nothing. Maybe the odd snippet—the tiniest fraction of a memory, like a rogue image here or there—but nothing that you can put your finger on." He paused, letting this sink in, before adding in a small voice, "You normally get to read the results of your actions in the papers the next day, when some poor soul gets found with his throat torn out." He shook his head. "But as I said, there are advantages to being in a pack."

The old man waved his fingers in the air before him. "All of my memories of being a Wolfan—all of the emotions and experiences that I've just described—are from Changes that were *not* during a full moon." He stopped, waiting for an interruption that didn't come. "That's only possible in a pack because the members of a pack can induce the Change in each other whether the moon is on the wax or the wane. Day or night, they can become lycos."

Trey stared at his uncle, trying to take this in. "So it's like having the amulet, it's like—"

"No, it's nothing like that. We were still Wolfan, still animalistic in our needs and urges." He stopped again, trying to find the best way to explain. "It's as if the pack exerts a mass will. We discovered it quite by chance. A few of us found each other over the years. We kept in touch and became friends, sharing experiences and concerns. Eventually, some of us—those first few, back in 1978—decided to get together at a full moon for the Change, have a group lockdown, as it were. We found a strong room that was large enough to take us all and we settled in together for the night. It wasn't until the next morning, when we were all talking, discussing how frustrating it was not to be able to remember and wishing that we could, that it happened. We began to morph. All of us. All at the same time. But it wasn't like it was the night before, the pain was nowhere near as bad or as long, and afterward we could . . . remember. We were able to remember what had happened." He shook his head, recalling. "That first time . . . it was out of this world. It was the most exciting thing that I'd ever experienced.

"I had a bit of money back then. Some of the others pitched in with what they could, and eventually I bought this place. A huge swath of land that we could live on. We fenced it off to keep out intruders, and we all moved here and set up a community by the lake. We had cabins built. We were happy . . . really happy."

"What happened?"

"Nothing at first. Like I say, we were happy. But then we had a few problems. A few . . . breakages of the rules."

"Rules?"

"Yeah, we had rules. You can't have twenty lycos living together in a community without rules. So we had specific days that we would set aside to morph as a pack. Nobody was allowed to go off in a splinter group and do their own thing. You need a minimum of three, you see? Three is the magic number."

Trey shook his head. "Three what?"

The old man shook his head and sighed as if he were in the presence of a simpleton.

"You need three or more lycos to enforce the Change, and they need to be in close proximity to one another. A pair of lycos can't get it to happen."

"What other rules did you have?"

"We could date outsiders—non-lycos—but they weren't allowed anywhere near the community on one of these set days." He nodded as though remembering the importance of this rule. "Anything on four legs was fair game as far as hunting was concerned, but there was a strict rule on never killing anything on *two legs*—if you know what I mean. And finally, we were still to lockdown during the full moon—we were very strict on that."

"Which rules were broken?"

"All of them," he said and looked away.

"All of them?" Trey said, thinking about the third rule. "People were killed by the pack? Hunted?"

His uncle batted the questions away. "Bad things happened. The community went into meltdown. I blame your father."

Trey blinked, surprised by the way that Frank had casually thrown this remark in at the end. "Why do you blame my dad?"

"He undermined me. He came to visit me with his new girlfriend, your mother, Elisabeth—they weren't married then. Said that he wanted to see what we had set up over here. He was being nosy, sticking his muzzle in where it wasn't wanted. He threw the whole community into disarray."

"How?"

"That thing around your neck for one. Some of them had heard about the amulet and the powers that it gave to the lyco wearing it. I guess it must have seemed strange to them that it had passed to my younger bother, and not me. His presence undermined my authority as the Alpha. Oh, he never made any attempt to displace me or anything . . . not openly. But Daniel had a way about him—he was so confident and sure of himself that some of the pack thought that maybe *he* should be the Alpha. Your father said that he had no intention of staying and taking over as the pack leader, but I think he was lying. The pack started to in-fight and it was impossible for me to stop it." He stopped and sucked at his teeth, considering how to go on. "Then there was the incident with your mother."

Trey held his breath, waiting. The clock ticked loudly on the wall.

His uncle lifted his glass, finishing off the last of the whiskey. "She was walking down by the lake one evening when she was attacked. She was lucky to survive." He shook his head, letting the statement hang in the air between them. "Nobody admitted to doing it. It wasn't a day when the pack had planned to hunt, so there shouldn't have been any

Wolfan about. Like I say, you need at least three lycos to force the Change, and everybody could account for their whereabouts at the time of the attack. Everyone except your father, that is. People said that it might have been an accident, that something had gone wrong and that he attacked her; others said that he had planned it, that he wanted to turn her—make her into a female lyco so that he wouldn't have to endure the curse alone. I think that it *was* an accident, that he lost control over the werewolf inside him and attacked her."

Trey looked over at the old man, his vision blurred by tears, unable to take in what had just been said.

"But he had the amulet . . . he had control over his powers."

His uncle set the glass down, shrugging as he did so. "What can I say? *Maybe* that amulet he and your grandfather were so damn keen on isn't all it's cracked up to be? Maybe we lycos are so dangerous and unstable that even if you're wearing a thing like that, you're not safe to be around. Maybe it's love that makes the thing go haywire because love makes you vulnerable, protective, threatened. Maybe love takes charge of the most primal and base emotions and overrides the influence of that thing around your neck?" The old man turned his face toward Trey's, his upper lip lifting in a sneer. "I wouldn't know. I never got a chance to wear it."

Trey was glad that his uncle could not see the tears that flowed freely down his face.

"It was decided that your father was trouble. He was banished, and he took your mother home to France." His uncle stopped and frowned, the silence seemed to press in on Trey from every angle. "Luckily for her, and for you I guess, Elisabeth survived her injuries." Frank nodded as if answering some unspoken question.

The ticking of the clock seemed to have grown so loud that Trey thought he could feel the molecules in the air jump each time the hand leaped forward another notch. He shook his head and stared at the carpet in front of him, unable to believe what he had just heard.

"You *did* know that, didn't you? You did know how your mother came to be one of us?"

"No. No, I didn't."

"Aw, kid, I'm sorry. I thought that you must have known. I thought that someone—your friend Lucien, maybe—would have told you."

"No."

His uncle shook his head. "Well, I'm sorry that you had to hear it like that. At least you now know what your father was and what he was capable of."

Trey looked over at his uncle. Despite what the old man had said, Trey doubted that he was at all sorry for telling him what had happened all those years ago. He hadn't sounded sorry. Trey stood up.

"What happened to the pack?" he asked, his voice cracking with emotion as he struggled to get the words out.

"We disbanded not long after your mother and father

left. The whole thing had gotten out of hand and there was none of the unity that we had had when we first formed. People were forming their own groups—Changing in small packs and hunting when they shouldn't. A few of them refused to lockdown, and then people on the outside started to get killed. The whole thing went to hell in a handcart, so I threw the worst offenders out and disbanded the pack."

"But there's a new pack now," Trey said. "Ella told me that there was a new pack and a new Alpha, Jurgen. If everything went so wrong with the original LG78, what would possess you to allow a new pack to begin again here?"

"Money." The old man let the word hang in the air between them. "That's right, money. This Jurgen guy approached me about a year ago, telling me that he wanted to try and form a pack again. I told him that it was futile, but he was pretty insistent. He's a rich kid, and when I say rich, I'm talking *seriously* wealthy. His dad used to be a member of the original pack, but he didn't stick around—went off to Russia and made a fortune in natural gas. Anyway, the kid offered me a load of cash if I would let them use the land in the same way that we used to. There's elk and moose here to hunt, the cabins are all down by the lake, and the fences are still up to keep out intruders. His dad had told him stories about the old days, and this Jurgen fell in love with the whole idea. He even wanted to keep the old name. For old times' sake, he said, he still wanted to call it the LG78. They've been here for about six months now."

Trey stared at the old man in disbelief. "Ella. The girl

99

that came here yesterday. She's a Bitten. She was attacked like my mother." He waited for a reaction. "Did that happen here?"

Frank let out a long sigh, puffing out his lips as he did so. "What can I tell you? History has a way of repeating itself, kid." The old man reached for his bottle, frowning when he discovered that it was empty. "While you're up, how about getting your uncle a fresh one, huh?"

Trey looked down at the old man, glad that his only living relative could not see the look of hatred on his face. "Get it yourself," he said and turned, heading for the front door.

# 13

Lucien filtered out the noise of the train driver's announcement that came through the speaker above his head. His eyes were screwed shut, and he hunched forward in his seat, willing the train to start moving again toward the next station so that he could get aboveground and call Tom to come and get him.

It had been two days since the incident in his office, and he hadn't been back to the apartment in all that time. Instead, he'd spent the days cooped up in another place he had in Mayfair and the nights walking the London streets, deep in thought about what was happening to him. Yesterday he'd called Alexa and Tom to let them know he was OK, and that he just needed some time alone. It wasn't unusual for him to go off like this, but with everything else going on right now, they were keen for him to come back.

The train had been stuck in the tube tunnel now for a little over fifteen minutes and this announcement—like the last two—was another apology for the delay. Opening his eyes, he glanced at his watch again trying to calculate how long it had been since he'd left the place in Mayfair. He must have been walking for a very long time—too long. His stomach twisted again and he hissed through his teeth in pain. He kept his head low and his eyes fixed on the dirty floor at his feet, knowing that if he looked up his eyes would be drawn to the two other night owls who shared the carriage with him, on their way home from whatever late pursuits they had been involved in. His fellow travelers had thankfully taken seats as far away from him as possible, but he was aware of their furtive glances in his direction. It was understandable—if he'd stepped onto a train late at night and seen somebody like him in the carriage, he'd have found a seat well away from them too. He tried to force himself not to think about them—it was too dangerous.

He had no idea what had made him come down into the underground system. He'd been walking, oblivious to everything around him. He'd made up his mind that he needed to talk to someone, or something, about what was happening to him and had been mentally going through a list of possible candidates. He'd been completely unaware of where he was. And somehow he'd ended up here on this train. Of all the places that he could have found himself right now, a train was not one that he would have picked. He looked at his watch again. His blood delivery was due any moment now. He'd redirected the courier and they would leave it for him, but . . .

He took his handkerchief out of his jacket pocket again, using it to wipe away the perspiration on his top lip. Another cramp jarred through his body and this time he was unable to stifle the low groan that escaped his lips. He'd asked for his daily delivery of blood to be increased from two to three bags, hoping that more of the stuff might help stave off some of the desires that he'd been having. He'd left with the intention of being back at the apartment in plenty of time for the delivery. And now here he was, on a sealed tube train compartment with a blood lust building inside him by the minute. He tried to block out any thoughts of the two humans in the carriage. But that was impossible.

When he was younger he would have killed them, torn through the train like the wrath of God and taken blood from anyone on board, leaving their dead and mutilated bodies for the authorities to find. He screwed his eyes shut tight, trying to dismiss these terrible memories. He could not allow himself to think like this, not here, not now.

He forced himself to concentrate on other matters. He wondered if Alexa had been successful in recruiting the Ashnon, and if he should not have sought out the creature himself. They needed the demon on their side if his plans for the Necrotroph were to be realized. If she had failed, he would take over from her and force the demon to see sense. And then there was Trey. The boy had not been in contact again since the first message that had been relayed to them via Galroth. Lucien would have to discuss with the demon the possibility of dropping in on the boy again. He would see to these matters as soon as he got back to the apartment—put his mind and efforts toward something concrete.

He relaxed a little. Puffing out his cheeks, he unclenched the tight knot of flesh and bone that he had made of his hands.

A breeze blew into the carriage from the window in the door at the far end. His body instantly stiffened again. He could smell them.

The woman's scent was the strongest—a mixture of sweat and perfume and stale alcohol that excited him. He thought again of the delicious thrill that had rippled through his every cell as he'd sucked the blood from the bag the other day, imagining the metallic taste on his tongue again. He breathed in deeply through his nostrils, mixing the smell of the woman's scent with the memory of that taste. He had no idea what she or her companion looked like, how old or young they might be, but it was of little consequence. If he did not get off the train soon, they would look like all of the others that he had killed throughout his earlier years—wilted husks of corpses lying in a pool of their own blood.

The speaker crackled to life above him. The driver apologized again in a voice that sounded anything but apologetic, and informed them that they might be stuck for some time yet due to a problem in the tunnel up ahead.

A groan escaped Lucien. He couldn't stay on this train any longer.

He rose to his feet and glanced toward the sliding doors to his right. He stumbled in their direction, trying to keep his eyes glued to them and not let them drift over to the couple sitting in the seats at the periphery of his vision.

He failed. His eyes tracked to the side and he took in the warm-blooded creatures.

They sat and giggled at each other, speaking in whispers. A loud squeal of delight came from the woman, and she looked up in Lucien's direction. The laughter died in her throat as she caught sight of the tall, bald man glaring at them both through baleful eyes that seemed to blaze with a golden light. The woman's smile was replaced by a look of pure fear, and she cut her eyes toward her male companion, hoping to find some reassurance there, but seeing only the same doubt and panic that she herself felt beneath the vampire's terrible stare.

Through his eyes, Lucien no longer saw them as people. Right now they were little more than meat to him. The woman's earlier excitement had caused the hot blood to flow quickly through her veins and arteries, and to the vampire, these bloody highways appeared as an intricate map of black roads just beneath her skin. His eyes were instantly drawn to the fat motorway on her neck that was her carotid artery as it pulsed and bulged with every pump of her heart.

He remembered his youth again and how he had fed upon countless young women like her. His tongue snaked in his mouth, the tip seeking out the area where his fangs had once been before he had had them removed. In truth, the act of being defanged was more a gesture to himself—a symbol—rather than any real attempt to remove a danger, and he knew that he was more than capable of tearing these

105

two people apart with his bare hands to sate the desires that boiled within him.

He swallowed loudly, averting his gaze from the blood map on the woman's skin and forcing his attention back to the carriage doors. In the blackened windows his reflection stared back at him, and he recognized himself as the monster that the woman had seen.

His hands were trembling as he reached forward. He jammed his fingers between the black rubber seals between the two sliding doors, and forced his hands apart, his colossal strength easily opening the doors to reveal the filth-encrusted, black tunnel beyond. Ignoring the loud alarm that filled his ears, he took in a huge lungful of the cold, rank air of the tunnel, and jumped down out of the carriage into the space at the side of the train. He turned and began to run, the complete darkness no problem to him as he made his way back along the underground channel deep beneath the streets of London. He needed to get back to the station that the train had come from. He needed to call for Tom to come and rescue him.

"What were you thinking, Lucien?" Tom said from the front of the car that he was driving back toward home.

He had received the call from the vampire and sped through town collecting more flashes from speed cameras than he could possibly count.

"It was a mistake," Lucien said from the backseat. He had

drunk his fill from the bag of blood that Tom had brought with him, and he was beginning to feel a return to normality.

"You don't make mistakes," the Irishman said, catching sight of his boss in the rearview mirror. "I have *never* known you to make a mistake."

Lucien closed his eyes and allowed his head to fall back against the headrest. Tom carried on talking, but the words were nothing but a background noise to Lucien as he tried to get his thoughts and emotions back in check.

What was happening? Why would he allow himself to lose control and put himself in the position that he just had? To risk everything that he had struggled to achieve?

He thought of his young ward, Trey, and how he'd told the boy of the need to master his own powers. How he should not, could not, be ruled by the creature that lived inside him. And he remembered how the teenager had described the feeling of being truly *alive* when he had first morphed into his werewolf state, how the strength and the might and the power had felt so . . . *right*.

Lucien had sworn that he would never return to the thing that he had once been—a taker of lives, a harbinger of death that fed upon the blood and misery of others. And yet tonight he had acted in a way that suggested that a part of him at least still yearned for that *rightness of being* that Trey had described.

He opened his eyes, catching Tom looking at him in the rearview mirror, and turned his head to stare out the window, looking out as the darkened London streets slipped by. He realized how exhausted he felt. His shoulder ached.

"How are Alexa and our guest?" he asked.

"They're fine. The Ashnon has been in contact again. It said to tell you that it was hungry."

"Good. Then we shall see to it that the creature's appetite is well and truly sated," Lucien said, regretting the choice of words as soon as they'd left his mouth.

# 14

Ronald Given sank back into his bed and stared up at the ceiling. He had been feeling unwell all day. A black, nagging pain seemed to emanate from his stomach and spread out to every part of him. He grimaced again, screwing up his eyes and hissing as another hot knife of pain stabbed through his abdomen, his hand automatically clutching at his midriff.

Something moved there. Something shifted beneath his hand, squirming away from his touch. He gasped in horror and sat up in the bed, looking around him in the darkness. He had to warn Lucien. He had to tell his boss that . . .

The thought dispersed and dissolved; despite his attempts to fix it in his mind, it dissipated away into nothingness. He lay back down again, frowning to himself and trying to remember what had just happened. A pain lanced through him, but he ignored it this time, as if it were not his pain at all, but that of someone else.

Ronald Given stared up at the ceiling through eyes that no longer communicated with his brain, entering a deep catatonic state.

The Necrotroph cursed its sloppiness and closed down all the nonessential systems inside the host body. It took complete control again and erased the thoughts that the man had just experienced.

The demon could not afford any more errors—*not after what happened in the Seychelles with the human Martin Tipsbury and his daughter.* The vampire lord, Caliban, had promised that the price for failing to re-infiltrate Lucien's organization would be a long and agonizing death at the hands of some hell-beast or another.

It was the girl who was playing on its mind, the girl who was causing it to make stupid mistakes by allowing its concentration to slip. Caliban did not know the Necrotroph had failed to extinguish Philippa Tipsbury in that boat on the Indian Ocean.

The Necrotroph had not heard back from the demon that it had sent to kill her at the hospital. More worryingly, nobody had seen hide nor hair of the Incubus since. It should have gone itself. It needed that girl dead. It needed to be sure that the worrying feeling that it had been experiencing since the Seychelles—the feeling that it was being watched—was not something to do with her. Because it did feel that it was being watched, a feeling that was uncomfortable for a creature that thrived on being undetectable to both human and nether-creature alike.

If anything became capable of detecting its movements, of knowing where, and who, it was . . . The demon shuddered to think what the outcome of that little scenario might be. But it couldn't shake the nagging doubt that something was wrong, and that it was something to do with that girl.

That damn girl who had refused to die. The demon tried to steer its thoughts to other matters—it needed to go through the next stage of its plans so that nothing would be left to chance.

The demon knew that it had done well to get this far undetected. It had needed to make some swift transfers to get into this body, and it thought that it was now only two more steps away from being at the heart of Lucien Charron's empire again. The older man that it currently inhabited worked for the vampire. He had access to most of the staff's cars and, as a result, was on friendly terms with the head of security, the Irishman Tom. The demon snickered at its audacity. It would take some effort to pull it off undetected, but it needed something big like this to show its master that it was still an essential cog in Caliban's plans—it never did to have the boss uncertain of your worth. So it had decided to do what it had not dared the last time it was on the inside of the organization—go straight to the person closest to Lucien Charron, his friend and confidante, the human Tom O'Callahan.

It knew that if it could get the Irishman away from the vampire for a while it could take him over. It would need to be sure to be on guard at all times, and completely suppress the Irishman host. It would use the mechanic to get the Irishman away from the building, making up some story about needing to take his car to his lock-up garage and needing a lift back. Then it would strike. And when it did, it would make its way back into the soft underbelly of Lucien

Charron's empire where it could help its master to destroy it forever.

The Necrotroph settled the current host down into the bed, allowing itself to relax a little and savor its impending triumph. It would soon be able to dispense with this body and take control of a key player in Lucien's organization. It smiled to itself and considered the havoc that it could wreak once its plans came to fruition. It closed the human's eyes and settled back to rest.

*I can sense you, Necrotroph.*

The body of Ronald Given sat bolt upright in the bed, his eyes scanning the darkness.

The voice seemed to whisper into the human's mind, and the sound sent a cold shudder of fear through the demon. It recognized the voice. Indeed, it should, it had spoken with that same voice for a while. It was the voice of the Tipsbury girl—the girl that it had left in the hull of a boat in the middle of the Indian Ocean.

*I might not know exactly where you are right now, but I can sense that you are out there.*

A bead of sweat trickled down the human's forehead, and he blinked as the salty liquid found its way into his right eye.

*I thought that I was mad. But I'm not, am I? You changed something inside of me forever, and now I can sense you out there. There are people who are interested in finding you, Necrotroph. People who came to visit me at the hospital. They saved me from the assassin that you sent to kill me, and now they are keeping me safe. Keeping me safe so that I can*

*help them find you. And I believe that I will be able to find
you, demon. I can't quite yet, but soon I think that I will be able
to do just that.*

"Bitch!" the demon hissed, rising to its feet from the
bed. "I'll kill you, do you hear me? I'll find you and tear you
apart from the inside." But the voice had gone. The demon
stared wildly around the room and smashed a fist into the
wall, closing off the pain receptors that screamed off elec-
trical signals to the brain as a result.

The human was panting. The demon had allowed its
control of the host to slip again, the host body was reacting
to the adrenaline coursing through its bloodstream. The
Necrotroph quickly took control and calmed the host down.

It needed to act quickly. It needed to get inside the vampire's domain as quickly as possible and get rid of the girl.

Ronald Given sank back down onto the edge of the bed,
his head in his hands. The Necrotroph knew that if the powers that the Tipsbury girl had described were real, then they
would indeed become more acute and that she would be
able to find it anywhere in this world or the demon realm. It
couldn't allow that to happen. It couldn't allow Charron to
know where it was, or it was doomed.

It needed to get at the girl. And quickly.

# 15

They'd all gathered in the living room to watch Alexa perform the magic that enabled her to speak to the Necrotroph through Philippa's voice. The young sorceress had sat on the settee with the other girl by her side. They held hands as Alexa spoke the words in a long-dead language, putting the girl into a deep trance.

Alexa looked at Philippa on the seat next to her. The girl's body was set rigidly, as though all of the muscles had locked at once, giving her an inelegant, mannequin-like appearance. The sorceress smiled sadly across at her, lifting her hand to push aside a strand of hair that had fallen across the girl's face. She glanced up at her father who responded with a swift nod of encouragement. He had been in a strange mood all day. He and Tom had arrived home late last night and he had hardly said a word to her all day, choosing to lock himself in his office instead. She had the distinct feeling that it was not her that he was avoiding, but the girl currently sitting by her side. As if, for some reason, he felt uncomfortable in her company.

She pushed these strange thoughts away, concentrating on the task at hand.

She closed her eyes, allowing the magic to enter her. It

was the first time that she had attempted this spell, and it would need all of her skill and focus to pull it off. She felt a part of herself reach out toward Philippa, nudging at the girl's consciousness and feeling a grudging resistance. A frown briefly flickered across her brow, and she tried again, pushing harder, and this time she felt the girl's opposition begin to give a little.

And then suddenly she was in—inside Philippa's mind.

She gasped. It was like swimming, swimming through a sea of somebody's life—a billion thoughts, feelings, emotions, and experiences were there, all clamoring for her attention. In her mind's eye she imagined them as an infinity of tiny fish, a curtain of color that shimmered and parted in front of her as she slowly made her way through them. It was beautiful. She was moving through another person's mind, and she reveled in the experience. The initial euphoria and wonder that she felt was almost too much for Alexa, but she slowly managed to pull herself together and began to move her way deep inside Philippa's psyche to locate the part that she was looking for—the region of her brain that had been irredeemably changed by the demon.

And then she sensed it up ahead, sensed it before she saw it—a darkness in among the twisting, iridescent world before her. Alexa knew that the black, festering mass had no right to be inside the girl, and she had to fight the urge to attack the thing in some way, to remove the foul tumorlike object that represented the dark magic of the nether-creature. But to do so would damage Philippa. Besides, they needed it—it was their only hope of finding and stopping the creature responsible for it being there. So she *swam* toward it, knowing that through it she would be able to locate the Necrotroph.

The magic was exhausting, requiring Alexa to form a huge envelope of energy around the two of them. In addition she was using another person's body as a conduit for the magic, and it required every inch of her strength and skill and concentration. She tried not to think of the toll that this was taking on her, or how long it might take her to recover from it once it was all over. Such thoughts were counterproductive right now and could jeopardize what she was hoping to achieve.

She hesitated in front of the thing, not wanting anything to do with the dark magic that it represented. Then she dived into the black morass, and as soon as she did so, she could sense the Necrotroph. It was terrible and terrifying being inside that dreadful blackness, but she spoke to the nether-creature, delivering the speech that she and her father had cooked up together, pleased when it reacted in the way that they had hoped it would. The nether-creature's anger and fear were almost palpable, and she reveled in its discomfort.

When she finally freed herself from the spell, she slumped back into the cushions, letting out a great sigh of exhaustion and relief that it had gone as they'd planned. She felt Philippa stirring next to her and realized that she still had her own eyes closed. She opened them, surprised at the effort that even this simple action required.

"How did it go?" Lucien asked, offering his daughter a glass of cold water. "Was our fish hooked?"

She smiled wearily back at him, gratefully accepting the proffered glass—magic required, and created, huge amounts of energy. Many spells, like the one she had just cast, created heat; others created cyclonic winds or bright lights, telekinetic forces that caused items to fly around the room, and some created powers so strong that only the greatest mages were able to perform them without themselves being torn apart. Alexa drank greedily from the glass, her hand raised in front of her to indicate that she would answer as soon as she had slaked her thirst.

"The Necro freaked out. It started screaming and shouting about how it was going to find Philippa and tear her apart. I'd say that the bait was well and truly taken."

Lucien nodded and turned to Tom, who was standing at his side. "You see? The demon is convinced that Philippa will develop the ability to locate it. It will need to make a move against her sooner rather than later." The vampire smiled reassuringly at Philippa. He leaned forward and gently placed his hand on her shoulder. It was the first time since they had met that she had not drawn back from his presence, let alone his touch.

"You are not in danger, Philippa. I will not allow any further harm to come to you. All we need to do is keep the

117

tension on the line, and we can catch ourselves a particularly nasty little nether-creature."

The last person in the room grunted something unintelligible, and shifted against the leather seat. Lucien turned to look at the Ashnon, which dipped its head in the vampire's direction, flashing a fierce smile.

Tom looked across at the thing as it sprawled back into the cushions. The Ashnon had been with them for the entire day, but the Irishman's brain could not comprehend that the figure sitting opposite him was *not* Maude Turner, the member of Lucien's staff who he had known for so long.

"What do we do now?" Tom asked, still staring at the old woman on the settee.

"Now? We wait," said Lucien. "We wait and see what the Necrotroph's next move will be. It will be forced to take action against Philippa here. It needs to remove her as quickly as possible. Remember, it doesn't know that we are aware of whose body it currently inhabits. My guess is that it will make its move in the next day or so."

"Poor Ronald," Alexa said.

"Indeed," Lucien replied. "But the demon had already taken control of his body when we found out. There was nothing that we could do to save him. But we *can* stop this demon from ever doing it to anyone else."

"Another family destroyed by that . . . thing," Philippa said, speaking for the first time since they had all gathered together.

They turned and looked at the girl, noting the tears that snaked their way down her cheeks.

Alexa squeezed the girl's hand. "There have been thousands of families destroyed by that creature, Philippa. But we are here to stop it. For good. And we are only able to do that because of you and the unique power that you now have."

"Ahem, aren't you forgetting that you need my help in all this?" The Ashnon raised an eyebrow and clicked its teeth together—an action that looked completely out of place when performed in the body of a seventy-year-old woman. The demon was in a temporary body that it had *borrowed* while they made their preparations. Maude Turner was an elderly tea lady who had worked for Lucien for a number of years. It had been Lucien who had approached her to discuss the possibility of the body swap. She had recently been diagnosed with cancer, and the deal was an easy one for her to agree to—she lent the Ashnon her identity for a few days, and when she came back to this realm, it would be in a body that was completely cancer free. It would bemuse and befuddle the doctors; they had told her that she had only a matter of months to live.

"Of course," Lucien said, turning and grinning in the old lady's direction. "The real work of permanently removing the Necrotroph will be done by our friend here."

"And how exactly will you be doing that?" Tom asked.

The Ashnon grinned back at the Irishman, meeting his stare with its own. "You just leave that to me, OK? Think of me as pest control. If there is one thing that we Ashnon are good at, it's removing vermin like that Necrotroph—it's what we were created for." The old lady turned to look at Philippa, smiling kindly at the girl who somehow managed to return the smile despite her fears.

"Now then, my dear," the demon said. "How do you fancy a trip of a lifetime to the Waldorf-Astoria hotel in New York?"

# 16

Trey slammed the front door behind him and stood on the porch sucking in great, burning lungfuls of cold air. He tried to calm himself down, blinking away the tears that welled up and blurred his vision. He stepped off the wooden platform and onto the hard-packed mud that constituted the driveway, making toward the woods. He had no idea where he was headed, but right now he just wanted to get as far away from the house and his uncle as he could.

A burning, rolling sensation churned in the pit of his stomach, and he repeatedly swallowed the watery spit that formed in his mouth in an effort not to vomit.

He couldn't shake loose the picture that persisted in his mind's eye. He could see his mother lying on the grass, covered in her own gore as his father stood over her in his werewolf form, wiping her blood from his face. Trey stopped and closed his eyes, pressing the pads of his thumbs against his eyelids, but the picture was still there, waiting for him. He shouted out in frustration and kicked at a small rock, sending it spinning off into the high grasses that led up to the edge of the forest.

He wanted to hit something. In his anger and frustration he fell to his knees and pounded the earth, ramming his fists into it time after time, beating it into submission. The news had confirmed all of his worst fears, everything about himself that he had feared might be true: that he might never be able to fully control the powers that he had inherited from his parents, that he might somehow tip over the edge and do something truly horrific that would make him no better than Caliban and the other nether-creatures which sided with him. And if he did that, what was left for him? To leave the human world forever and live in the Netherworld with the other creatures. Creatures like him? If his father—who Lucien had described as having complete control over his powers—was capable of attacking his mother in that way, what hope was there for Trey?

He climbed to his feet again and walked on as if in his sleep; his feet on autopilot as they carried him up the grassy slope. His uncle's revelations had made it clear that his lycanthropy was capable of rearing its savage head at any point, and that even the amulet—whose powers he had come to trust and rely upon—might not be capable of controlling it. He stopped, screwing his eyes up as another terrible vision formed in his mind's eye, a hellish image that caused him to utter a small whimper of despair. The picture was similar to the one he had just had of his mother, except this time it was Alexa on the ground, her throat a ruined mess of long, bloodred ribbons that trailed out onto the grass beside her, and it was Trey, not his father, who stood over her with the taste of her blood in his mouth.

The tears flowed freely now and he stumbled on. He'd

entered the woods at the top of the slope and the temperature was much lower here, the cold air eddying around his face like an invisible specter. Through the trees off to his left he could just make out the sun as it began its final journey toward the horizon, surrendering the last of its light. Soon its cousin would take its place in the night sky, and it would be a full, unadulterated moon that looked down on the earth tonight.

Trey's breath hung momentarily in the air before him, and he shoved his hands into his pockets, hunching his shoulders, lost in thought.

He wished he had never come here. It had seemed so important to him when he had first found out about his uncle's existence. He'd blamed Lucien for keeping secrets from him, and had rushed out here to seek out the only living member of his family, hoping to find somebody who could help him to cope with everything that had happened to him. It had not occurred to him that there might be secrets he'd be better off not knowing. Lucien had, as always, simply had Trey's welfare in mind; he knew what Frank was like, knew what he was capable of. He'd tried to shield Trey from this, tried to warn him without insulting or abusing the teenager's uncle. But Trey had ignored him and come anyway.

Trey snorted at his foolishness. He'd come thousands of miles around the world to find his family without seeing that he'd already found it. Tom and Alexa and Lucien had taken him in and given him everything that he could possibly have wanted and needed. They'd made sure that he'd been able to cope with his lycanthrope powers, and made sure that he had learned to control the impulses that came with them. They'd taken him into their home and made him a member of the family. And yet Trey had spurned all of it, leaving them to come out here.

And now, with everything that he had just found out, he realized that he could never go back to that life now. He couldn't return to London. Could not go back to Lucien and Alexa and Tom—to the people who really cared for him—because he could not, and would not, put them in the danger that his mother had unwittingly been in when she had been with his father. They were too precious to him. *They* were his family, not a hate-filled old drunk who derived some kind of sick pleasure out of tormenting him.

He felt beneath his shirt at the amulet that hung around his neck. Up until now he had felt safe with it on; safe from the madness that the moon brought about in his kind. But he had been fooled. It was not some panacea that protected him from the beast within. If anything, it was more dangerous than giving in to his true self, because while he wore it, he was fooling himself that he was not dangerous to be around, that he was in control. He reached under his shirt and grabbed the amulet, lifting it up and pulling the long chain that it hung from over his head. He looked down at the small silver fist, drew back his arm, and threw the chain deep into the woods where it fell somewhere in among the deepening shadows.

He turned back toward the house, steeling himself to face his uncle, when a twig snapped somewhere behind him. He spun around, looking in the direction of the sound, scanning the gloom for any sign of what might have made the noise.

Ella stepped out from behind a tree. She took a step in his direction, an enigmatic look on her face.

"Trey," she said, nodding in his direction.

A puzzled expression flashed across her features, and she took her eyes off him for a second, cutting them in the direction that he had just hurled the neck chain. He followed her look, wondering if she had seen him discard it, and realized that he didn't care.

"I'm surprised to see you out here on your own. It's not long until moonrise." She cast her eyes toward the sky, but it was impossible to make out the heavens through the overhead canopy.

"I could say the same thing about you, Ella. Shouldn't you be back in your cabin with the other members of the pack?" He spat the last word out, a sudden feeling of anger coming over him at the thought of the group that had re-banded on his uncle's land—as if they were somehow to blame for the horrifying news that had been revealed to him that afternoon.

Ella's smile didn't falter. "There's no need for me to go anywhere, Trey, the pack's right here."

She turned her head slightly and the remaining members of the LG78 emerged from the shadows of the woods. They walked up to stand beside her, looking at him with interest.

Trey studied the other members of the group. They were all male of course, the werewolf curse being passed from father to son, but he was surprised by how young many of them seemed to be; they were all older than him, sure, but not by very much. There were only six of them, and he guessed that the average age of the group must be about eighteen or nineteen years old. He frowned to himself. He didn't know why, but he'd expected them to be older. Lucien had told him Caliban had hunted down and killed most of the werewolves, and yet here was living proof that he had not been as successful in this venture as Lucien had believed.

Trey's eyes drifted down to the ugly scar on Ella's forearm, and he wondered which of the group had attacked her, turning her into the thing that she now was: a Bitten.

The largest male stepped forward. He was tall and muscular-looking beneath the thick sweater that he wore, and a neatly kept short beard adorned his chin, black like the hair on his head that was tied back in a ponytail. He exuded an aura of power and confidence, and Trey instantly knew that this must be the pack leader, the Alpha, Jurgen.

There was something about the man that made Trey immediately feel uncomfortable and he had to force himself to stand his ground as the larger man stepped closer to inspect him.

"So you're the new boy?" Jurgen said. His accent was similar to Ella's, and again Trey thought it sounded Scandinavian in origin.

126

"That depends on what you mean by 'new boy,'" Trey answered. An uncomfortable burning sensation rose in his stomach and he had begun to sweat despite the cold air that surrounded him.

Jurgen looked back at him, his expression impossible to read. The irises of his eyes were very dark and seemed to merge with his pupils, which were fully dilated in the low light of the woods. The smile on his face was anything but friendly. "Isn't it time for all good little Wolfan boys to be locked up? Didn't your uncle tell you that it's dangerous for you to be wandering around outside on the night of the full moon?" Some of the members of the pack snickered at this, and Trey cut his eyes toward them, trying to work out what the pecking order was within the rest of the group.

"The same could be said for you," Trey said in a voice that he hoped sounded a lot braver than he felt. "Surely it's time for you guys to crawl back to your own cages."

Jurgen took another step closer, forcing himself deeper inside Trey's personal space. The big man looked down at the teenager, the cruel smile on his face widening. "You're assuming that we are *good*," he said in a low voice. If he was trying to unsettle Trey, he was doing a good job.

"But then again," he continued, "I have made the same assumption about you. Maybe that's it? Maybe you don't want to be locked up in a metal pen all night. Maybe, like us, you think that is wrong."

Trey shook his head. "No, that's not it at all."

Jurgen glanced back at the others before returning his attention to Trey. "Then what are you doing out here?"

"I was just on my way back." Trey took two backward steps, keeping his eyes on the pack. He didn't want to turn his back on them. In particular he did not want to turn his back on the Alpha, Jurgen. There was something about him that Trey found particularly unnerving, like a dog that you think might just take it into its head to bite as soon as you look away. But he had little choice if he was going to make it back to the house. The uncomfortable feelings in his chest and stomach were getting worse. A knife of pain shot through him, and he let out a small gasp. Looking at the rest of the group he could see that they too were in discomfort, some of them grimacing and hunching their shoulders. Only Jurgen stood rocklike, still glaring at the youngster.

Unable to stand it any longer, Trey turned on his heel and began to walk away. Knowing that he had little time left, he lengthened his stride into a jog, and then a run as he hurried back in the direction of the house.

He was almost halfway between the woods and the house when the volcano in the pit of his stomach erupted. He cried out, clutching his hand to his abdomen, trying to force his legs to keep going. His skin began to feel incredibly hot, and the uncomfortable pulling sensation had begun deep inside his bones so that within no more than a few more strides he was moaning in pain each time his feet made contact with the ground. He forced himself onward, gritting his teeth against the pain that was growing to an unbearable level.

He'd cleared the long grass of the slope and was now on the flat ground that led up to the house. He couldn't run any longer. He stumbled on the uneven ground, losing his footing and falling headfirst. The pain was in every part of him, and while he had experienced the agony of the Change before, he had always had the amulet, so it had been mercifully short. This, however, was like a long, slow, exquisite torture, unrelenting in the agony that piled in on top of itself by the second. A terrible animal-like mewling sound came from somewhere deep inside him, a cross between a whimper and a scream. He tried to stand, almost getting to his feet when another grenade of pain exploded, dropping him to his knees again. He was aware of a high-pitched tinnitus sound in his ears. His body was shaking all over, huge tremors that caused his arms to fly out from his side. Red-hot nails had been jammed into every square inch of his flesh and it suddenly occurred to him that the tinnitus that he had imagined was in fact the sound of his own screams. He looked toward the house that was no more than twenty meters away, knowing that he would not make it back there now. He raised a hand as if he could grab the house and pull it toward him and saw that his hand had begun to change—the fingers shortening and appearing to retract into a palm that was already thickening and swelling into a paw. Hairs formed across his burning skin and Trey sank to the floor, hoping that something, anything, would put a stop to the agony that he was experiencing.

The Change happened there on the ground in front of his

uncle's house. The last of the human was driven out of the teenager's body, and Trey let out one last high-pitched scream as he transformed into the huge Wolfan beast. His final animalistic wail was answered by the howls of the pack from the woods as they celebrated the joining of their newest member.

After that, there was nothing but blackness for Trey Laporte.

# 17

The coppery smell of blood filled his head, making his stomach somersault. The biting cold that ate through his skin and into his bones made the teenager clamp his arms around his torso to try and keep in any hint of heat trapped inside him. Trey slowly opened his eyes, scanning his surroundings and hoping to discover where he was and why he was lying on an icy cold floor surrounded by the stink of blood. He was naked and the spasmodic shudders that wracked through his body shook the leafy mattress beneath him. He slowly got to his feet, wincing at the aching in his bones and muscles, his body feeling as if he had gone twelve rounds with a pickup truck. He blew warm breath into cupped hands and clapped them together against the cold, jumping with fright as a large ugly-looking magpie took off from a branch just over his head, cawing at him in protest.

He looked down at his hands and noted how they were covered in the coppery brown of dried blood. Frowning, he made a brief mental check to confirm that he himself was not injured. He reached up and touched his head, thinking that this much blood must have come from a scalp wound, and his fingers encountered stiff, matted hair that also seemed to be covered in the stuff.

But he was sure that he was unhurt.

Certain now that none of the blood was his own, his stomach contracted again, and this time he gagged, spewing hot vomit onto the floor, where it sat in a steaming puddle. He walked around in a tight little circle, filling his lungs with cold, fresh air and swallowing the bile that rose up to his mouth.

He looked around again without a clue as to where he was or how he had got here. He hoped that he was still on his uncle's land, but with no break in the trees for as far as he could see in any direction, there was no way to tell, and a feeling of panic began to creep over him at the prospect of wandering around in these woods on his own. He needed to get warm and acquire some clothing because he was certain that he would die very shortly if he did not.

He spun around at a sound from behind him, and saw Ella peering at him from behind a large oak tree. He felt his face burning a bright scarlet as he covered his modesty with his hands.

"Ella," he said, nodding his head in her direction.

She nodded back at him, smirking at his embarrassment. "It's cold, isn't it?" she said, grinning.

Trey flushed red again. "Where are we?"

"I have no idea," she said, looking around her. "The kill is over there and the others are just waking up. I've already seen Jurgen; he's always the first up in the morning after a full-moon Change. He'll get the others together shortly, and then we'll head off home."

Trey frowned at her, casting his eyes behind her at the dense woods. "I thought you just said that you didn't know where we were."

"And that's true, but once we're all together, we can Change again and then follow our own trail back home. It's either that, or we wander around helplessly until we all die of exposure." She looked at him, smiling kindly at the consternation on his face. "It's what we always have to do following the night of a forced Change. We might have wandered several miles away from where we started out the night before, and our only hope of getting back is—"

"I couldn't go through that again," Trey said, cutting across her. "I'd rather die out here than experience that agony again."

Ella stepped out from behind the tree and walked toward him, seemingly unperturbed at her own nakedness. Trey didn't know where to look. At first he gawked at her as she slowly approached him, taking in the white, goose-bumped skin of her body. He swallowed, the action sounding incredibly loud in his own ears, and he could feel the heat burning on his face. Eventually he fixed his eyes on a large clump of earth at his feet. She was close to him now, too close for him not to take in her body as she stood in front of him, and suddenly she leaned forward to give him a friendly bump on the head with her own.

"Come on, silly, it's not like that was the first time you've been through it. You must have had quite a few full-moon Changes at your age?"

Trey mumbled something under his breath, still not knowing where to look.

Ella leaned forward and nudged his head again. Trey thought it a strange action—something between a playful bump and a nuzzle. "Anyway," she said, "it isn't like that when we *choose* to Change as a pack. The violence of the forced Change during a full moon is pure, unadulterated agony for us all, but it will be nothing like that, I promise. It will be a wonderful experience for you. You'll never look back, Trey. You are one of us now. You're part of the pack."

Trey considered this. He thought about how he had transformed into his bimorph werewolf state under the controlling influence of the amulet. Then, the Change had been mercifully swift, one huge supernova of exquisite agony and then it was over. But the long, all-consuming torture that he had undergone yesterday had scared the hell out of him, and he shuddered when he remembered it. He now understood what his uncle had meant when he'd told Trey how he wished for death as a respite from the agony of the Change during a full moon. He looked up into Ella's blue eyes and hoped that she was telling the truth. He had little choice. He would either have to agree to transform with the rest of the pack, or be left out here to die of the cold.

"Is this blood?" he asked, noting how Ella's face and hands were also smeared with the dried gore.

She didn't say anything; she just stood there looking back at him.

"Where did it all come from?"

To his surprise she smiled back at him. "Come with me," she said, turning away from him. She walked back in the direction she had come, and Trey was forced to follow.

They came to a small clearing in the woods where the other members of the pack were now up and about. They nodded in his direction as he entered the area, and Jurgen came up to him, a broad smile on his face. He clapped a hand on Trey's shoulder, squeezing the boy's flesh harder than was necessary. "Well, well," he said in a voice loud enough that the others could hear, "our little wolf cub is here at last. We thought that we'd lost you."

Trey looked past the big man at the bloody carcass lying in the grass. It was a huge elk of some kind. Or it had been. Now it was a grisly mess, its innards strewn out about it, one dead eye staring up at the blue sky overhead. He noted how it had been half eaten, great rents visible in the flesh where hunks of meat had been torn loose, especially around the hindquarters where the damage was greatest. Trey tried not to imagine himself with his head buried in that bloody mess, but the evidence caked over his skin suggested that that was exactly what had happened, and he knew that he'd taken part in the creature's demise just as much as the others.

Jurgen followed his gaze and then turned and walked toward the crimson chaos. He bent down, picked up a torn length of the creature's intestines, and threw them in Trey's direction so they landed with a wet thud at his feet. "Maybe you'd like some breakfast before we start off back home?"

Trey turned quickly, bending at the waist, and vomited

on the grass. The other members of the pack laughed at this, and Jurgen in particular seemed delighted with the boy's discomfort.

"It seems the youngster doesn't like his meat too rare," he shouted, joining in with the laughter at his own joke.

Once the hilarity had died away, the mood sobered as if by some invisible signal. The other members of the group stared at Jurgen, and they began to approach the big man, forming a loose circle. They joined hands, glancing around at one another with a look of eager anticipation. Ella looked at Trey, and smiling her reassurance, she nodded at him to fill the gap in the circle beside her. The teenager could feel the tension that had suddenly built up among the other members—it was almost tangible. The look on all their faces was the same—an excited expectancy.

Jurgen was almost directly opposite him in the circle. Trey could hardly take his eyes off of him; that same unsettling look that he'd witnessed the night before was on the Alpha's face again: hungry and angry and, to Trey's mind, more than a touch psychotic. It was the face of a drug addict preparing for his first fix of the day. But if the other members of the pack noticed, they chose not to draw attention to it.

Trey slowly linked hands with Ella on one side and a tall, ginger-haired teenager who Trey guessed to be about seventeen years old on the other. As soon as the circle was joined, he could feel it. The power that passed through him was something that he had felt before, and he waited for the Change that he knew was coming.

It was mercifully short. Like the other transmogrifications that he had experienced before coming to Canada, the group Change from human to Wolfan was intense, but short-lived, and when he opened his eyes he looked about him at the giant wolves that made up the pack.

They were huge creatures: great solid slabs of muscle and sinew that moved around each other warily, eyeing the other pack members, their movements and body posture instantly displaying how they were feeling. For Trey it was as if his mind had simply switched to "wolf." He could instantly tell who were the more dominant members of the pack, noting how these members approached the others with an upright posture, and how the more submissive pack members would lower their own bodies in response. Jurgen-wolf was by far the largest of the animals; his great black pelt seemed to suck in the light, creating some great living wolf shadow that padded noiselessly on the leafy carpet. The Alpha paraded among the others, pacing about high on its paws, tail held straight out behind it. As it approached the members of the pack, they would sink down in front of him. One wolf, presumably the weakest—the Omega wolf—lay down on the ground as the pack leader approached, turning on its back so that its belly was exposed to the huge black beast in a display of complete and utter supplication. Trey knew that the subordinate wolf had been the tall ginger-haired boy who he'd linked hands with only moments before.

The animal that had been Trey Laporte took all of this in without question. He was no longer human, and yet in some part of his wolf brain there remained a tiny element of his human self that seemed to be looking in at the whole thing from the outside—just as his uncle had described it. Trey took in the smells and sights and sounds of the forest, his brain decoding the stimuli in a way that it had never done before. He caught the scent of a rabbit brought to him on the faintest of breezes, and he knew that the creature was no more than forty meters away off to his right. The overriding stench of blood from the animal carcass caused a shiver of excitement to pulse through him and his mouth filled with saliva. He could sense the same exhilaration in the other members of the pack as the smell of death stirred them, wanting nothing more than to feast again on the dead body. But they had to wait. Wait until the Alpha had started. Trey eyed the dead body hungrily, so caught up in his thoughts of sinking his teeth into the meat again that he missed the Alpha's approach.

The black werewolf slowly walked toward the newcomer, its dark eyes never leaving the youngster as it did so. It stopped no more than a couple of meters away and looked hard at the new pack member, its head cocked slightly to one side as if puzzled by something that it saw. At the last moment the new pack member became aware of the dominant Alpha and turned to face it, too slow in showing the subordination that was expected of him. The pack shifted in anticipation of the Alpha's response, knowing that violence would ensue.

The werewolf that had been Jurgen bristled its pelt, the

raised hackles making it appear even bigger than it already was. Its eyes took on an angry look and its lips peeled back to reveal the teeth and gums. A low rumbling growl issued from the huge creature's chest as it prepared to attack the impertinent young upstart.

Trey knew that he didn't stand a chance against a beast that was almost twice as big as he was. His rewired wolf brain took over, instinctively bending his front legs in a bowing motion that lowered his head below that of the Alpha. He kept his eyes glued to the other wolf's, sensing that the attack would come anyway, that the Alpha would need to prove his dominance over him to the other pack members and reassert its number-one rank within the group.

When the attack did come it came fast and hard, and took Trey by complete surprise. His eyes were still fixed on the great black head of the Alpha when the white-furred bitch bowled in low from his side, biting into his shoulder and causing him to cry out in pain and shock. Trey turned to face his attacker, backing away to keep both her and the male Alpha in his vision. Ella-wolf growled back, revealing rows of teeth, some of which were still stained with his own blood. Trey recognized the signal and lowered his head in acquiescence.

The huge black Wolfan that was Jurgen eyed the scene, weighing up its options. Eventually it turned its back and walked away, seemingly satisfied that the female Alpha had dealt with the matter.

The situation diffused, Ella-wolf approached Trey, and

the youngster moved forward and licked her on the muzzle, thanking her for her intervention, which had spared him from the much worse savaging that the pack leader would have meted out. They moved against each other, their bodies pressing together at the flanks, sharing scent and reinforcing their friendship.

Jurgen-wolf approached the dead elk and sniffed at the blood on the ground. The others started to move toward the corpse, but the pack was not to eat that morning. The Alpha turned to look at them, its eyes resting on Trey again, taking him in. Suddenly the black wolf turned away and sprang forward into the forest, leading the way for the others to follow.

They raced between the trees on paws that barely stirred the mulch beneath them. They were like one unified beast as they ran, each knowing the others' position, and taking it in turns to lead, then follow. Their scent from the night before was unmistakable, but they hardly needed it to find their way back through the forest. Some wolf sense had kicked in, and each and every member of the pack instinctively knew the way back to their own territory. For the creature that had been Trey, the world was a tsunami of sounds and smells and sights that were woven in and through each other so that he believed he could have closed his eyes and still run through the densely wooded landscape without colliding with anything in his path. He was a creature in complete unison with his surroundings, tuned in to everything around him and part of an even more perfect entity—the pack. He was in ecstasy. Later, he would remember this feeling of pure elation, the feeling of the *rightness* of what he now was.

They emerged from the woods, eating up the ground that led down to Frank's cottage with huge, loping strides, before coming to a halt, circling each other, rubbing their flanks against one another, and exchanging scents. Eventually Jurgen-wolf turned from the group and looked away at the trees in the direction of the lake and the cottages that they inhabited. Trey looked off in the same direction, and even though he sensed it was some distance away, thought he could detect the smell of the lake on the air.

Trey knew that they were about to leave him, and he sounded out his dismay at the prospect of this. Once again the white-furred Ella-wolf was the one to come over to him. She used her muzzle to push Trey in the side, ushering him toward the building and letting him know that this, at least for now, was the way that it had to be. He turned and looked at the wooden building again, taking his eyes off the other creatures for a second, and as he did so he *felt* the pack start to leave. He could feel the power and magic that had united them begin to ebb away as they moved off. He threw back his head and howled, his wolf voice turning into a strangled human cry as he transformed back again. There was no answer from the pack this time.

He looked about him. He was alone and naked and standing in front of his uncle's house.

# 18

Philippa woke up and slowly opened her eyes. The room she was in was nothing short of spectacular, and she propped herself up on one elbow to stare about her in wonder at the opulent surroundings. She had no recollection of getting here. The Ashnon had told her that this would be the case, and that she would feel disoriented for the first few hours. She glanced across at the digital alarm clock on the bedside cabinet—it was a little after five p.m. The bed that she was lying on was unimaginably large and she had to roll over twice to get to the edge, where she let her feet hang down and gently bounce against the deep pile of the carpet. She was incredibly thirsty. Looking about her for some sign of a drinks cabinet or fridge, she stood up and padded over to a walnut cabinet that looked as if it might conceal a refrigerator, her face breaking into a broad smile as the interior lit up when she opened the door. She grabbed a large bottle of sparkling water and a chocolate bar and carried them over to the window.

Park Avenue was the bustling mass of life that she had always imagined it to be. The view from her window was not what she had hoped or expected, and she was disappointed that she could not see any of the more famous buildings and monuments that she associated with the city. Everything was hemmed in; huge buildings stood shoulder to shoulder in the street opposite, and even from this height, they obscured the view that the hotel must have once commanded. She reached forward and grasped the handle of the window, hoping to open it to allow the sounds of the city, which she could just make out through the glass, to enter the room. But the handle wouldn't budge, and the angry horns of the taxis as they pushed their way through the mass of moving metal below remained muffled and indistinct. She sighed. She'd always wanted to go to New York. She'd watched countless films and television series that had featured the city as a backdrop, and she had always hoped that her dad might take her there one day so that she might see it for herself. The unbidden memory of her father darkened her mood and she had to fight back the tears that inevitably threatened whenever he wandered into her thoughts.

Her father would never be taking her anywhere again; the Necrotroph had seen to that.

That was what she was doing here—in this mirage that looked and sounded, and no doubt, smelled like New York, but was really . . . she shuddered. She didn't want to think too closely about what and where this place really was.

The Ashnon had told her that she was perfectly safe here, describing the safeguards and sorcery that kept its guests completely protected while they were in its charge. Protected that is, as long as they stayed inside the hotel and did not venture outside. If they did that, the demon was powerless to help them.

"Think of it as one of those all-inclusive resorts that they have in some of the less pleasant destinations," the demon had said, sounding like some kind of supernatural travel agent. "Everything is on tap at the resort, and you're perfectly safe—as long as you *stay* on the resort complex. Go outside, and the bad guys might get you."

"It shouldn't be for very long," Alexa had added, shooting the Ashnon a withering look. "You'll be out of there and back with us before you know it."

Philippa took a big gulp from the water bottle, enjoying the feeling as it fizzed in her mouth. Her head felt weird, as if it were stuffed full of cotton, and she thought that it might be a good idea to lie down for a while. She reached out, taking hold of the curtains to draw them against the world, and as she turned her head to do so, the scene outside the window changed. It was quick and almost imperceptible, but it made her heart jump in her chest, and she stopped, freeze-framed with her arms spread wide to the world outside. It seemed to her that, for the tiniest fraction of a second, from the periphery of her vision, she had caught a glimpse of the real world on the other side of that glass, a world that was darker than anything she could imagine. It was no more than a flicker caught from the corner of her eye, and was gone almost as soon as it had appeared, but for that fraction of a second she knew that she had somehow caught a glimpse of what lay beyond the illusion, and that glimpse was enough to send a knife of the purest terror through her.

She became aware that she was holding her breath, and she let it out, breathing rapidly in time with her heart, which was galloping away inside her.

There had been something else. In that momentary flash she had seen something—no, not seen, but *sensed*. Something in the shadows opposite the building. There had been something lurking in the shadows, and it seemed to her that it had been looking up at her window.

She pulled the curtains shut and looked over at the phone on the bedside table. Alexa had given her a number that she could call in an emergency. In reality, it wasn't a number at all—any more than the telephone was a real telephone—but a spell that was activated by her performing a certain action in this realm, and Alexa had thought that a phone call would be the simplest thing for her to remember.

She looked down at her hands and saw that they were shaking. She was spooked. No, more than that, she was terrified by what she thought she had seen in those shadows because she *had* seen something outside the window. She told herself to calm down, to get a grip. The situation didn't really constitute an emergency, not yet, and she remembered how Alexa had told her to use the spell only if she had to—as a last resort. She pursed her lips and chewed at the inside of her mouth, something she always did when she was nervous, and forced herself to turn away from the phone.

She wished that Alexa were here. She'd grown to like

her and thought that they were becoming good friends. She was somebody who seemed so normal, and had managed to cope with all the crazy and terrible things around her in a way that Philippa didn't believe that she would ever be capable of. She looked down at the water bottle in her hand and thought of how Alexa would react in this same situation. She wouldn't make the call.

Resolving to try and be a bit more like Alexa—to stop being so weak and helpless—Philippa took a deep breath and started to hum tunelessly to herself. She would take the nap that she'd planned. Then, when she woke up, hopefully with a clearer head, she'd work out what she was going to do with her time here.

When she woke again it was morning. After the window incident she remembered getting changed into a pair of light blue pajamas that she'd found in a drawer. The drawers were rammed with clothes of every type, all her size, with a note on top of the wooden chest of drawers from someone called Hugo, who had been assigned as her personal shopper and who would, at her call, happily get anything for her that she wanted in order to make her stay here more comfortable. She'd laid down on the bed, not believing for a second that she would sleep, and now here she was having dreamlessly slept her way through to the next day.

She threw the covers back and got up, cautiously approaching the window. Wrenching the curtains apart in one large, quick movement, she stared out at the view.

It was pouring. Great sheets of rain were blowing up the street and the sound of them against the glass was like somebody throwing handfuls of grit against the hotel's exterior. If anything, there were even more cars on the roads than she had remembered from the evening before. She experimentally flicked her eyes to one side, expecting to catch a glimpse of the black and malevolent world that she had seen last night, but the scene didn't change. New York, or this version of it, stayed as New York.

She was on edge, every nerve in her body tightly wound to breaking point. *Get a grip,* she told herself, moving back away from the window. She needed to keep control of herself. She couldn't afford to freak out at every little thing that she saw, or thought that she saw. She had agreed to do this. She'd listened to the Ashnon and Lucien, and she'd told them that she would do it—convinced them that she *could* do it—that she wanted to help. It was a chance for her to exact revenge on the *thing* that had tried to kill her and had killed her father.

They had told her that she would only be here for a matter of days. That they were confident of getting this mess sorted out quickly so that she could come back and start to live her life again.

"I can do this," she said to herself.

She picked up the telephone by the side of the bed and hit the button to connect to reception.

"Yes, Miss Tipsbury. How can I help you?" The voice on the other end of the line was light and airy, and went some way to calming her.

"I wonder if I could get some books?" she said, fighting to keep her voice calm and steady.

"That won't be a problem at all. If you make a list of the authors you like, or what type of books you enjoy, I'll send somebody up to your room to collect it. It shouldn't take us anytime at all to acquire them and have them brought up to you."

"I'd also like an MP3 player . . . and a laptop. You do have wireless broadband here, don't you?"

"Of course, madam."

"And can I rent DVDs for the player in here?"

"We have an extensive list of films available for our guests to rent. In addition, we have the pay-per-view option that—"

"I don't suppose I could get a couple of game consoles and some games?" she interrupted.

"Just add it to your list, Miss Tipsbury."

The receptionist acted as though this were the most normal request in the world. "Is there anything else?"

"Yes, please. I'd like some breakfast sent up to my room. I'd like poached eggs on toast, some melon and strawberries, a jug of iced tea, and chocolate . . . I'd like *lots* of chocolate."

"I'll have it brought up to your room immediately, madam."

"Afterward I was thinking of using the gym."

"I think you'll find that the health and fitness facilities on the fifth floor are very well equipped, Miss Tipsbury. We could arrange a personal trainer for you if you would like?"

"Yes, that would be perfect. Thank you."

She hung up and looked around her again. She'd call back in a minute and get some flowers delivered to the room, lots of them, like she'd seen in the hotel rooms of pop stars on the TV.

If she was going to be holed up like a prisoner in this place for a while, she might as well make the most of it.

# 19

"The most practical solution is to kill the host body," Tom said between mouthfuls of an apple danish that he was devouring. "We know that the Necrotroph will leave him for dead anyway." He pointed with the blunt end of the pastry in Lucien's direction. "It's the simplest, most expedient method available to us. You can't deny that. For the first time, we *know* where that foul creature is and who it is inside. You told me yourself that nobody survives after the creature transfers to a new body, so Ronald Given is little more than a walking corpse. Now, I like old Ron, don't get me wrong, but if that thing is—"

"Philippa did," Lucien said, stopping his friend mid-flow.

"What?"

"Philippa survived. Damaged, yes, but she survived."

"Yes but—"

"You know why we can't do what you suggest, Tom," Lucien said, looking at his friend from beneath his eyebrows, a small smile playing at his lips.

"I could. And knowing Ron as I do, I'd bet my back teeth that he'd want me to. I'd want *you* to do it to me if that thing had possessed my body—"

150

Lucien raised a hand, cutting off his friend. "You know that I have vowed never to take another innocent human life. I cannot, and will not, destroy what little chance this unfortunate man has of surviving this ordeal for the sake of . . . *convenience.* He is already the victim in this affair, and yes, his chances of survival are negligible, but his death will not be at our hands. We will do everything we can to help Mr. Given survive this, regardless of how beneficial his death might be to us at the moment."

Tom took a gulp of tea from his mug and ran his hand over his short cropped hair. When he looked up again, he let out a long sigh. "You're right. I'm sorry." He placed the hot drink on top of the sideboard beside him. "It's just that we have been trying to find this bloody Necrotroph for so long now, and when we do finally find it we're forced to wait around. I feel that we should be doing something."

Lucien swung around in his seat and looked out the window to his left, choosing his words with care, knowing why the Irishman was behaving in this way. "You must stop blaming yourself, Tom. It was not your fault that the Necrotroph made its way into our organization, and you were *not* to blame for Alexa's abduction. Neither was the damage that has been done to Philippa nor the death of her father your doing. My brother, Caliban, is to blame for all of this, not you."

The Irishman looked down at his feet, and when he spoke again it was in a low voice. "I should have known."

"How?"

"For crying out loud, Lucien, I'm supposed to be the head of security for this place. You placed your faith in me and my team to keep this building and the people in it safe, and I allowed that creature to just waltz in here and—"

There was a small cough from the doorway and they both turned around to see Philippa Tipsbury's doppelganger standing there looking back at them.

"It's what they do," the demon said in the girl's voice. "They're so very hard to spot. Plus they're pitiless in who they use to achieve any goal that they have. That is why they have survived for so long." The girl smiled in a way that sent a cold shiver down Tom's spine. "But this one's time is up. This one has been careless and showed us its hand." The demon gave them both a little nod before stepping into the room to stand by Tom's side. The grim and determined look set into the teenage girl's features looked out of place and Tom had to remind himself for the umpteenth time that the girl standing next to him was not a girl at all.

"My apologies for the interruption," the nether-creature said. "I did not intend to eavesdrop on your conversation. I merely came to inform you that the Necrotroph is on the move. Alexa is tracking the host body from next door and—"

"She needs to be careful not to let it become aware that it's being followed," Tom said, talking across the creature.

"She knows that," the Ashnon answered, smiling back at the Irishman. "She's using a magic spell that I have suggested to her. It's like a form of remote viewing, allowing her to watch the car that the host is driving. We discussed this at length, and despite it being a rather cumbersome method, it is the one that gives us the biggest chance of remaining un-detected. For added safety, one of Lucien's people is following in a car." The demon held up its hand, cutting off another in-terruption that Tom was about to make. "Yes, they are being extremely careful not to be spotted. They are just there for insurance, in case Alexa should somehow lose contact. It's like a police operation: Alexa is the 'eye in the sky' keeping the driver in touch with everything that she sees."

"Well, you seem to have everything in hand," Tom said, the unmistakably peeved tone in his voice raising a small, guarded smile to Lucien's lips.

"I think we should go and see how Alexa is getting on," the vampire said, standing up and coming around the desk to his friend. He placed a perfectly manicured hand around the Irishman's shoulders and gently steered him toward the door. "Tom, is there any chance that I could trouble you to make me one of your fabulous cups of tea?"

Alexa sat stiffly in the chair, her spine perfectly straight as if some wooden board had been placed down the back of the black and gray vest that she wore over her T-shirt. Tom bent forward and placed a cup on the table in front of her, but one look at the girl told him that she was completely unaware of his presence. Her eyes had taken on an eerie silvered sheen, giving them a strangely insectlike appear-ance, and they stared off unblinkingly into the distance.

"Is she . . . OK?" Tom asked in a hushed tone, studying

the girl with concern. "She looks like some kind of bloody zombie or something."

"I can hear you, Tom," Alexa said, although there was no hint of emotion in her voice—the words coming out in one long monosyllabic drone.

"She has to go into that state for the spell," the Ashnon said from the couch on the other side of the room. The demon was lounging back against the pillows and leafing its way through a celebrity magazine. "Alexa is perfectly safe, but she is having to work incredibly hard at the moment." The demon looked up, casting its eyes in Lucien's direction. "I'm impressed. She is turning into a very talented sorceress. She reminds me of her mother."

There was a stillness in the room. The demon found the vampire staring back at it. It flicked its eyes in Alexa's direction.

"When was the last time you saw Gwendolin?" the Ashnon asked Lucien. "It's just that the last time that I was in the Netherworld there was talk that—"

"There is always talk in the Netherworld," Lucien replied. "Nether-creatures like nothing more than to gossip and speculate. The clever ones are those that know when to hold their tongue. Those that don't often find that they no longer *have* a tongue to hold."

The vampire's eyes shone for a second, burning with a ferocity that sent a chill running up Tom's spine as he looked between the two of them.

The Ashnon swallowed loudly, and a nervous smile

154

flickered across its lips. It looked down into its lap at the magazine again, suddenly finding something fascinating to fix its eyes upon. "I meant no offense, Lucien. Forgive me."

"It's coming here," Alexa said into the empty space ahead of her. "The Necrotroph is heading straight this way."

# 20

Jurgen paced the floor in front of the large stonework fireplace that dominated the main living area of the cabin. Marcus sat in a fireside chair and watched him, careful not to stare too openly at the pack Alpha and run the risk of Jurgen interpreting it as some kind of open challenge.

For the last few months the pack had witnessed Jurgen change into the edgy, paranoid, and volatile person who stood before him now, and Marcus knew that the tiniest thing could send him hurtling into a terrible rage. These rages had escalated too, and the violence that accompanied them was getting too much for everyone to bear.

Marcus had no idea why he had been summoned, and he knew better than to ask. Past experience had taught him that it was better to just sit and wait until Jurgen was ready.

They'd arrived back at the lake after leaving the new boy at his uncle's house. Marcus had no sooner showered and changed into a fresh set of clothes when his walkie-talkie had squawked: Jurgen informing him that he wanted to see him in his cabin, immediately. The second in command—the Beta—had wanted nothing more than to curl up on his bed and sleep, but he'd gone over, knowing from the sound of Jurgen's voice that whatever it was he was being called for, it wasn't going to be good.

He'd entered the simple accommodation to find Jurgen standing alone in front of the unlit fire as if he had taken up the position for dramatic effect. Marcus was greeted with a nod in the direction of a chair, and obediently took up his position. That had been a little more than fifteen minutes ago, and not a word had been uttered between the two of them since. Jurgen had taken up an incessant pacing, his heavy boots marking a monotonous bass beat as they crossed the hearth, leaving Marcus to simply sit and wait.

Eventually Jurgen stopped. Placing a forearm on top of the mantelpiece, he turned around to look at his deputy, a frown beetling his brow, as if he'd forgotten that he'd summoned Marcus and was surprised to find him there. The look of confusion disappeared, replaced by the familiar, hostile glare that always seemed to adorn Jurgen's features these days.

"What do you make of him?" Jurgen finally said, breaking the silence.

"Who?"

Jurgen waited, the small muscles at the sides of his jaw bunching up as he ground his teeth in impatience.

"The new guy?" Marcus added.

Jurgen glared back at the other man.

"He seems OK. Why?" Marcus glanced at Jurgen's hands as he repeatedly clenched and unclenched them into fists.

"I don't think he is *OK*. There's something not right

about him. Something that he's not telling us." Jurgen turned to gaze into the ashes of the dead fire, as if the answers he sought might somehow be contained therein.

*Tephromancy*, Marcus thought. That was the name for divination through ashes: tephromancy. He chastised himself for letting his mind wander—it wouldn't pay to drop his guard when Jurgen was in this kind of mood. He wondered what it was that had set the Alpha against the newcomer so quickly. He himself thought that the kid had seemed fine, but it wouldn't pay to disagree with Jurgen. Then again, if he said nothing the situation was apt to escalate out of all proportions.

"What do you base these . . . *feelings* on?" Marcus asked slowly.

Jurgen turned and looked down at his second in command. His eyes scanned the other's face before a small smile crept into the edges of his mouth.

"He's keeping something hidden from us."

"He's just a kid, Jurgen. Mixed-up and afraid like the rest of us were when we were his age and found out what we'd become—what we'd inherited from our fathers."

The Alpha returned his attention to the ashes. "How did you feel the first time that you Changed with the pack?" he said. "I mean, how did it feel to know that you could be the wolf that lay dormant inside of you *when you wanted to*? To truly experience what it was like to be a werewolf for the first time?"

Marcus considered the question. "It felt incredible," he

said, remembering. "Exhilarating and enlivening and breathtaking and—"

"Did you see him when we Changed in the woods this morning? Did you look at him at all?" Jurgen turned to face the other man.

Marcus shook his head.

The Alpha leaned forward, bending at the waist so that his face was no more than a hand's width away from Marcus's. "I did," he said. "I was watching him. I always watch them the first time. I like to see their reaction when they first realize what is happening to them, that dawning realization followed by the ecstasy of the moment. Do you remember the first time Ella Changed? The way that she sprang around for an age before sitting back on her haunches and howling with the joy of it?"

Marcus smiled at the memory.

"This kid did nothing." Jurgen straightened up and wandered over to the window, replaying the scene in his head. "He Changed as if nothing at all had happened. He took in his surroundings and then just looked at the rest of us, waiting to see what was going to happen next. It was like he'd done it a thousand times before. Water off a duck's back. Piece of cake."

"Are you sure that you're not just imagining that. Different people react in different ways, and—"

"Yes, I am sure that I am not just imaging it, Marcus!" He crossed the room in a beat, looming over the chair, so that he stood before Marcus, his fists clenched again. This time Marcus had to force himself to maintain eye contact, trying not to back down too easily in the face of this aggression. Eventually Jurgen pulled back and resumed his position in front of the fire.

"There's something up with that kid, I tell you."

"OK, Jurgen. What do you want to do?"

Marcus waited, watching the Alpha's face lose the red flush that it had filled with seconds before.

Jurgen nodded to himself. He took a deep breath in through his nostrils, holding it for a second. "Go fetch Luke. Bring him here. We're going on a little trip."

Marcus reluctantly stood up. "Where are we going?"

The smile on Jurgen's face was unsettling. "Don't bring Ella," he said by way of an answer.

# 21

Trey lifted the large, weed-filled terra-cotta pot with one hand while his fingers blindly groped in the dirt underneath until they came to rest on the key. His uncle had had the forethought to tell his nephew where he kept the spare key, and Trey was glad to find that it was still there. Letting himself into the house, he closed the door as quietly as possible behind him, holding the latch in his fingers and leaning his weight into the wood so that it engaged silently with the frame. He needn't have bothered. Billy came flying down the hallway, his claws skittering on the wooden surface, and he gave Trey a short bark of welcome. The teenager couldn't help but smile down at the little tattletale, and bent down to give the dog's ears a brief rub.

"Shh, Billy, there's a good boy."

He couldn't hear his uncle. There was a perfect silence in the house, and Trey walked up the short hall, poking his head around the door to find that the living room was empty. He thought for a second, then tiptoed over to the far wall, carefully turned the door handle, and peered through into the back room. His uncle was asleep on the floor of the cage. He was curled up on the mattress on the floor, and his snores bounced back off the bare walls, filling the room. Trey backed out, pulling the door shut behind him, pleased that he did not have to face his uncle right away.

He went back down the hallway and entered the room that had been offered to him as a bedroom during his stay. It was little more than a repository for his uncle's junk. Great, sprawling heaps of what looked to Trey like jumble, covered almost every inch of floor space.

On his first evening in the house, Uncle Frank had led him to the room, opening the door and waving his hand in the general direction of the rear wall.

"There's an old army camp bed in there somewhere," he'd said. "I have no idea how the thing goes together anymore, but knock yourself out, kid." He'd backed out, leaving Trey the task of finding the bed, and the even more difficult job of trying to clear a space in which to put it.

The teenager walked over to the bed now and lowered himself onto the creaking frame. He pulled an old blanket up around him to keep the cold air from his flesh, and thought about everything that had happened. He had it in his mind to sleep. All he wanted right now was to curl up under the covers and sleep.

His head simply had too many thoughts and emotions jostling and elbowing at one another, and he found it almost impossible to think clearly. He couldn't shake the feeling of elation that he'd felt when he'd been running with the pack, that feeling that they were one huge organism, greater than the sum of their parts. But he also knew that he had lost most of his humanity. He'd been utterly animalistic: a throwback

162

to the way that mankind must have been when they were both hunter and hunted, relying on their instincts and senses to stay alive. He remembered how his heart had sunk as they'd emerged from the woods and he'd caught sight of this house again, how Ella had come over to him, rubbing her flank against his and reassuring him that everything was going to be all right. He inhaled, realizing that he could still smell her scent on him.

An image of Alexa suddenly flashed into his mind, and his face flushed with shame at how he had momentarily forgotten her. He thought of how concerned she had been for him before he'd left, picturing her sitting next to him on his bed back in London, quizzing him on when he might return. A wave of sadness filled him—the perfect counterpoint to the ecstasy that he had recalled moments before.

He knew that he wouldn't be able to go back.

Frank's revelations about his father's attack on his mother had reinforced doubts that Trey had always had about his powers. Despite everything that Lucien had told him: how he believed that Trey was destined for greatness, and how he believed the boy would fulfill an ancient prophecy that would lead him to defeat a vampire lord and restore peace between the Netherworld and the human realm. Despite Lucien's insistence that Trey *could* control his lycanthrope powers, Trey had always felt there was some part of him that had the capacity to go wrong—something that might be triggered at any time and lead him to do something terrible. Something like his father had done. Another terrible thought entered the teenager's mind: What if his father had done it on purpose? What if he'd deliberately attacked his mother, turning her into a lyco so that he could have a full-blood werewolf child? What if Lucien had encouraged him to do that to try and realize the prophecy?

He shook his head, sighing at the mess that he found himself in.

Whatever the truth was, there was one thing that Trey now believed: He was not safe to be around, even with the amulet. And he would not risk the lives of the people he'd come to care about. He forced all thoughts of returning back to England from his head, screwed his eyes shut, and allowed the tears of frustration to snake down his cheeks and onto the rough surface of the blanket.

He jumped as a loud clanging sound filled the house, as if two metal trash can lids had been crashed together like cymbals. The sound was answered by excited yaps and barks from Billy, who, from the sounds of things, was running around the house in a state of euphoria. He guessed that the timer that kept the cage door locked had tripped, and that the old man's incarceration was over for another month.

Trey listened as the old man began to move around the house. He could hear the shuffling gait approaching his door, and he lay perfectly still, holding his breath and staring at the wooden surface.

"Are you in there, Trey?" his uncle asked.

Billy let out a short woof and scratched at the door.

"I'm going to cook some breakfast for us," Frank continued.

"I know that you're still sore at me, Trey, and I can't blame you for that. I shouldn't have said those things that I did. I blame it on the whiskey. I'd had too much to drink." There was a long pause then, and Trey resumed his breathing, thinking that the old man had given up and gone. "No, that's not right," his uncle said in a soft voice that Trey had not heard since his arrival. "I can't blame it on the drink. It was me. It was wrong of me to say those things to you."

Trey wiped at his eyes and raised himself into a sitting position, the bed moaning in response. He let the silence hang.

"Well," his uncle said, moving back a little from the door. "I'll pour you a coffee, dish everything up, and you can make up your own mind if you want to join us or not. C'mon, Billy."

Trey listened to the man shuffle away, wanting some time on his own before deciding whether to face him or not.

Frank was sitting at the table nursing a mug of coffee. The food that he had made them was still hot—the early morning sunshine highlighting the wispy tendrils of steam rising from the plates.

"Good morning," he said, as Trey, fully clothed now, took the seat opposite him.

"Morning," he replied before starting in on the plate of fried food.

As a rule he hardly ever ate cooked breakfast, preferring a bowl of cereal and a couple of glasses of fruit juice, but as soon as the first forkful of greasy bacon and egg landed on

165

his tongue he realized that this was exactly what he needed, and hungrily followed it up with another.

He realized something else—his uncle was sober. He watched as the old man sat listening to him eat, holding the mug of coffee in front of his face, enjoying the feeling of heat on his skin.

He let the boy eat in peace, not wanting to disturb him as he refueled his body. But eventually, as the gaps between the sounds of the fork hitting the surface of the plate grew further apart, he spoke. "You didn't come back last night."

Trey placed his utensils on the plate and looked up again, wiping his lips with the back of his hand.

"No. Sorry."

Frank shook his head. "No need to apologize. You ain't beholden to me in any way."

"That may be, but I said that I'd be here with you for the Change, and I wasn't. I—"

"Believe it or not, kid," his uncle interrupted, the familiar harsh tone creeping back into his voice for a moment, "yesterday was not the first time I've been through the night of a full moon on my own. I'm quite used to looking out for myself. I didn't ask you to hang around here; you invited yourself, remember?"

Trey nodded, then realizing that his uncle would not have seen the response, he added, "Sure."

His uncle took a sip of coffee. "Where d'ya go?"

"Out. I needed a walk, time to think, you know?"

"All night? That's quite a walk."

"I needed to get my head around what you'd told me about my father. I'd been foolishly kidding myself that I had this werewolf thing under some degree of control, but when I heard what he'd done to my mother—"

"Trey—"

"Let me finish. Now I know that it's all just been a lie. Everything Lucien told me about my father and how he'd used his powers to fight evil. Everything he told me about how he loved my mother. Everything he told me about being a lyco and the Amulet of Theiss. It's all just lies." The words poured out of him in a torrent.

"Listen, Trey, there are some things that you—"

"I met up with the pack," Trey cut across the old man, annoyed at the continuous interruptions. "I think that they were waiting for me. They were in the woods at the same time that I was." He looked over at the old man and was glad that those blind eyes were unable to see him as he fought to hold back any more tears from falling. "I'm moving out. I'm not going back to England. I'm going to join the pack and live with them in the cabins by the lake."

He expected the old man to say something, but his uncle just sat there, unmoving, deep lines forming harsh valleys in the flesh of his forehead. Trey stood up, his chair scraping across the floor tiles like a band saw. As he turned to leave the kitchen his uncle finally spoke.

"You Changed in front of them?" he said in a small voice. "You Changed into your werewolf form in front of the pack?"

Trey stopped in the doorway. "I Changed *with* them."

Frank lifted his head to look toward the sound of the boy's voice. His eyes were dancing in their sockets and his head was shaking in little movements from side to side.

"But the amulet. The amulet stops you from changing into one of us; it changes you into a—"

"I don't have it anymore."

Frank got up on his feet. The swift movement unbalanced him for a second, making him lean into the kitchen table that almost tipped over as a result. "What do you mean, you don't have it? You stupid child! What have you done with it?"

Trey was already down the hallway. He grabbed his coat from the hook by the front door and twisted the door handle to open it.

"I don't want it anymore," he shouted over his shoulder.

"Trey, wait—" the old man shouted from the kitchen doorway.

"If you want it as much as you seem to, go get it; it's in the woods over there someplace. Good luck finding it." He turned away, pulling the front door closed behind him and shutting off his uncle's protests.

# 22

He hurried down off the porch at the front of his uncle's house and turned to his left, setting off through the long grass in the direction that the pack had taken after leaving him. He filled his lungs with the sweet, oily smell of the pine trees that carried on the late morning breeze. Something small and nervous broke into a desperate run in the long grass just ahead of him, and he stopped, scanning the ground to see if he could make out what it was.

He took a look back toward the house, regretting not having stopped long enough to grab some of his stuff before leaving. It meant that he'd have to go back sooner than he would want to, but not now. Right now he just wanted to get away away from his uncle Frank and the poison that surrounded the old man like some toxic gas. He pushed ahead, taking big strides and enjoying the emptiness and solitude. He started to ascend a low hill leading up to the trees that marked the start of the forest, a not unpleasant glowing warmth starting to build up in the muscles of his thighs. He congratulated himself for having the foresight to put on the Timberland boots that he wore beneath his jeans. He had no idea how far away the cabins were and realized that he didn't care—he'd walk all day and night if he had to. He stopped just before the entrance to the trees, slowly turning on the spot to take in the magnificent countryside that surrounded him. In the distance he could make out a mountain range rising up over the tops of the trees behind his uncle's house, the purple and brown ramparts giving way to the snow-covered peaks. He hadn't really taken any time to admire the beauty of this country; his head had been too full of other things since his arrival. He took another deep breath, suppressing the sadness and regret he felt, and tried to cheer up a little by telling himself that if he was going to be forced to live somewhere as a prisoner of circumstance, there were far worse places to do so.

The Range Rover jostled and bounced its occupants out of their seats as it negotiated the uneven ground. They'd taken an alternative route—a shortcut that avoided the main road—but the terrain was atrocious, the ride unimaginably uncomfortable. Jurgen drove, his mouth set in a pinched slit as he concentrated on the ground ahead. Luke, in the back, was getting the worst of it—the Range Rover was an ex-military vehicle equipped with inward-facing bench seats in the rear and no seat belts or anything to hang on to. The rear passenger was being thrown around like a rag doll.

"How much longer?" Luke shouted. "I'd like to think that I'm getting out of this thing with all of my limbs still attached."

Jurgen ignored the youngster, setting his jaw and glaring at the road in response.

Marcus turned in his seat to look back at him. "Not much farther," he said, nodding at the exasperated looks the teenager shot in his direction. Luke was a hothead who liked to use his fists a little too freely, a habit that had caused a number of run-ins with other members of the pack. But he was fiercely loyal to Jurgen and was afforded greater leniency from the Alpha as a result.

The car bounced out of another depression in the ground, and Luke was slammed into the side of the car again, Jurgen laughing loudly at the boy's dismayed cries.

A few moments later the car stopped, Jurgen killing the ignition and peering forward out of the front windshield. They were on a ridge overlooking the clearing that Frank's house occupied. Luke leaned over the front seats to get a better look.

"What are we doing here?" he asked.

"We have some business with the new kid," Jurgen said, not taking his eyes off the house.

"Couldn't we have taken the normal route on the road through the woods? It would have been a hell of a lot more comfortable. These seats in the back of this thing are absolutely—"

"When I want your opinion on which route to take, I'll ask you for it. Now I suggest you shut up."

A silence descended over them all, broken only by the

sound of a woodpecker drumming on a tree and warning off any trespassers with its loud *tchur-tchur* call.

The engine ticked slowly as it began to cool down.

"How do you want to do this?" Marcus asked eventually.

"Do what?" Luke said from behind them.

Jurgen turned in his seat, giving the youngster the full benefit of his stare. "We are going down there to have a word with the old-timer and his nephew. I want to find out what makes the boy tick."

"Tick?"

"There's something about that boy that he's keeping from us. He's up to something, maybe something that could endanger the pack. And as Alpha, I am responsible for the safety of the pack."

"And what is it that you think this youngster is up to?" Marcus asked. He looked across at the man in the driver's seat, uneasy at the feral look on his face and the white-knuckle grip that he had on the steering wheel. He wanted to try and talk to Jurgen about his fears and suspicions—to try to calm him down and get him to consider what he was doing. But he knew that it was pointless. Jurgen had shown all too often recently that he did not take kindly to any opposition to his leadership. Right now, it was better to play along with him and try to be the voice of reason if things got out of hand.

Jurgen opened the door and began to climb out.

"What if they refuse to tell you anything?" Marcus called out, opening his own door.

"Then I'll find a way of asking the question that ensures that they will."

The three gathered together, Jurgen clapping the other two on the shoulders. Marcus forced a smile, and tried not to notice the simmering rage that seemed to burn off the man by his side.

"Let's go," Jurgen said, and started off down the hill.

# 23

Philippa toweled off the sweat from her forehead and took another swig from the isotonic drink that she'd bought. She'd pushed herself extra hard on the cross-trainer, pumping her legs while simultaneously pushing and pulling the upright handles of the equipment until she was panting for breath. She reasoned with herself that she owed her body this, to make amends for all of the chocolate that she'd eaten that morning. Raul, the personal trainer that the hotel had assigned to her, came over, giving her a thumbs-up as he approached. He was a tall, olive-skinned hunk of sculpted muscle, and he flashed her a grin made up of perfectly white and symmetrical teeth. It occurred to her that he would not have looked out of place on an advertisement for male underwear.

"You're really going for it, huh?" he said, nodding in her direction. "You work out a lot back home?"

"Not as much as I should," she said, stepping down off the machine. "Thanks for your help, Raul. You've been great."

"Hey, don't mention it. You coming back in tomorrow? I've got a great abs workout that I'd love you to try. It's great fun."

"I guess I could. Although my experience of gyms

suggests that anything described as 'fun' tends to result in a whole lot of pain."

"Come on. No pain no gain, huh?"

"OK, you're on."

"See you tomorrow," Raul said, turning away from her and walking toward the little desk that occupied a corner of the room.

Philippa watched him as he went. He was fit—in all senses of the word. She raised the towel again, burying her face in the soft cotton cloth and enjoying the feeling of it against her hot skin. She took a deep breath and was overcome by a sudden feeling of giddiness.

When she looked up again, the world had been turned inside out.

Her eyes opened on to a gym from hell. It was the antithesis of the clean and sterile and harshly lit place that she had just spent the last hour and a half in. The walls and ceiling might once have been white, but now black spores grew on their surface—wet, fetid, living tapestries that filled the room with a cloying stench strong enough to make her stomach heave. Hundreds of small yellow stalactites hung from the ceiling, depositing whatever foul liquid that had accumulated within them onto a floor that appeared to be made of the same black substance amassing on the walls. She looked around in short, panicked glances, finally stopping when her eyes took in the machinery that she had just been using. The cross-trainer that she had been exercising on was in fact a living creature: a nightmare beast from hell that was chained to the floor, lying on its back with its extraordinarily long arms held straight up before it by chains that hung from the ceiling. Its scaly head, chest, and hips were secured to the floor by great metal strips, and the beast's short, stumpy legs were curled in front of it, held there by some kind of sprung harness. On top of the legs someone had fastened small wooden boards that appeared to have been nailed into the flesh below. A shuddering breath escaped her as she realized that she had been standing on those boards and gripping those arms while performing her exercises.

The rest of the gym was no better. There were machines that looked more like torture devices than anything that you would use to improve your health. The middle-aged man whom she had watched working his cardiovascular system with some heavy hitting on a punching bag was in fact a grossly fat demon creature with skin the color of raw salmon. The flesh was bloated and distended, like a balloon that has been over-inflated and is about to explode with a bang. Despite this, the demon moved with a swiftness that Philippa would not have thought possible, punching again and again at the creature that was hanging from the roof in front of it. The victim of the abuse was a great sluglike creature that groaned in pain as each blow connected with its body—the impact making a low, dull thump as the demon's fists sunk into flesh.

The black-skinned creature with the rows of deadly-looking teeth began to rise up out of its chair behind the desk in the corner and move toward her.

Philippa felt her knees give, and she shot out a hand, grabbing at a pole on the wall to stop herself from falling. She *blinked* and the world flipped back. The walls were once again a boring shade of magnolia and the punching bag was nothing more than a sand-filled leather cylinder.

"Are you all right?" Raul said, halfway across the room now.

Everything that she had seen, she had seen in a fraction of a second. But she knew that *that* had been the reality of where she was right now, and that the pictures and smells and sounds that were being relayed to her brain *now* were false.

She turned her back on the demon and ran.

# 24

Some part of Philippa's brain—she guessed it must be the part that had been irrevocably changed by the dark magic left behind when the Necrotroph had departed her body—was unable to sustain the Ashnon's carefully constructed illusory edifice that she was supposed to be experiencing. It was similar to the time that she had woken up with Lucien sitting next to her in the hospital for the first time: She had simply *known* that he was a vampire. And now that she'd seen a glimmer of what was really behind the New York facade, her brain was unable, or unwilling, to maintain the illusion.

The hotel corridor flickered in and out of reality and unreality as she ran headlong down it. Most of the time it appeared as the long, straight corridor of the Waldorf-Astoria, but occasionally—as if some part of Philippa's brain were toggling a light switch, alternating between what she was supposed to see and what was really there—it would transform into a terrible, dark tunnel. Loud sobs escaped her as she plunged forward, not knowing or caring where she was going. She glanced behind her, checking that she was not being pursued, and took some small solace from the fact that the corridor was empty.

*For now,* she thought.

She knew that she was in danger of coming unraveled, of losing her mind completely if she could not find a way to stop the hellish visions. But they seemed to be coming with more regularity now, and she instinctively knew that this was a result of the panic that swelled, unchecked, inside her. The small part of Necrotroph that had been left inside her was causing the Ashnon's magic to malfunction, and she instinctively knew that the more afraid she became, the more this would happen. She couldn't stay here any longer.

She'd fled the gym and turned left, running headlong down the hotel corridor with its tasteful wall lights and plush carpeting. She didn't know how she'd managed not to scream in the gym—how she'd stopped up the horror that had consumed her. She wanted to scream now—to run and scream and never stop.

The toe of her sneaker caught on the carpet and she stumbled forward, her arms flying out ahead of her to break her fall, but she maintained her balance. The risk of the fall made her slow down, and she finally came to a halt, looked about her, and sucked in great gulps of air to feed her burning lungs. She was disoriented and couldn't remember where the elevators were. She shook her head, blinking away the tears that were blurring her vision. Now that she had stopped running, the pure white panic crept in again, forcing itself upon her.

She was sweating, her skin beginning to chill now that

she'd stopped, and her legs, already aching from her earlier exertions, were now cramping up.

She blinked and the wallpapered corridor was gone. A black tunnel of cold stone stretched out before her disappearing into the distance. To both sides, at regular intervals, the tunnel branched off into sub-arteries of pure blackness, and it seemed to her that *something* moved about in that darkness, something that was aware of her. She gave in to the panic and screamed.

The world inverted again, and the hotel corridor was back.

She stood looking around her, slowly unclenching her hands, which she'd scrunched up into tight balls of flesh and bone.

*Please stop this from happening,* she begged silently. *Please, please stop all of this.*

She slowly and deliberately closed her eyes, screwing them shut so that they creased at the sides and a deep frown formed on her brow. She quickly opened them, her pupils dancing from left to right as she took in her surroundings. Nothing.

"You need to contact Lucien," she said aloud to herself. She was way beyond the point of caring that someone might catch her talking to herself. "You need to get to your room and use that emergency number that Alexa gave you and ask him what you should do. He'll know. Lucien will know what to do."

She swallowed, the action sounding loud in her ears. She nodded, confident in the course of action that she must take.

She took another deep breath and started off down the corridor at a jog.

She slowed as she approached the elevators. There were six dull metallic elevator doors, identical triplets that eyed one another from opposing walls. She jabbed at the button to call one, and stood back, trying to calm her breathing and keep herself together.

The low chime announced the elevator's arrival, and she looked up to see which of the cars it was. Stepping forward to the doors as they slid open, she stopped. The elevator was occupied. An old lady looked out at her, and nodded in acknowledgment. Music drifted out into the foyer, the bland instrumental music intended to calm seeming at complete odds with the fear that gnawed through every part of her. The old woman placed her finger on the button that held the doors open.

"Are you going up?" the pensioner asked, smiling pleasantly back at the girl.

Philippa stood gawking at the figure. She had no idea what the real creature inside the elevator looked like, but she had no wish to get in and then blink "one of those blinks" and find out.

She shook her head, her lips clamped together as she concentrated on keeping her eyelids apart, forcing them wide-open and ignoring the stinging sensation that had already started up at the edges of her eyeballs.

"Suit yourself," the old lady said, and pressed another button, causing the doors to slide shut.

Philippa glanced around her. She didn't want to summon another elevator for fear that there would be more creatures inside.

She stopped then. Her body stiff and unmoving. She didn't have her room key. She slowly moved her hands up and patted at her tracksuit jacket pocket that wasn't there: She'd left it hanging somewhere in the torture chamber that she had been using as a gym. She couldn't, wouldn't, go back there to get it. Her mind raced as she worked out what she must do. She'd have to go down to the main lobby to get a replacement key, and that meant talking to the receptionist, and that meant not blinking in case the blink turned out to be a *blink*.

She shook her head, knowing that there was no alternative.

"Stairs, Philippa," she said aloud to herself in a voice that she hardly recognized. "Nobody takes the stairs, so you won't bump into anyone." There was a small door to one side of the elevators with a green sign above it indicating that it was to be used in case of a fire. She headed toward it, pushing against its weight and stepping into a sickly lit stairwell that ran up and down through the heart of the tower.

"You can do this. Go down there, get a key, get back up to your room, and call Lucien."

She hesitated, her heart thumping in her chest.

"C'mon, Philippa. You *can* do this."

She grabbed the handrail and let it slide through her hand as she descended, turning her body to one side and taking the stairs three at a time, not caring if she turned her ankle. The gym was on the fifth floor, so it wouldn't be any great hardship to get down to the lobby. Getting back up to her room on the eighteenth floor was not going to be a barrel of laughs, though, but it was that or take one of those elevators.

A blink transformed the staircase. She was on a stone spiral of steps that wound down through a shaft that appeared to have been hewn out of the black glassy rock face all around her. The water dripping from a roof somewhere high overhead made loud plinks as it landed, the sound amplified and echoing around the passage. She glanced at her hand on the rail and instinctively snatched it away. The scales that were carved on the surface felt, for a horrible second, all too real, and she was loath to reach out and touch it again.

"You can do this, Philippa," she repeated the now-familiar mantra.

She took a breath and, taking hold of the rail once more, began to descend.

"Can I help you, madam?"

The man standing behind the reception desk beamed at her, his head angled slightly to one side. He looked immaculate in his uniform, the light from the ornate lamps that lined the long wooden reception surface reflecting back from the gold buttons of his jacket.

"I . . . I've lost my key," Philippa said.

"That shouldn't be a problem . . . Miss . . . ?"

"Tipsbury, Philippa Tipsbury. I'm on the eighteenth floor

in room—" She realized that she had no idea what room number she was in. "I'm afraid that I can't remember the number."

The receptionist stared at her. He had a kind-looking face that was now lined with concern. "Is everything all right, madam?"

She knew what she must look like, standing there drenched in sweat, staring back at him with her eyes held open impossibly wide. An itching sensation began at the corner of her right eye. She tried to ignore it, repeating her newfound mantra over and over in her head, but the itch wasn't listening to anything she had to say; it had set up residence now, and wasn't moving until it got the attention it felt it deserved. It got worse and was now a burning sting that made her clamp her jaws together in an effort not to give in to its demands.

"Madam?"

"I'm fine, thank you. I'd just like my key." She shifted from one foot to the other, tapping her hands against her thighs in tight, fidgety rhythms. "I'm in a hurry," she added.

"Of course, madam. I'll just find it for you."

He turned away from her and tapped on a keyboard to his right.

She blinked. It was impossible for her not to. She sucked in a great breath as she did so, her heart slamming into her chest. But the reception stayed as a reception. She turned around and looked at the foyer, blinking quickly to irrigate her eyes, unable to stop now that she had started. With each blink she steeled herself, expecting the worst. But it didn't come. The huge, ornate brass clock continued to dominate the lobby space, faces of long-dead American presidents peering back at her from around its base. The old men sitting in the leather seats reading their papers to her left were just men, and the world on the other side of the revolving doors appeared to be New York on a rather wet and dreary day.

She was about to turn back to the receptionist when she saw him. He was standing on the other side of the revolving doors, looking in at her, and as she saw him he smiled, raising his hand in a gesture that was all too familiar to her.

After everything that had already happened that morning, it was almost too much for Philippa. Her knees gave a little, and she staggered for a second, struggling to stay upright as she felt the world slip away beneath her. She pulled in a great, shuddering breath, and the oxygen went some way toward providing her with some much needed equilibrium. She took a step toward the doors.

Her father mirrored her action, approaching the portal that separated the inside from the outside, a look of elation still on his face. He took another step and then frowned, turning his head quickly as if hearing something from behind him. As he turned, she caught the look of panic on his face, and this was enough to send a shiver of ice running down Philippa's spine. She had never seen that look on her father's face before. Something had scared him terribly. He looked back toward her, torn between her and whatever it was that threatened him from behind.

Philippa broke into a run, the rubber soles of her shoes making loud chirping noises as she sprinted toward the doors. She had to get to him. She had to get him inside and away from whatever it was that was endangering him.

She was almost there, her long legs gobbling up the ground in front of her. The polished brass and tinted glass of the huge revolving doors loomed in front of her, and she could still make out the figure of her father through the glass. All sense and reason had been erased from her mind. Some part of her desperately tried in vain to remind her that her father was dead, but she blocked out that unwelcome voice, stifling it and denying it. Because he was here, in this world that was made to look like New York—he was somehow here, and she had to get to him.

The receptionist shouted at her from behind. His voice sounded harsh and panicked, completely at odds with the smooth and polished demeanor that he had exhibited only moments before. He must have jumped over the reception desk to pursue her, because she could hear his footsteps gaining on her. She was at the doors now, her pursuer no more than three or four strides from catching her. She urged her aching legs forward in one last effort, stretching out her arms, palms turned up to hit the brass bars of the merry-go-round that led to the world outside the hotel. The doors gave way with surprising ease, swinging around their central column and issuing a weird hissing noise.

And then she was out.

She'd fallen, stumbling as the door behind her hit her in the back and sent her sprawling into the blackness where she collapsed, hitting her head painfully on the ground. Slowly raising herself up onto her hands and knees, she looked down at the cold, black rock beneath her. The hard, rough surface had grated the skin from her palms, and a hot, stinging burn had already started up. The rock seemed to radiate a black energy that made her feel desperately scared, and she blinked, pressing her eyelids together before letting them spring open, hoping to turn the black rock into the gray, regular paving slabs she'd spied through the hotel doors.

From somewhere behind her she became aware of the muffled cries of the receptionist. His voice sounded incredibly distant as though he were shouting at her from inside some giant goldfish bowl. She couldn't make out what he was saying. She did recall the warnings that he had screamed at her as she had hurtled through the lobby. How he had told her not to leave. How he had begged her to stop.

It was too late now.

She slowly raised her head, looking out from between the strands of hair that hung over her eyes at the lightless landscape before her.

There was no New York.

There was, and never had been, any sign of her father.

There was nothing out here in this pitiless landscape except for the huge, winged demon that was laughing down at her. Its great black tongue lolling from its mouth as it eyed the foolish human whom it had so easily lured from the Ashnon's protective custody.

It reached down and effortlessly picked her up in its clawed hands, cruelly digging the talons down into the soft flesh of her torso until she screamed. The demon threw the girl over its neck. Leaping into the air, it beat its great leathery wings and carried its prey off to its master.

# 25

"What is he doing here?" Jurgen said, the words harsh and sharp as he barked them out in the close confines of the kitchen.

There was no answer.

"Hit him again," Jurgen said with a nod of his head.

"Jurgen, don't do this." Marcus's voice was small and quiet from behind the larger man.

Jurgen ignored him. "Hit him again, I said."

Luke looked at the two of them, his eyes flicking between the two faces. When his eyes finally settled back on Jurgen's baleful glare, he balled his hand into a fist and punched Frank in the side of the head. A small shower of red flicked up into the air, landing in neat, crimson circles on the door of the fridge before growing tails that slowly tracked their way down the white surface. More blood, mixed with spit, hung from the old man's lower lip, reaching down toward a widening pool of the stuff that had already soaked into his shirt.

"You need to stop this," Marcus said from behind Jurgen. He looked down at the crumpled figure of the blind man and shook his head. "This isn't right." He reached out a hand and took hold of Jurgen's elbow.

Jurgen spun around to face him, his eyes blazing with a ferocity that made Marcus back away a step. "I told you that I was coming down here for some answers." He motioned with his head at the man strapped into the chair behind him. "He can give me those answers."

"He's an old man."

Jurgen stepped back, his eyes scanning Marcus from head to toe, as if sizing him up. "I expected more from you. I thought you understood the importance of the pack, the importance of keeping it safe. I was wrong about you— you're weak. If you don't like what is happening here you're free to leave." His eyes flicked for a second toward the kitchen doorway. Marcus didn't move; he stood eyeing Jurgen, considering what was the best course of action. When Jurgen spoke again he spat the words in an open display of contempt. "Or perhaps you think you can stop me in some other way? Maybe you think you should be the pack leader? Maybe you think it's your time?"

The silence in the room was broken only by Frank's ragged breathing. Marcus cut his eyes in the man's direction, inwardly wincing at what he saw there and wishing that he had the courage to take up the challenge and help him in some way. But Jurgen seemed to have lost his mind, he was uncontrollable right now, and Marcus knew that he stood little chance up against him in a straight fight. He met the Alpha's eyes again.

"I want nothing to do with this," he said. He looked over at Luke for a moment, but knew that the youngster was too terrified of Jurgen to come with him. He shook his head and, keeping his eyes fixed on Jurgen, backed out of the kitchen doorway, before turning on his heels and hurrying down the hallway to the front door.

Jurgen spat in the direction of the retreating Marcus. As the other man opened the front door, the crazy little dog came bundling in past him, racing up the hallway to get to its owner. Jurgen slammed the kitchen door on the creature, leaving it to yap and scratch and bark on the other side.

He turned back to the scene of the interrogation, walking over and bending at the waist so that his head was on the same level as Frank's.

"I'm losing my patience," he said in a whisper. "I suggest you wise up and start to tell me what I want to hear. So I'll ask you again—what's the boy doing here?"

"I've told you," Frank said, although he was having trouble forming his lips around the words. "He's visiting me. He's my brother's kid."

"How come you never told me about this *brother* before? You said that you had no family. You told me that if I set up on this land I wouldn't be getting any unexpected visitors. We pay you for the privacy and freedom and protection that this place allows us. We pay you very well. How come you forgot to tell me that you had a brother, huh?"

Frank raised his shoulders for a second before letting them sink back down. "I got a bad memory."

Jurgen sighed and stepped back, nodding at Luke who swung again, this time aiming at the stomach. The blind

191

man's breath burst out of him accompanied by a great "Ooof!"

The dog's barking increased in volume, as though it could somehow sense what was happening on the other side of the door.

"Well, we'd better see what we can do to help you with your memory problem."

Frank's head was slumped forward now. His arms were tied behind his back with duct tape, his legs strapped to the wooden chair in the same way. A wet cough brought up more of the blood and he spat it onto the floor between his legs.

"Where's this brother now?"

Another cough and another gob of red on the floor.

"He's dead. Been dead for years."

"And yet suddenly his kid turns up here. Why?"

Frank shrugged. Luke went to hit the old man again, but was stopped by a shake of his leader's head.

"Where did he come from?"

"I've told you."

"Tell me again. It seems like my memory isn't that great either."

"London, England."

"And you've never met him before? Your own nephew?"

"I didn't even know the kid existed."

"What's he doing here?"

There it was—that question again. Frank couldn't get his head around what was going on. Jurgen and his guys had broken into the house through the front door, smashing the small window at the side of it and reaching through to un-lock it. They hadn't even knocked. They'd gone through the house, shouting up a storm, going from room to room.

They'd hurt Billy. Frank had heard the dog howl in pain. Then the front door had slammed and Billy could be heard scratching at the wood, still barking wildly in frustration, trying to get back in. Frank had been in the pantry, fetching a fresh bottle, and he came out shouting into the darkness, demanding to know who was in his house.

They'd surrounded him, asking him where Trey was. He'd asked where his dog was, what they'd done to Billy. Jurgen had laughed at him then and started to push him around, asking again where Trey was. And Frank had told them all to go to hell.

Jurgen had come up to him then, standing so close that Frank could feel the guy's hot breath on his cheek. He'd told him that he'd give Frank one last chance to tell him where the boy was. Frank had told him where to go again, and pushed the punk away, yelling at them all to get out of his house. It was then that Jurgen had taken the bottle out of his hand and hit him in the side of the head with it. It wasn't like the movies. The bottle hadn't broken into a thousand pieces and sent Frank staggering about, it had stayed intact, mak-ing a horrible thunking sound as it connected with the old man's skull, and he'd collapsed in a heap on the floor.

When he'd come round, he was tied into the chair. He'd gotten real mad then, cursing them and telling them all what he thought of them, their parents, and anyone else who might have ever had anything to do with their miserable lives. They'd laughed at him for a while, expecting him to let up, but when it became clear that he wasn't going to, when they'd become tired of his cursing, Jurgen had ordered the youngest one to beat him. Frank thought back to when he could still see; he'd been in quite a few scraps in his life, and being hit was never a good thing. But when you couldn't see when the blow was coming, couldn't prepare yourself in any way for the impact, it was terrifying. He was damned if he was going to show these lowlifes how scared he was, but he *was* scared—mostly by the sound of the uncontrolled menace in Jurgen's voice.

"I asked you a question, Frank," Jurgen said, pulling the old man out of his reverie. "What's he doing here?"

"Visiting. He heard what nice company I keep, so he thought he'd drop by and see for himself."

Jurgen smiled. To Luke, who hadn't taken his eyes off the pack leader since they'd set foot in this house, there was something terrible in the way he looked down at the old man.

"You sent for him, didn't you?" Jurgen nodded, answering his own question. "He's here to try and take over the pack, isn't he? You called your nephew over to do your dirty work for you. You want a Laporte to be the Alpha of the LG78 again, don't you?" Jurgen's voice had risen and had taken on an almost hysterical quality now, and Frank didn't like the sound of it. He knew he should shut his mouth and let the kid get it all out of his system, let him talk himself out.

Instead he retaliated in the only way he could. "You

really are one crazy son of a bitch, aren't you? Where the hell do you get such an insane idea as that?"

There was a silence in the kitchen then. Frank braced himself for another beating, but it didn't come.

"He's Changed in company before," Jurgen said close to Frank's ear, making the old man jump in spite of himself; he hadn't even heard the wacko cross the space that had been separating them.

"What are you talking about?"

"Last night he ran with us. We got deep into the forest and had to get back this morning. This kid, your nephew, Trey, he joins us near a kill that we've made. Ella tells him that we've got to Change to get back, and he hardly reacts. Imagine that—she tells him that he's going to Change in daylight for the very first time, and this kid doesn't even blink. At first I thought he was just doing some great job of trying to be ultra-cool about the whole thing. I thought to myself, 'That's it, kid, you're doing a good job of pretending now, but once you Change with us in a second, once you Change and can feel what it's like, to know what it's really like to be a Wolfan, we'll see how cool you'll be then.'"

Jurgen moved away, stepping back but remaining directly in front of Frank. "But that didn't happen. I know, I was watching him. I always watch them when they first Change. Watch them freak out and jump about like crazy little cubs, howling with joy." He stopped for a moment as if waiting for Frank to say something.

"But this kid didn't do any of that. He Changed, looked

around him a bit, sniffed the air, and then was ready to go. Just like that. Just like it was *nothing* to him."

Jurgen put his foot on the seat between Frank's legs, resting the sole of his black cowboy boot on the wooden edge. He leaned forward and tipped the old man's head up so that he could get a good look at the bloody mess.

"Do you know what I think? I think that the kid's part of some other pack. A pack that you know about, and have kept secret from us." He waited, before continuing. "Some pack of Wolfan that is looking to expand? You brought him here to infiltrate us. He's here to take over my pack, isn't he?" He stopped then, a new thought freezing him in position until the muscles at the side of his jaw tightened and he slowly turned to look at Frank again, his eyes burning with an accusatory ferocity. "You told him about Ella, didn't you? You told him that there was a female Bitten here. He's here to try and take her away from me, isn't he?" His voice had risen to a shout now, and the sound was painful to the blind man's sensitive hearing.

"Do you know what I think?" Frank said. "I think that you might just be the most paranoid, crazy, out-of-his-tiny-mind freak that I have ever met. You proved that when you did that terrible thing to that poor girl. Insane doesn't even begin to describe how messed up you are, and if someone doesn't take over as the Alpha of this group before the next full moon, I'll eat my—"

The roar that came from Jurgen filled the room. He bent forward and lifted the chair with the old man strapped into it as though it were a child's toy. Spinning on his back foot, he heaved it across the room, slamming it into the far wall with a sickening crash. Frank's head connected with the hard surface and his whole body was already limp before the mangled and shattered mess crashed to the floor.

The room was perfectly still for a moment. Luke was the first to react, running across the kitchen to the figure of the old man lying in a rapidly widening pool of blood that seeped from the wound on his head. He knelt beside the figure, ripped the tape from around his wrists and ankles, and pulled the man out of the chair. He pressed his ear to Frank's chest, and when he looked back at Jurgen, his eyes were wide with fear.

"He's barely breathing," he said in a small voice. "And look at all this blood. My God, what are we going to do? He might die."

Jurgen was staring out the window, his eyes gazing off into the distance.

"Let's go and find the nephew," Jurgen said. And turning on his heel, he walked out of the room.

# 26

Marcus climbed in behind the wheel of the Range Rover, relieved to find that the keys were still hanging from the ignition. He paused for a second, glancing through the windshield at the house at the bottom of the hill. He told himself that there was nothing he could do, trying not to imagine what might still be going on in there, but the terrible mix of guilt and shame that he felt stopped him from turning the key to start the engine straightaway.

*It's not my problem,* he thought. *And pretty soon I'll leave this mess behind me for good.*

He blew out his cheeks and started the engine, crashing the car into reverse and pulling away from the clearing and the house, heading back to the cabins. As he rounded the first bend, the merest hint of a smile briefly touched his features when he thought about how Jurgen would react when he came out to find that the car was gone.

*Let the psycho and his weak-willed sidekick walk back to the lake,* he thought.

He had no intention of being around by the time they got back anyway. He'd had enough of this place and the pack leader who seemed to have lost whatever grip on reality that he might once have had. It was time to get out now while he still could. Get out and stay out.

The car bounced around on the uneven ground even more than it had before when it had had the additional weight of the other passengers, and he had to take it slower than he would have liked to avoid the risk of a puncture or worse.

His thoughts once again turned to Frank, back there with that maniac. He hoped to God that Frank had wised up and told Jurgen what he wanted to hear. He didn't want to imagine the alternative.

He swung between two trees, bounced through a drainage ditch, and came out onto the road that led to the lakes. He relaxed a little, putting his foot on the accelerator and speeding up, blinking against the sun that dappled the windshield now that he was out from under the thick overhead canopy.

He turned a bend and pressed his foot down on the brake, bringing the car to a skidding halt. He was at the top of the road that wound its way around the basin in which the lake and its community of little wooden cabins sat. The sunlight washed the scene with a wonderful golden hue, and Marcus reflected on how they had all stopped at this point when they'd first come here, looking down on the same scene, full of hopes and dreams about the adventure that they were about to start out on together.

They'd met via the Internet; Jurgen had traced some of them through his father's contacts, and they'd set up a private forum where they could talk to one another. It was Jurgen who had told them about the ability to enforce a Change in a group, and he'd suggested that they should try and meet up. His father's wealth made it easy for him to facilitate this meeting; he'd even paid for their airfares to Russia where they'd been transported to a huge villa. Jurgen was a different person then—laughing and joking the whole time, full of enthusiastic plans for the group. It was such a relief for the young men to be able to speak openly of the curse that had blighted them all since the beginning of their teenage life, when puberty had revealed to each of them what they were to expect for the rest of their lives. Most of them had led a nomadic life, moving from place to place to keep out of reach of the vampire Caliban and his spies. So many of their fathers' generation had been hunted down and killed by the vampire lord that their sons had learned to keep hidden, especially during the full moon. So when Jurgen had suggested they travel out to a wood on the outskirts of the town to try and make that first group Change they'd initially balked at the idea. But Jurgen had been so persuasive, so adamant that they should try it, that eventually they'd all agreed.

None of the group was comfortable with the idea of going through a Change out in the open. They were always scared of being detected by creatures that monitored for signs of nether-creatures in the human realm; the notion of transforming into a werewolf in daylight was something that none of them had ever dreamed about. To do it outside was unimaginable. But again Jurgen had taken the lead, assuring them that they would be safe, and that they could outrun, and if necessary outfight, anything that might be sent to confront them during daylight hours. Most of the lycanthropes that had been killed through the years had been dispatched at night, when Caliban and his minions were free to roam and hunt within the human realm.

They'd gathered in the wood, all very embarrassed when Jurgen had told them that they should strip down to their underwear and hold hands. That first Change had been amazing. The five male werewolves had roamed the woods, hunting together and sharing the joys of the kill. They all felt alive for the first time—alive and free. And by the end of the week, having Changed on three of the seven days they were together, an inseparable bond had been forged between them. In particular, Jurgen and Marcus had become very close, and Marcus felt like he'd found the brother that he'd always wanted as a child.

At the end of their time together Jurgen had sat them down and told them about the land in Canada, and how his father had informed him that the man who owned it, Frank Laporte, had somehow arranged for the place to be protected against vampires so that it could be a haven for a werewolf pack. He told them of his plans to go there and how he wanted them to join him.

They'd agreed, and two months later they'd all flown out to Canada.

Things went well at first. They spruced up the cabins, Jurgen paying for any work that was needed to make them habitable again. Those first four weeks in Canada had been wonderful. They'd reveled in the freedom that they were afforded by the place, Changing whenever the fancy took them and roaming far and wide through the forests that made up the land. But it all went terribly wrong when Jurgen invited his girlfriend, Ella, to visit for a weekend. Childhood sweethearts, they'd been going out, off and on, for years, and Jurgen believed that they were meant for each other.

They'd all met Ella at the airport. She hugged them each in turn as Jurgen had made the introductions, and then she'd fallen into her boyfriend's embrace, holding him close to her for what seemed an age. That night they'd had a small party. They'd sat around a large open fire by the lake. It was nighttime, and everyone had drunk too much. Ella asked Jurgen when he was going to come back home—when he was going to stop playing frontiersman in the woods and come back to his friends, family, and the playboy lifestyle that he'd always enjoyed. He'd reacted angrily, telling her that he'd brought her out here to show her what was important to him now. How his old life and his father's money wasn't what he wanted anymore. And then he told her that he wanted her to stay with him, to make a new life here together.

The rest of the group watched in astonishment as he told her what they were—a werewolf pack.

She'd laughed at him, telling him that he was clearly drunk and possibly more than a little delusional. Then he'd demanded that Marcus and the other members join hands with him in a circle around Ella, telling her that he'd show her just how delusional he was. Reluctantly the others obeyed, and they Changed in front of her.

She'd screamed and tried to run, but the pack had kept her hemmed in, backing her up toward the lake like a sheep being herded by a farmer's dogs. When there was nowhere left for her to go, Jurgen had stepped forward. The great wolf looked up at her, its eyes blazing in the firelight. Ella raised her hands, pleading with the nether-creature not to kill her. Then it bit her. It lunged forward and bit into her arm, opening up a large wound that painted the surrounding grass a deep red.

It was part of a plan that Jurgen had not revealed to the others. That had been five months ago, and it was the beginning of the end for the Alpha. Ella stayed—she had little choice now—but she never forgave Jurgen for what he had done to her, the love that she once felt for him began to slowly turn into resentment, and this seemed to tip the pack leader over the edge.

A crow cawed loudly in a tree to his right, and Marcus shook his head, clearing it of the memories. He couldn't afford to idle around daydreaming. He put the car into gear and sped down the hill toward his cabin, eager to be gone from this place as soon as he could.

Ella looked up from the book that she was reading at the sound of a car's tires skidding to a halt somewhere outside. Getting up from her chair, she crossed the room to the window beside the door to see Marcus climbing out of the Range

Rover. Something about his demeanor bothered her—he seemed agitated, looking behind him at the woods before hurrying over to his cabin and ducking inside.

She frowned. She'd heard the Range Rover leaving a little more than an hour ago, peering outside to see the back of the vehicle disappearing off up the road. She'd thought it odd at the time that anyone should be going out. Usually on the morning after a Change the members of the pack were very subdued, lounging around by the lake all day or simply taking to, and staying in, their beds. It was unusual for anyone to be seen out and about, let alone getting in the car and driving off into the forest.

Her interest piqued, she placed her book facedown on the table and went outside.

The cool air made her shiver involuntarily and she folded her arms in front of her. She stared into the woods, wondering what it was that Marcus had been looking for there. A duck came flying in at an oblique angle, skidded to a less than graceful halt in the middle of the lake, and caused an uproar of disgruntled quacking from those residents already present. Ella turned to her left and walked the short distance to Marcus's cabin. She gave the door a cursory knock, pushing against it as she did so. She blinked in surprise, and shoved a little harder when it refused to give way—nobody locked their doors during the day; everyone came and went between one another's cabins freely, without announcement. She frowned and knocked again, louder this time.

"Who is it?"

"It's me, Ella. Are you OK, Marcus?"

When there was no reply, she tried again. "Marcus, are you all right?"

She started to move away toward the window, when she heard the sound of a bolt sliding free of the lock on the door. Marcus opened the door a fraction, peering out at her through the gap.

"I'm busy," Marcus said with a glance over her shoulder.

"Busy doing what?" She waited, noting the anxious look on his face. "Look, I'm not going to go away until you tell me what's going on, so you might as well open the door and let me in."

He stared at her, willing her to leave, but she met his eyes with a look of determination. Eventually he sighed, shook his head in exasperation, and stood back, opening the door to let her in.

The suitcase on the couch was already half full with clothes that appeared to have been tipped straight into it from the drawers stacked on the floor. Another smaller bag containing Marcus's personal items was just inside the door.

"Where are you going?"

"Away. I'm leaving, Ella. Today."

"What brought this on? Why would you suddenly decide to pack your stuff and leave like this?" She waited for a response. "If it's about that silly argument that you and Jurgen had last week, I'm sure that—"

"The silly argument in which he threatened to take me over to the lake and drown me if I didn't shut up, you mean?"

205

"He was just kidding, Marcus. You can't possibly think that he meant anything by that."

Marcus stood perfectly still, studying her. He stared at the scar on her forearm, and when she realized what he was looking at, she let the arm drop down by her side, hiding the ugly pink flesh.

He shook his head, his jaw set determinedly. "Perhaps his breaking Lawrence's jaw for disagreeing with him doesn't mean anything. Because it sure as hell means something to Lawrence—it means that he'll sound like he's speaking with a mouth full of marbles for the rest of his life."

"What is all this?"

Marcus turned his back on her and continued to throw clothes into the suitcase. "He's lost it, Ella. He's so far gone that I doubt there is any way back for him. He's dangerous. Paranoid. It's only a matter of time before he does something else that will end up with somebody, probably one of us, losing their life."

"He's made some mistakes, I grant you—"

"Mistakes?" Marcus turned to face her, an incredulous look on his face. "Of all the people who should be able to see him for what he really is . . ." He stopped, trying to calm himself before carrying on. "Ella, he's like a rabid dog, and right now he's got it into his head that this new boy, Trey, is some kind of impostor, that he's here to try and take over as the pack Alpha. That's why he is, at this very moment, beating the hell out of a blind old man to try and find out what is going on."

206

Ella stared at him, looking for some sign that he was joking. "He's doing what?" she finally said.

Marcus looked down at the crumpled shirt in his hand. He put it in on top of the other clothes and began to close the suitcase. "You heard me."

Ella turned and headed for the door.

"You're not taking the car," Marcus shouted after her, his voice a mixture of malice and fear.

She stopped, outlined in the rectangle of the doorway against the bright sunshine outside. She spun around and faced him, her face a mask of fury.

"Oh, yes I am, Marcus," she said. "And *you* are going to help me stop this. If you want to leave afterward, fine. But you are going to come with me to Frank's house." She looked down at the suitcase on the settee and then back at Marcus, her piercing blue eyes never wavering from his.

After a second, he looked away, wondering if she had sensed the shame that he felt.

"OK," he said in a small voice. He puffed out his cheeks, grabbed hold of his jacket, and crossed the room, ushering her out. "But I'm warning you, Ella. I don't see any way back for him this time."

# 27

The Necrotroph sat in the car in the underground garage, the engine still idling. The demon was steeling itself for what lay ahead, playing over in its mind the various scenarios that might present themselves and not liking any of the options. It *had* to re-infiltrate Lucien Charron's organization, and quickly. Caliban had tried to make contact the night before, and the Necrotroph had had to make up some cock-and-bull story about why it was taking so long to find a suitable host. The entire situation was a mess, and it could see no way of achieving what it needed to. Because of that damned girl.

She was the demon's top priority now—the Irishman would have to wait. The demon replayed the scene when she had spoken to it through the host that it was currently inhabiting.

*I might not know exactly where you are right now, but I can sense that you are out there,* she'd said. And then much more worryingly, *I believe that I will be able to find you, demon. I can't quite yet, but soon I think I will be able to do just that.*

Lucien's organization had the girl, and they were hoping to use her to find out where the demon was hiding. If they succeeded, the Necrotroph was doomed. How much time did it have? It doubted that it had very much.

The problem was this stupid body that it found itself in now. It couldn't think of any way that it would be able to get to the girl from within the body that it currently occupied. The mechanic was perfect when the plan had been to take over the head of security, but there was no way that it could hope to get access to the teenager through it.

It thumped the steering wheel, jumping in alarm when the horn sounded in the enclosed concrete space. Finally realizing that the engine was still running, it turned the key. The demon twisted in its seat, looking around to see if anyone might be in the garage and if they had been alerted to its presence by the sound.

The Necrotroph needed to find an interim host. It would use up precious time, but it could think of no other way. It would have to possess someone inside Lucien Charron's organization who would stand a better chance of getting to the girl. But this increased its risk of exposure, as the Tipsbury girl now seemed to know when it was transferring between bodies.

Damn it all! It needed that blasted girl out of the way as soon as possible.

Ronald Given's hand stretched out to remove the keys from the ignition. He opened the door and climbed out, straightening up and stretching his back with a slight wince.

The demon walked around to the back of the car to fetch the human's work things from the trunk. It looked up at the pinging sound that announced the arrival of the elevator, and watched as the doors in the far wall slid open, blinking in surprise when it saw who the two occupants standing in the brightly lit interior were. They stepped out of the elevator and began to walk toward it. The Necrotroph couldn't believe its eyes—although strictly speaking they weren't *its* eyes at all—it was as if all of its prayers had been answered: the Irishman, Tom O'Callahan, and the Tipsbury girl were coming this way. They were walking straight toward it, as if the devil himself had delivered them into its arms.

It steadied itself, taking complete control of the host body, suppressing all nonessential parts of the brain to avoid any mishaps that might alert the girl to its presence. It stood by the car and waited for them, a big welcoming smile plastered on the Given man's face.

"Ronald," O'Callahan called across to him. "Good to see you back. I understand that you've been ill for the last couple of days?"

"Yes, I've had some kind of virus. Just haven't felt myself, you know. But I'm OK now."

"That's grand. Good to have you back with us."

The Necrotroph nodded in their direction, smiling all the while.

"Are you two off somewhere?"

"Yes, I'm taking this young lady to meet someone. Sorry, how rude of me. Philippa, this is Ronald. He helps keep all of Lucien's cars on the road and is a dab hand at fixing anything that you can take a screwdriver to. Ronald, this is Philippa Tipsbury. She's helping Lucien out with something."

"Pleased to meet you." The Necrotroph held out its hand and shook the teenager's. A small bead of sweat ran into Ronald Given's eye, and he blinked the salty liquid away.

"Well, we'd better be off." Tom moved toward the black BMW that was parked in a bay off to their left. He stopped, patting his pocket, a deep frown creasing his forehead. "Ah, crap. Would you believe it?" he said, shaking his head and looking at the girl. "I've left the keys upstairs in the apartment. We'll have to go up and get them." They started to move back in the direction of the elevator.

"I could take her wherever she needs to go," the demon said, wincing inwardly when the words came out too quickly and eagerly. It looked between the girl and the man. "I mean, if you wanted me to, I could take her. My car's just here and—"

"Ah, no thanks, Ronald. I'm to take her in person. Lucien's orders."

The Necrotroph knew not to press the matter. It would only draw suspicion on itself if it continued to act in any way that seemed out of character, but it couldn't believe how close it was to its quarry. Cursing its bad luck, the demon shrugged and turned away, opening the trunk. It looked down at the toolbox and briefly considered simply taking out a hammer and eliminating the two of them. But he knew that the Irishman would not be dispatched so easily. It lifted the box out and set it on the floor.

"I tell you what, though," Tom said to him, stepping forward and speaking in a conspiratorial tone. "You could do me a huge favor by waiting with Philippa here for a second while I shoot up to the top floor to grab my keys." He turned and spoke to the girl. "If that's OK with you, Philippa? Just wait here with Ron while I shoot up in the elevator? I'll be back down in just a few minutes."

The girl glanced between the two of them for a second. The Necrotroph held its breath, not daring to move.

Eventually the girl nodded. "Yeah, fine. I'll just wait here with Ronald until you get back."

# 28

The demon watched the elevator doors close, returning the little wave that the big, dumb Irishman gave them both from between the rapidly narrowing gap. It counted slowly to ten in its head to make sure that the doors weren't going to slide back open. When it was certain that they were alone, it turned to face the girl.

She nodded. A polite smile momentarily flashed over her lips before she returned her attention to her feet, nudging a small stone back and forth with the toe of her Converse sneakers, the tiny staccato sound the only break in the oppressive silence of the garage.

The demon also stared down at the stone, lost in thought.

"So you fix Lucien's cars?" she asked, glancing up for a brief moment.

The demon had no idea how long it might have, minutes at most. It would have to act quickly. There was nothing for it—it would have to do what it needed to out here in the open. It was high risk, but the stakes were so critical that it felt anything was justified right now.

"Yes, I look after the entire—"

The mechanic stopped, a look of fear and astonishment on his face. His eyes opened impossibly wide and then screwed shut. He sucked in a harsh and ragged breath and clutched at his chest, fingers curled into claws as they grabbed at the flesh beneath his shirt. He bent forward at the waist, a hoarse hissing sound escaping his lips until he lifted his head and looked up at her, his eyes beseeching her to do something. The terrible gray color of his face perfectly matched the concrete walls behind him.

"Mr. Given, are you OK?"

She watched as he sank to his knees, his eyes still locked with hers. He couldn't speak. His mouth was turned down in a ghastly grimace and tears made their way into the creases that lined the corners of his eyes. That terrible sound came out of his mouth again, and he fell over onto his back, still clawing at his chest with his fingers.

The girl moved to stand over him, looking down at him with a mixture of pity and terror. She glanced back at the elevator doors for a moment before returning her eyes to the dying man.

She sank to her knees beside the man's body, her hands fluttering in the air over his chest, as if unsure what to do.

The demon looked up at her through the dying man's eyes, willing her to come forward just a little closer, knowing that it had her now. If it could lure her in just a little more and make the transfer to her body as quickly as possible, it would be able to use the apparent heart attack and her subsequent attempt to revive poor old Ronald Given as the perfect cover, and not have to worry about hiding the man's body.

The man was trying to say something. His mouth was

still set in that ghastly upside-down grin but she couldn't make out the words. The girl leaned farther forward to hear him better.

Ronald Given grabbed the girl's head between his hands, forcing her closer to his own and opening his mouth as he did so. Her eyes opened wide in terror but she didn't pull away. She too opened her mouth to shout for help, and in that moment the demon seized its opportunity.

The Necrotroph's head suddenly appeared in Ronald Given's mouth, which had stretched open impossibly wide to accommodate it. The creature's black eyes momentarily took in the girl's face and then the whole thing shot forward, the glistening wormlike body thrusting itself across the gap between them. Tiny, armless hands that stuck out from the side of this body grabbed on to the girl's mouth, pulling against the lips viciously and forcing the head deep inside the open orifice. The demon felt the girl reach up with her own hands and wrap them around its body, and it prepared itself to shock the girl with the row of spiked tentacles arranged along the length of its body.

But something strange happened, something that it had never experienced before. Instead of trying to pull the demon free from her throat and mouth, as so many countless others had, the Tipsbury girl forced the demon deeper inside, grasping the slippery body and pushing it toward her own face in an effort to get the Necrotroph inside her as quickly as possible.

It occurred to the demon that something was wrong;

something was terribly wrong. It tried to resist, shocking the girl's hands again and again in an effort to make her stop. But it was too late. The last of its body slid down the esophagus and the demon was inside the Tipsbury girl. It swiveled around in the stomach and briefly considered what had just happened. The former host body was almost certainly dead now. They invariably died during the transfer process; those that did not die were left as nothing more than gibbering lunatics.

It sent out tendrils into the girl's body—great, rapidly elongating things that started hooking into the parts of the brain and spine to enable it to take complete control of the body and mind of this new host. But as it did so, there was a dawning realization that this thing that it was now inside was not the Tipsbury girl. It was something far worse than it could ever have imagined.

Lucien and Alexa stepped out from the shadows of the garage and rushed to where the body of Ronald Given lay. Alexa knelt down and placed her fingers against the man's neck, frowning and shaking her head when she couldn't find a pulse.

The doors to the elevator opened again, and Tom ran across to join them, having stopped the elevator from ascending as soon as the doors had closed earlier.

The Ashnon got slowly to its knees. It seemed incapable of even the simplest movement, and as it got one foot under it, it listed to one side, almost falling to the ground again. Three pairs of hands shot out together and they helped the demon to its feet, where it wavered on the spot like a drunkard.

Lucien stood in front of the figure and spoke, not to the demon before him, but to the demon that was now inside.

"At long last we meet," he said. The vampire's golden eyes bored into those of the thing in front of him, blazing with a ferocity that was enough to send a shudder down Tom's spine. "I know that you can hear me in there, and I wanted to tell you that your time is now over. You have taken over your last human body, and now it is time for you yourself to be consumed."

The facsimile of Philippa Tipsbury's body jerked suddenly, one hand going to her stomach while the other clamped firmly over her mouth. A muffled heaving sound came from behind the hand over her lips, but the Ashnon's eyes were full of humor as it looked back at Lucien. There was another jerk of the body and the Ashnon buckled at the knees, almost falling to the floor. When it looked up at Lucien again, the vampire knew that it was time. He nodded his thanks to the demon and stood back a little.

The Ashnon shot its eyes quickly to the other members of the group, still keeping the hand clamped over its mouth. It nodded once to each and then closed its eyes and tipped its head back slightly. There was a fizzing sound in the air like rain on overhead power cables, and Tom, Alexa, and Lucien felt themselves pulled forward toward the nether-creature, having to rock back on their heels to avoid over-balancing in that direction. Then a hugely powerful but brief

217

wind blasted outward, taking their breath away and throwing them back a step or two. When they opened their eyes, the Ashnon was gone.

"Is that it?" Alexa asked, looking up at her father.

"Yes, that's it. The Necrotroph's fate is sealed. The Ashnon has returned to the Netherworld, and the demon inside it will be consumed. Philippa will be returned to us shortly. We must find out from her what she wants to do with her life now, and help her in any way that we can."

Tom nodded in Lucien's direction. "I'll take care of Ron. I'll make sure that he's seen to and that the necessary arrangements are made."

Lucien glanced down at the prone body. "Thank you, Tom. Make sure that any family that he had are well looked after, and that they get anything and everything they need." He took his daughter's arm and walked back toward the elevator.

"You still haven't heard from Trey, have you?" she asked as the doors slid open in front of them.

They stepped inside, Lucien pressed the button to take them back up to the penthouse apartment. The look on the vampire's face matched the worried expression on his daughter's.

"No. It's been three days now, and despite the message from our friend Galroth to the contrary, I *am* worried about the lack of any contact. If Trey has not called by this evening, I will send someone over to his uncle's place to check that he is OK. Depending on the feedback, Tom will decide whether he should go over to Canada."

He turned to look at her. She realized that there was something else troubling him.

"What is it?" she asked.

"Alexa, I too have to go away. Now that this unfortunate business is over, I need to leave you and Tom and Trey for a while."

"Where are you going?"

"Away." He held up his hand to stop her protests. "I have something that I need to do."

"But surely you need to wait and see that Philippa and Trey are both—"

Lucien reached out and gently took his daughter's shoulders. "I cannot wait any longer, Alexa. There is something wrong with me. Something terribly wrong. If I don't get help, I believe that I might do things—horrible things that I swore I would never do again. And I may hurt the people that I love and care about. I have tried to fight it, but it's no good—it's getting worse. If I can't stop these . . . inclinations, I'll become the thing that I most despise. I'll become my brother again."

The elevator announced its arrival at the apartment, but they stayed where they were, looking at each other.

"I have left instructions for you all while I am away. Philippa will be fine. I would have heard if she were not."

"Where are you going?"

Lucien smiled a sad smile. "I'm going to find a friend of Trey's. The battle angel, Moriel."

# 29

Jurgen and Luke left the house and walked out into the bright sunshine, shielding their eyes against the glare and staring up toward the ridge where the car had been parked.

"Marcus," Jurgen hissed through his teeth. He spun on his heels, looking about him wildly as if expecting to see someone or something pointing and laughing at his inability to appreciate the joke. "I'll kill him," he muttered under his breath. He stopped and noticed the path trodden through the grass off to the left of the house, the tall grassy spines all bent and flattened in the same direction. "He went that way," he said in a low voice.

"Marcus?" Luke said.

The pack leader turned on the younger man, pressing his face to the other's and glaring at him. "The boy! The Laporte boy. That's the direction he took when he left the house."

"Jurgen." Luke looked nervously back toward the house. "The old man . . ."

"Let's go," Jurgen said. Without another word, he loped off in the direction of the tracks.

Trey came out of the woods. He was on a high ridge that looked down at the wooden cabins littered around the edges of the lake below. It looked idyllic now, almost a picture postcard, but he guessed that in the middle of winter it didn't look so cozy.

He made his way down the slope, turning sideways to negotiate the gradient, grateful once again for the sturdy boots on his feet. It was treacherous going. The mud gave way underfoot, sending mini landslides down the hill in front of him, and on more than one occasion Trey fell, throwing out an arm to stop himself from tumbling headfirst and helter-skelter down the steep incline. At some point there must have been trees on the hill because here and there weathered old stumps poked their heads out of the ground, their gnarled roots providing yet another obstacle to avoid. By the time he got to the bottom, Trey was completely out of breath. He stood with his hands on his thighs, hunched over, inhaling great lungfuls of air.

When he finally looked up, he was struck by the beauty of the place.

It was quiet by the lake. A few waterbirds made the odd honk or hoot in his direction, but there didn't appear to be any people around. He looked over to the cabins on the shore to his left—about sixteen in all—and realized that he had no idea which of them might be occupied. He was hoping to find Ella, to explain to her what had happened between him and his uncle, and ask her to speak to Jurgen on his behalf. He couldn't imagine any reason why the pack leader wouldn't accept him into the group, but he was wary of the Alpha male—he seemed . . . unstable, and Trey thought that Ella would be his best, and least complicated, way in.

The ground was level now, and he strode toward the wooden houses. He slowed down as he approached the first cabin, calling out to anyone who might be inside, then knocked at the door. When it was clear that nobody was home, he walked around the building to take a look. A clothesline had been set up behind the cabin three down from where he was standing—the floral blouse and black leggings could only be Ella's, and he walked behind the cabins toward it. He hadn't gone more than seven or eight strides when a voice behind him stopped him in his tracks.

"What are you doing here?"

Trey turned to see the tall, ginger-haired youngster who had stood next to him during the Change in the forest earlier that morning. The boy was holding a shotgun, pointed in Trey's direction, and he immediately put his hands up. Ginger was terribly thin, his skin so pale that it almost blended in with the white T-shirt that he wore over his jeans. The sunlight was bothering him and he squinted in Trey's direction. There was something wrong with the kid's mouth, as if his jaw had been put on crooked.

"I asked you what you were doing here," the older boy repeated, tilting his head to one side and doing his best to look tough. He spoke in a mumble, and it was difficult to make out the words.

Trey knew that the teenager was the pack Omega—the lowliest wolf in the group. Ella had introduced him, and

Trey was wracking his brains to try and remember what the guy's name was.

"I want to see Ella. I saw the laundry on the clothesline, and assumed that that was her cabin." Trey motioned with his head at the building behind him. "You're Lawrence!" he said, pointing at the other boy. Despite being the one holding the gun, Lawrence took a step backward. "It's Lawrence, isn't it?"

Ginger nodded, his face still screwed up against the sun.

"Do you think you could point that thing somewhere else?" Trey said.

The other boy looked down at the rifle before lowering it to point at the ground.

"She's not here. They've all gone out somewhere. I'm the only one left here at the moment." The boy glanced over at Trey, tipping his head back and jutting out his chin, which only made his jaw appear even more grotesque. "That puts me in charge."

Trey had to struggle to keep from smiling. He guessed that the Omega was enjoying this opportunity to assert some authority for a change. "I guess it does," he said.

Lawrence nodded and drew himself up to his full height. "She left with Marcus a short while ago. To be honest, it's pretty rare for anyone to go out on the morning following a Change. Something big must have come up."

"Something big?" Trey said. "But they didn't take you along with them?"

"Like I say, someone has to stay back here to take charge."

"Do you know when she might be back?"

Ginger shrugged. "No idea."

There was a silence then, the two simply looking at each other.

"Well, is there anywhere that I could wait for her?" Trey finally asked.

The cockiness that Lawrence had tried so hard to maintain seemed to simply drain out of him. He frowned and looked about him as though the answer to the question might be lurking somewhere in the shadows cast by the wooden buildings. He looked over Trey's shoulder toward Ella's cabin, chewing at the inside of his cheek nervously.

"I don't—"

"I could wait for her in her cabin, maybe? I'm sure she wouldn't mind."

Lawrence was already shaking his head, stuttering his protests as Trey continued. "She's expecting me," he lied. "Both Jurgen and Ella are expecting me. But I could leave if you want me to, and you could explain to both of the Alphas how you felt it was better to ask me to leave." He eyed the other boy, before adding, "I'm sure that Jurgen would understand your decision. After all, you *are* in charge."

The mere mention of the pack leader's name was enough. Lawrence raised one hand, palm facing the younger man, as if stopping traffic.

"Hey, man, if you say they're expecting you, they're expecting you. It seems foolish for you to go and have to come back again, and I'm sure that it'll be fine for you to wait in

Ella's cabin." He nodded in Trey's direction, and began to move off toward his own dwelling. "Don't touch anything, though," he said over his shoulder. "Ella's very particular about anyone touching her stuff."

He was gone before Trey could reply.

# 30

The Range Rover's tires crunched to a halt, kicking up a small cloud of dust. Ella glanced at the house before turning her head to look at Marcus. He stared out of the front windshield, his eyes fixed on some invisible point in the distance.

"Well," she said.

Marcus chewed at his lower lip. Apart from that, no other part of him moved.

"We have to do this, Marcus." She opened her door and stepped out. For a terrible second she thought that he was going to drive off and leave her to sort this mess out by herself, but after a moment he switched off the ignition and climbed out, closing the door behind him.

They crossed the weed-strewn path to the wooden porch, worry lines etching Ella's face with each step she took. The front door was still open and she walked through it calling out, "Hello? Frank? Jurgen?"

She paused in the hallway, her vision temporarily made poor by the sudden transition from sunlight to the dimly lit interior. "Frank?"

The house was unnaturally quiet, and she'd taken no more than three steps when she saw the reason why. The tiny figure of Billy lay on his side, his body twisted at an impossible angle, back legs and front legs at odds with each other. His salmon pink tongue lolled from between his teeth, and his dead eye stared unseeingly at something on the ceiling above her.

She knelt beside the still figure of the animal, stroking at its coarse coat with the tips of her fingers. Tears ran down her cheeks, and she shook her head angrily. She turned her head and glared up at Marcus, with a look of pure hatred.

Marcus held his hands up in front of him. "He was alive when I left," he said. But he couldn't help feeling that the dog's death *was* his fault—the animal had rushed in through the front door as he'd opened it to leave.

Ella wanted to pick up the small dog, to carry it in her arms and place it in its favorite place on the settee, but she still had to find Frank.

She cocked her head at a sound from the kitchen, listening for it again. It was a small sound, little more than a sigh, a whisper. When it came again she stood, hurrying toward the kitchen door and pushing it open.

"Jurgen? Frank?"

A scene of horror greeted her. Blood spatters, with long crimson tendrils that reached toward the floor, adorned the walls and the doors of the kitchen cupboards in front of her. In the center of the room, having somehow dragged himself there, lay Frank, the bloody wash behind him describing the arduous journey that he had made to get that far.

She rushed over to him, kneeling down next to him, not knowing what to say or do. She shook her head, blinking

227

her eyes in disbelief at the sight before her. With shaking fingers she smoothed back a strand of gray hair that was plastered to a face that she hardly recognized, its features horribly bloated and covered with dried blood. She moved her fingers to his neck, not sure how to take a pulse there, but hoping to find one nonetheless.

"Oh, Frank, what have they done to you?"

A tiny rattling sound came from the old man's voice, and she stopped, staring down at the bloody mess, unsure if she had actually heard it or not.

"Bleeegh." A word this time. Nonsensical, but a word.

She looked up at the sound of the tap being turned on, and saw Marcus running a cloth under the cold water. He hurried over with it, handing it to her so that she could mop the old man's head. "Thank you, Marcus," she said, and as gently as possible washed away some of the blood and gore from the old man's face.

"Beeleeegh," he said again. And he tried to turn his head away as if looking for something with his sightless eyes.

She knew what he was trying to say, and who the blind man was asking for.

She shook her head and blinked away the tears that blurred her vision. "He's dead," she said. "Billy's dead."

A whimper came from between the split and ruined lips, and tears welled up in the old man's eyes. Ella fetched a glass of water, crouched down, and held Frank's head so that he could take a sip. He shook his head, but she held the glass there insistently until he managed to take some.

228

"I heard him," Frank managed to say now that his mouth had been cleared a little. "He was trying to get at them from the other side of that door." Still struggling to shape his lips around the words, he shook his head again. "Why did they have to hurt Billy?"

The old man lifted an arm, clawing at the air in front of her.

"Stay still, Frank. You're badly hurt and you need to—"

"Get me up," the old man said as best he could.

She looked down at him again, the hand still reaching out for her. She shook her head in disbelief. "Wait a moment," she whispered. She nodded at Marcus to fetch one of the wooden chairs. She placed it beside Frank, wincing at the stupidity of what she was doing and knowing that she should be seeking professional medical help for him right now. She gently took hold of the arm still held out toward her, Marcus moving around the other side and slipping his hands beneath both the old man's arms. They hoisted him up as gently as they could, off the floor and into the chair.

"Thank you, Ella," he said in a slurred whisper.

"Do you want some more water?" she asked, moving to retrieve the glass.

"Whiskey," he said.

"I don't think that's a good—"

"Whiskey," he hissed, raising his head in her direction.

She would have smiled if the sight of his face was not so horrific. Both eyes were swollen to such an extent that even if they had worked, they could not have seen much. His nose was a red mess too; one nostril had almost been torn off, and it hung down like a ragged piece of gristle. It was his mouth that was almost too horrible to look at—his lips had split open at several points, and the bottom one was purple and swollen to such an extent that his jaw could not close properly.

"Whiskey," he said again. "Please, Ella."

She went to the pantry and grabbed a bottle from one of the boxes. Hurrying back to the kitchen, she unscrewed the metal lid, letting it fall to the floor where it skittled around before coming to a halt under the chair. She poured the old man a large glass, reaching forward and guiding it into his hand.

Frank raised the glass to his lips and took a gulp, wincing at the burning pain it caused to his lips and gums. Lowering the glass, he dug around at the front of his mouth with his tongue, stopped, and spat a discolored, bloody tooth onto the floor. He finished off the rest of the glass and held it up in the air, waving for it to be filled again. Ella obliged and half filled the vessel again with golden liquid that the old man downed in two or three mouthfuls.

She watched as he tipped his head back, some of the tension in his shoulders easing just a fraction.

"What happened?"

"Ask your friend," the old man said, nodding in Marcus's direction. "Oh, he didn't stay to see the finale, but he was here all right." The old man lifted a trembling hand to wipe at his lips, wincing as he did so.

230

"Marcus came back to help," Ella said, taking the hand and holding it in her own. "Please, tell us what happened."

"Jurgen," the old man said as if that one word was all she needed to have as an explanation.

He tipped the glass again, but this time when he discovered it was empty he did not ask for a refill. Ella watched as the old man's forehead creased. He leaned forward, trying to stand. The unexpected movement caught Ella off guard and she grabbed the old man by the arm to steady him.

"Where's Trey?" the old man cried, struggling to his feet. "Where's my nephew?"

"You need to sit down, Frank. We need to get you an ambulance."

"Where is he?" he asked again.

"I have no idea," she said. "The pack dropped him off here this morning. I thought he was with you."

"He left. Came to see you, you and your *friends* down there by the lake."

The old man was still struggling to speak clearly, but Ella was struck by how much he had rallied since she'd given him the whiskey. She looked at the blood on the walls and floor, and reasoned that Frank's injuries must be a whole lot worse than she'd first guessed. Even so, she had to admit it—Frank Laporte was one tough old customer.

"Frank, why does Jurgen think Trey is a danger to him? Why would he beat you like this?"

"He's a mad dog, Ella." He shook his head. Lifting his hand in the air, he made a peculiar waving motion with his fingers. "I shouldn't have said those things to Trey. This is all my fault. All my stupid fault!"

"Frank?"

"Jurgen has guessed that Trey has a secret."

"A secret?"

"Nothing that would harm your precious pack, but yes, Trey has a secret. Jurgen thinks that my nephew is part of some plot to try and take over the pack." A short, derisive snort escaped the man. "As if the kid could give a damn about the pack!" The old man went still. "No, Trey has a destiny much greater than that, and thanks to me, he's thrown away the one thing that can help to protect him from those that would do him harm. People like Jurgen." The old man began to move forward, gently trying to push Ella's supporting hands away. "I have to find it somehow. I have to find it and get Trey away from this place."

There was a silence in the kitchen, broken only by the dripping of the tap.

"The necklace," Ella said eventually.

Frank stopped. "What? What do you know about it?"

"I saw him remove it and throw it into the woods. Last night before the Change. I saw him take it off and hurl it into the trees at the top of the ridge out there. I remember thinking at the time that it was an odd thing to do, and how upset he seemed. I would have asked him about it, but the next thing I knew, the Change was upon us."

Frank turned his head in her direction. "In the woods? Is

there any chance that you might be able to find it again? It's very important, Ella."

She looked down at the old man. His milky eyes stared back at her unblinkingly. She replayed the scene when she'd watched Trey in the woods, fixing his and her location in her head and recalling the direction in which he'd flung the silver chain. In her mind's eye she traced the arc of the object as it flew out of his hand toward a group of beech trees off to her right. There had been no sound when it landed, and she guessed that it must have fallen in the leaves near the base of the trees.

"Ella?"

Frank's voice pulled her out of the woods, and the hint of a smile played at the edges of her mouth.

"I think I could find it," she said. "But I'm not going to— not right now. If Jurgen has become . . . unhinged . . . If he's responsible for doing this to you, and if he's a danger to Trey, I think the best thing to do is to find him and try to—"

"There won't be any talking to him now!" Frank's voice boomed, taking Ella by surprise and making her jump in alarm. "He's flipped his lid. He's beyond all reason now."

"He's right, Ella," Marcus said in a low voice.

Frank started forward, wincing with the effort. He held out a hand for her to help him. "That amulet is the only hope Trey has. Give me a hand, will you?"

"Frank, I think that you should sit down. Even better, I think that you should go and lie down while we—"

233

"Shut up and help me, or leave. They're the options right now, girl. Choose." He held his arm up to her and it wavered in the air as though this simple act was almost beyond him.

She shook her head in disbelief, but reluctantly took his arm.

He gently took her by the shoulders and turned her body so that she was facing away from him. Placing his hand on her right shoulder, he gave her the slightest of nudges, and they walked out of the kitchen and down the hallway toward the front door, slowing down and treading carefully as they passed the prostrate figure of Billy on the way. Ella glanced down at the little animal again, for once thankful that the old man could not see. She let out a small sigh, and as if sensing what had caused her to do so, the old man gently squeezed her shoulder for a second.

"Let's go and find that amulet, Ella," he said.

# 31

They were almost at the wall of trees that signaled the beginning of the forest. Frank's breathing sounded more ragged and strained. He was not in great shape anyway, and the beating that he had taken earlier had clearly left him in an even frailer state.

Ella stopped, turned to face the blind man, and removed his hand from her shoulder.

"This is about as far as you go, Frank." He started to protest, but she continued in a firm voice. "I should not have let you come. Please. I want you to sit down here with Marcus and get your breath back. I'll go ahead and try to find the chain. I'm the only one who saw Trey throw it, and it makes sense for me to go and look for it alone. If I find it, I'll bring it straight back here to you."

The old man shook his head, but his chest heaved with the effort that he had already put in. He pointed a finger in Ella's direction. "You want to leave me here with one of the men that tried to kill me?"

"Frank."

He sighed in defeat. "Go on then. Go."

"I'll be as quick as I can," she said, nodding at Marcus. She paused, watching as the younger man carefully helped

Frank down onto the grass. Then she turned her back on them and entered the woods.

She ran through the trees. It was farther than she remembered, but eventually she slowed as she spotted the large oak tree up ahead. She ran her fingers across the rough, sharp bark as she rounded the trunk. She stopped on the far side, leaning out and looking back in the direction she had just walked, replaying the scene from the previous evening to pinpoint the exact location where Trey spun around once he'd realized she was there. When she had it in her head, she came out from the tree and went to stand in the same spot that he had occupied. She looked off to her left and saw the birch trees, their bleached bodies looking out of place among the gray and brown and green that surrounded them. She ran in their direction, trying to *feel* the speed of the chain as it tumbled through the air after being thrown. She slowed, imagining the deceleration and fall of the object, knowing that it had to have landed somewhere very close to where she was now standing.

She let her eyes scan the ground. The leaf mulch was thick here. The ground had not been disturbed in a very long time, and she knew that it would be all too easy to miss the thing that she was looking for if it had skidded beneath the old and rotting leaves that carpeted the floor. The light under the canopy was not great, and she cursed her luck. Her only real hope of finding the amulet was to catch a glimpse of the sun's reflection on its surface. She got down on her haunches and scanned the ground. Nothing. She turned slowly in a circle so that she could take in as much of the ground around her as possible, but something told her that what she was looking for was up ahead. She faced the birch trees again and started to circle to her left. She'd taken no more than five or six steps when something caught her eye. She stopped, holding her breath and letting her eyes wander over the surface again. The tiniest glimmer flashed at her through the undergrowth. She fixed her eyes upon it and crept forward.

She'd been lucky. Most of the necklace was buried, burrowed beneath the loose top surface of the forest floor as it had skidded to a halt. But a small section had caught upon a small stick, looping itself around the wood so that it peeked out from beneath the brown carpet.

She bent forward and picked up the chain, letting the full length of it hang from her hand. It was unusually long and she had to hold her hand high above her head so that the small silver amulet at the bottom could twist and spin before her face. It was a small fist. Pitted and scarred, it looked extremely old. She reached forward with her other hand to take the amulet between her thumb and forefinger, holding it still so she could study it more closely. She felt a cold shudder fork its way down her spine, and realized it was not just the coolness of the air beneath the trees that had caused it. There was something about the amulet—something that made her want to put the chain over her head and have that silver clenched fist close to her skin. To tuck it away and tell the old man that she hadn't been able to—

"I'll take that," Frank said.

She whirled around to see him standing no more than ten feet away, one hand on Marcus's shoulder, the other stretched out toward her—palm up. She hadn't heard them approach. She'd been so caught up with the feelings that the amulet had stirred inside her that she hadn't heard them walking up behind her. She shook her head in disbelief, frowning as she wondered how they could have followed her.

"How did you . . . ?"

"Your scent," Frank said, letting go of Marcus and taking a step toward her. "I couldn't sit around back there just waiting. Besides, I didn't know how you'd react when you found it. So Marcus led me into the woods at the point that you entered, and after that I followed your scent."

Ella glanced at Marcus who simply shrugged and nodded in confirmation.

"You smell good—like coconuts," Frank added.

She peered at him through the gloom. His face was in shadow, and in spite of his age and his injuries, she sensed a wolfish menace in him. She looked down again at the chain in her hand.

"The amulet, Ella," Frank said, inclining his head toward the outstretched hand.

They stood like that for a few moments, statue-like among the other living statues of the forest.

When she looked up again he was smiling at her through blood-caked lips. "It's beautiful, isn't it?"

That same cold shiver pulsed through her again. She

wondered what had made her want to keep it. Why she had considered lying to Frank about finding it despite his assertion that it was the only thing capable of saving Trey right now. She collected the chain in one hand, piling the links on top of one another until she had a small, metallic island in the center of her palm. She hefted it, surprised at the weight of the necklace, and then stepped forward and carefully transferred the tumbling links from her hand to Frank's.

He closed his fingers around the chain, a strange look on his face as he did so.

"If you had any idea how long I have waited to hold this . . ." His voice trailed off and Ella thought that she could see tears forming in the corners of his eyes. But she didn't like the way that the old man was clenching the necklace in his fist, the knuckles white with the pressure he was applying. She thought back to what Frank had said in the house—how the only thing to do would be to reunite Trey and the amulet and get him away from here as soon as possible. Looking at him now, she couldn't help but wonder if Frank was capable of giving up the amulet clutched so tightly in his hand.

"What are we going to do now?" she asked.

"Hmm?"

"What's next, Frank?"

The old man nodded to himself. "Now we're going to save my nephew."

# 32

Trey pushed the door open and stepped inside the cabin, gasping as a wall of hot air met him. He looked around for the source, spotting an oil-filled radiator in one corner that had been left on. Leaving the door open, he crossed the room to the heater and flicked the switch on the wall to turn it off. Removing his jacket, he hung it over the back of a chair, and walked over to the small kitchenette where he ran the cold tap, searching the cabinets for a glass.

He turned around, leaning his back against the edge of the metal sink, enjoying the sensation of the cold water on his mouth and throat as he drank greedily from the tumbler. He took in the immaculately clean and tidy room. It was open plan—the living area, dining area, and kitchen all housed in the same space. Only two doors came off the room, both set into the same wall to his right, and he guessed that these must be the bedroom and bathroom.

A large stone fireplace and chimney dominated the wall opposite him; two high-backed armchairs were arranged facing each other on either side of it. There was a small table between the chairs, and the half-empty cup of coffee that was left next to a facedown paperback book were the only clues that anyone had been in the room that day. Every item was tidied away, and there didn't appear to be a sign of dirt or dust in the place. It seemed that everything Ella owned was allocated a space, and everything was arranged with an eye to order and organization. She'd manufactured a series of long shelves against one wall, and these were filled with books. Hardbacks filled the uppermost shelf, displayed in size, from the tallest on the left to the smallest on the right. The other shelves were filled with paperback novels, and Trey knew without looking that these would be organized in some equally anal-retentive manner, probably alphabetized by author name, or something. He smiled to himself and finished his drink, turning to refill it from the tap and using the cloth he found neatly folded on the counter to wipe away the splashes that he'd made.

He glanced at the clock on the wooden mantelpiece, wondering how long he might have to wait for Ella to return. The temperature inside the cabin had fallen to a more bearable level now, cool air coming in through the door from across the lake and bringing with it the smell of the forest and the water. He crossed the room, pushed the door shut with his heel, and wandered over to the bookshelf. He smiled again when his suspicion about the arrangement of the books was confirmed. Spotting one of his childhood favorites, *Treasure Island* by Stevenson, he knelt down and eased it free of its companions. He took the book and settled down in the nearest armchair. If he was going to have to wait, he might as well make himself comfortable.

Jurgen emerged at the edge of the trees, no more than a stone's throw from where Trey had recently stood, and looked down toward the cabins. He wasted no time in scrambling down the slope, taking none of the precautions that his predecessor had in tackling the treacherous gradient, and hurtling head-long down the hill in great, bounding leaps. He heard a shout from behind him as Luke fell but he ignored the boy's cries, intent as he was on getting to the bottom of the slope as quickly as possible. The hill leveled out, and he'd started to make his way across the grassy open land that led up to the lake when Luke called out to him again.

"Jurgen, help me. My ankle. I think I've broken it."

Jurgen paused and slowed to a stop but didn't turn around to see what had become of the boy. He clenched his fists and swore beneath his breath. He'd leave the boy there, move on ahead to see what the newcomer, Trey, was doing in his camp. Luke would have to make his own way back as best he could—there was no time for him to play nurse right now. He started off, ignoring the cries behind him and scanning the area around the cabins for any sign of the four-by-four vehicle that Marcus had driven off in. He slowed when he saw that the car was not there. If Marcus wasn't around it might be difficult for him to do what he planned . . .

He stopped, turning to look back at Luke. The boy had slid feet first into a long-dead tree stump sticking up out of the ground like a gnarled old hand. He had both hands clenched around his ankle, and his eyes were screwed shut. A hissing sound came from between clenched teeth as he struggled not to shout out with the pain. Jurgen took a deep breath, trying to keep his anger at the boy's foolishness in check.

"Wait a moment," he said through gritted teeth. "I'll be right up."

The trip across the field took an age. They started out with Luke on his feet with his arm over Jurgen's shoulder, but the high grass kept snagging on the boy's injured foot, and he begged him to go and get the car.

"There isn't any car," Jurgen said, taking a grip on the other's belt and pulling him along with him again. "Marcus has not returned with it."

"How am I going to get to a hospital? How am I going to get this ankle looked at?"

"We'll find Marcus and the car and then we'll drive you to a hospital. But not right away. We've other fish to fry before we can worry about that. I need you back at camp with me right now." He moved forward again, pulling Luke along with him.

Luke began to cry. The pain was horrendous, and he couldn't keep his foot sufficiently high off the ground any longer; his thigh muscle was burning with the effort of it. After a few more minutes he stopped, refusing to go on any farther—the pain that he was suffering overcoming his fear of the pack leader.

"Just leave me here," he said. "Leave me here until you can come back with help."

"You're pathetic," Jurgen snarled, his face pressed close to Luke's so that the other could see the fury that burned in his eyes. "You're not fit to be part of this pack." He pushed the boy away and watched as he sprawled to the ground, crying out in agony as his foot jarred beneath him. "I thought Lawrence was the weakest member of the group. But I was wrong. You are a weakling. A pathetic weakling and I should never have let you join us."

"I'm sorry, Jurgen." The boy turned his face away.

Jurgen glanced across the remaining patch of land that they had to cross to get to the path around the lake and the cabins on the other side. He reached down and tugged on the boy's shoulder, forcing him to sit up. He might need him. He turned his back and crouched down. "Get on," he said, pointing over his shoulder with his thumb toward his back. "I'll carry you."

Jurgen straightened up and tipped his shoulders back, sending Luke sprawling to the ground in front of Marcus's cabin. He ignored the scream of pain and curses aimed in his direction as he glanced around him. Opening the door, he looked inside, taking in the suitcase and empty drawers on the couch. He stepped back outside, pulling the door shut, his hand resting on the handle as he stood stock-still, trying to figure out what had happened.

He was too late. The impostor, Trey, had already convinced

Marcus to join him. He must have found out about the argument Jurgen and Marcus had had at the old man's house. They were forming a new pack—a pack that he would lead and . . .

He looked over at Ella's cabin. What if the boy had managed to sway her too? What if he'd used the same conniving, scheming ploy to lure her away? He roared in anger and ran toward the cabin, shouting her name at the top of his voice.

At the sound of his pack leader's voice, Lawrence emerged from his cabin, looking around him to see what was going on. His was the cabin farthest from the others. He'd taken it because he liked to be away from the rest of the pack, especially Luke, who teased him constantly about his stature in the hierarchy of the group. The ginger-haired boy took one look at his pack leader running in his direction and knew that something was terribly wrong. Jurgen had blood all over his hands and clothes. It had dried to a coppery color, but it appeared to Lawrence that his Alpha had been attacked by someone or something. He remembered the newcomer's unexpected arrival earlier, and guessed that Jurgen's agitated state was something to do with the boy. He hesitated for a second, then set off in Jurgen's direction to see if he could help.

Jurgen looked up to see Lawrence running toward him. The boy was shouting something at him, waving his hands and pointing toward Ella's cabin. But Jurgen was too consumed with anger to hear him. The blood that rushed through his veins sounded like a torrential river in his own ears and he shouted out Ella's name over and over to try and drown out the sound. Something strange had happened to his vision—it had become blurred at the edges and a red veil had descended, as if there were blood in his eyes. He turned to look at Lawrence, who had stopped in his tracks, and was now slowly backing up, staring at him in horror.

That was when Jurgen knew that he wouldn't need the other two to force the Change. The anger that raged through him now was enough to bring the Change about. This had happened to him only once before when he'd been on his own, deep in the woods. There had been a trespasser and . . . when he'd come round again the hunter was dead.

He threw back his head and roared at the sky, welcoming the metamorphosis that would turn him into the Wolfan.

Trey stepped out of Ella's cabin, wondering what on earth was going on outside. Someone had been screaming her name, bellowing it over and over again.

He threw the door open and stepped outside to see Jurgen, who was kneeling on the ground with his back arched painfully behind him, bellowing like some madman. It had been the Alpha that had been roaring Ella's name. Trey could see in an instant what was happening—it had happened to him once. But unlike Jurgen, he'd managed to control the Change, using everything in his power not to give in to it and succumb to the beast within.

One look at Jurgen told him that he was too far gone to stop the transformation now. The Alpha had fallen forward onto the ground and his body was already horribly distorted. The bones made a grinding noise as they broke, stretched, and reset into a new skeleton on which the muscles were already growing and swelling. Trey stared in horror as the human body went through the grotesque Change. It was nothing like watching the pack transform together that first time; Jurgen's body was twisting and contorting in agony, the screams coming from his mouth inhuman and sickening to the ear. Jurgen's face was distending, the muzzle appearing to push its way out from the skull, the mouth stretched wide in agony as teeth erupted out of the jaws. Trey watched as fingers disappeared into huge clawed paws that tore at the ground as the pain continued unabated.

Trey caught a flash of movement from the corner of his right eye, and glanced in that direction, registering the look of fear on Lawrence's face as he sprinted back in the direction of his cabin. Behind Jurgen, another member of the pack was lying facedown on the ground, grimacing in pain and clutching at his foot. Trey's heart hammered in his chest and he was torn between the desire to go and see if he could help the injured man, and the stronger desire to stay as far away from the creature—that was almost fully transformed now—as possible.

The Wolfan finally lifted its head, and looked up to see Trey standing there. As soon as the creature's eyes fell on him, it let loose a roar that hurt Trey's ears and echoed around the lake, causing ducks and other creatures on its surface to take to the sky.

Something was wrong. Something about the way that the creature had looked at him sent a terrible cold shudder forking through him, and Trey knew that he was in danger. The creature was almost fully Changed. The last vestiges of the human that it had once been, all but gone. Trey stepped back into the cabin, slammed the door, and threw the bolts into place to lock it.

# 33

The four-by-four easily negotiated the large depression in the track, bouncing up the other side and throwing the three occupants out of their seats for a moment. Frank reacted with a low "Oof," and Ella apologized again for the uncomfortable ride. They'd taken the fastest route they could toward the lake, ignoring the main track, which was much smoother but which looped around the forest and took considerably longer.

"Please stop apologizing, Ella," Frank said. "You just concentrate on driving and leave me to worry about whether I'm ever going to walk again when I get out of this thing."

Marcus had accepted Ella's offer to drive, taking up a seat in the back of the vehicle, where he'd sat silently throughout the journey. Ella had checked on him in the rearview mirror a few times during the trip, but he'd always been in the same position—sitting, staring at the floor between his feet, deep in thought. He spoke now, his voice low and difficult to hear over the noise of the tires on the track. "So what's your plan, old man?"

"Huh?"

"Your plan. I assume that you have one, and one that

involves the necklace that you were so keen to retrieve. I think that Ella and I have a right to hear what it is."

Frank squeezed his fingers around the silver chain in his fist, but remained silent. Ella glanced across at him for a second, unwilling to take her eyes off the road for any more than that.

"I'm going to do what I should have done from the start—I'm going to get my nephew out of this godforsaken place. I'm going to reunite him with this amulet and send him back to England—to be with people that care for him and can look out for him. I don't know what I was thinking, letting the lad stay here in the first place. This place has always been bad news."

"And you think he'll go?" Ella said. "Just like that?" She turned the wheel sharply to avoid a large hole in the road, throwing everyone around in the car like rag dolls. "What makes you think you can persuade him to go?"

"He'll go when he's heard what I have to say to him," Frank said in a voice so low that Ella had to strain to hear it.

"He came out here to be with you, Frank. You're the only family he's got."

"Hungh," the old man grunted. "Some family I turned out to be." He tilted his head back to let it rest against the head support on the back of the seat.

"What about the pack?" Marcus asked.

Frank sniffed and wiped his face with the back of his hand. "To hell with the pack," he said. "It's finished. You two are going to have to deal with that lunatic, Jurgen. If he goes quietly, I won't press charges. If he kicks up a fuss, I'll have the police here to arrest him on an attempted murder charge." He was silent for a second, before adding, "If it was up to me, that son of a bitch would be made to pay for what he's done. He killed Billy . . ."

Marcus looked up and met Ella's eyes in the rearview mirror. The look they shared suggested that neither of them believed it was going to be that easy to get rid of Jurgen and dissolve the pack.

Ella swung the steering wheel around and they cleared the last of the trees, pulling out onto the top of the slope that swung around the lake and down to the series of cabins on the far side. She slowed down a fraction, taking in the view below them as she always did. Her heart filled with the same feelings of excitement and eager anticipation that it had when Jurgen had first brought her here on this same road. Then something caught her eye. Something down by her own cabin, and she stepped on the brake, bringing the car to a complete halt as she peered down at the scene.

She shook her head, as if doing so might shake loose the images that were being relayed to it from her eyes. "Oh my God," she said softly.

"What?" Frank said, his head turning in the direction of her voice. "What is it, Ella?"

Marcus had come off his seat and was leaning between the two of them. He looked out, following the direction of Ella's eyes, seeking out whatever it was that had caused her to freeze in this way.

"What can you . . . ?" he began, but then he too saw it, and the words caught in his mouth.

The huge black werewolf lifted its bloody face from the dead body on the ground. Gore hung from the sides of its jaws and it turned its head very slowly to look back at the car that it had sensed through its acute hearing. Its pink tongue flickered out from between massive jaws, cleaning the mess of blood and flesh that surrounded its mouth. To Ella it appeared that the huge wolf-creature was grinning at them. Then it rolled its head away to take in the wooden structure that was Ella's cabin. Turning its huge and powerful frame, it approached Trey's hiding place.

"Who is that on the ground?" Marcus asked.

"I think it's Luke," Ella said in a hollow voice.

"Will somebody please tell me what the hell is going on?" Frank shouted out. The desperation in his voice brought Ella around and she quickly regained her senses. She released the brake and pushed her foot down hard on the accelerator, sending a cloud of dust and stones flying into the air behind them as the car lurched forward down the hill.

"It's Jurgen," Ella shouted over the roar of the engine. "He's Changed. He's killed Luke. I think that Trey must be down there somewhere."

"Hurry," Frank said, as he looped the silver chain over his head. "Get us down there as fast as this heap of junk can go."

# 34

Trey looked out the window, holding his breath as he waited for the huge nether-creature to reappear. The Wolfan had already killed the poor guy with the damaged ankle, Trey was sure of that. To see if his fears were confirmed, he craned his neck again, pressing his face against the glass window-pane, trying to see out beyond the field of vision offered by the window.

Trey had not witnessed the attack, but he'd heard it. The young man's screams echoed around the grassy bowl that the lake sat in, a high piercing screech that was suddenly cut short. For Trey, the silence that followed was even worse than those terrible cries.

The Big Bad Wolf was coming, Trey didn't doubt that. And *he* was the piggy in the house made out of sticks. He shuddered, trying not to think about how that had turned out for the poor little porker.

He looked at the security bolts on the door, knowing that they would not withstand an attack from the nether-creature outside. Even if they could, there were the windows to consider—the Wolfan would think nothing of hurling itself through the glass to get at its prey. He was trapped. Dead if he ventured outside the door, dead if he stayed put. Neither option was very appealing.

He looked around him for a weapon that he might try to use to fend off the huge beast, but nothing looked even remotely fit for the purpose. The knives in the kitchen block, even the largest ones, all seemed tiny and insignificant when he thought of using them to defend himself against the creature. His options were extremely limited: beheading, drowning, or fire were the only three surefire methods of dispatching a werewolf, and Trey couldn't imagine a single way of employing any one of them without first being torn to pieces. A small whimper escaped him, and he turned back toward the window, pressing his face against the glass again and peering as far to his left as he could, in the hope that he might be able to catch sight of the nether-creature. His breath, coming fast as his lungs worked overtime to fuel his panicking heart, misted up the pane, and he had to go up on tiptoe to find a clear spot on the glass to look out from.

It was then that he caught sight of the movement on the ridge up ahead of him. His eyes switched to the road that wound down from that direction, and for one second he thought that he'd imagined it—his eyes playing tricks on him in this moment of desperation. But then from behind a row of large bushes that grew up alongside the road, the Range Rover emerged. It was traveling quickly, too quickly to be safe, and Trey guessed that the occupant had seen some of what had happened outside and was coming to help him. It had to be Ella. She'd been to Frank's house, talked to him, and had come back here to try and make peace between uncle and nephew. She must have spotted Jurgenwolf from the ridge and was now racing to Trey's rescue—to get him away from the creature and—

Something black ran past the window. Like the shadow from an airplane momentarily blocking the sun, it was gone in an instant but the briefest glimpse of it had caused Trey's heart to jam into his chest, halting his breath.

Ella wasn't going to get to him in time.

Trey knew that the Wolfan would be in the cabin any second now. It might choose to come crashing through glass or through wood, but it would get in somehow, and it would kill him as it had killed the injured teenager outside. He would be defenseless against it.

If only he had the amulet. If only he hadn't been so reckless in throwing away the power that his father had bestowed upon him. He'd done so in a fit of rage, but unlike Jurgen, whose anger had turned him into a mindless, bloodthirsty killer, Trey's moment of anger and frustration had resulted in leaving him as nothing more than a pathetic and defenseless target. How could he have been so foolish? The amulet's powers had saved his life on more than one occasion, and Lucien had stressed to him the importance of never removing it. And yet he had simply discarded it. Thrown that protection away. Did he really think that he would be safe here from Caliban? Indefinitely? No, the vampire would have found him eventually. And even the pack would not have been able to save the teenager from the vampire lord's murderous intentions. Trey had signed his own death warrant. A short snort escaped him when he thought how his imminent death would not be at the hands of the vampire—instead it would be at the hands of a creature much closer to home.

Trey moved to the door, hoping that he might be able to put his weight into it if the Wolfan decided to try to enter that way, and at the same time knowing that it was the quickest way *out* of the cabin should Jurgen choose another means of entry.

He concentrated on the spell that his friend Charles had taught him. It was a spell that allowed Trey to speak directly into the mind of another person. He silently intoned the words of the incantation, concentrating on a mental picture of Ella at the same time.

*Hurry, Ella. I'm in your cabin. Jurgen is going to kill me. I'm by the door and—*

The glass in the window at the back of the room exploded and the huge black shadow that poured into the room landed among the broken shards. The Wolfan shook its head, sending more glass slivers skittering across the wooden floor in every direction. Yellow eyes looked up from beneath the creature's brow and took in the boy with his hand upon the door. A trickle of thick saliva, tinged pink with blood, hung from one side of its vast jaws, and lips peeled back to reveal rows of deadly teeth.

Trey held his breath, the nether-creature that was Jurgen seemed even bigger than he had remembered from the

256

woods that morning. Then, he too had been Wolfan, and while Jurgen had been the biggest wolf in the pack, Trey had not been that far behind. But looking at the creature now, the vast blackness of it filling the room, Trey suddenly felt very small—a mouse staring up into the face of a cat. From outside came the sound of a car skidding to a halt. Trey didn't hesitate. He turned to the door and threw back the bolts that moments before he'd hoped would hold it in place. Wrenching the thing open, he ran out of the cabin toward the car.

# 35

The glass from the window saved him. Trey had thrown the door open but had not even taken his first step across the threshold when he'd caught the sound of the werewolf's claws gouging at the wooden floor as it sought some kind of purchase. The thousands of slippery glass shards denied the pads any sort of grip and the frustrated roar that had followed Trey out of the door hurt the boy's ears. He looked up, saw the car, and sprinted toward it. He willed his legs, which suddenly felt as though they were filled with cotton, to move faster. He wasn't going to make it. The nether-creature at his back would be upon him any second to tear and rip at his flesh. The car was no more than ten meters away but it may as well have been two hundred.

He looked ahead of him, his eyes wide and filled with panic. Ella was already out of the car, as was the other man, Marcus, who'd climbed out the door at the back of the vehicle. Despite the all-pervading fear that flooded every part of him, Trey noticed that the front passenger door was also open, but that there was no sign of whoever had occupied that space in the car.

The world around him seemed to have slowed down to half speed. His breathing and heartbeat were impossibly loud, filling his ears and blocking out everything else. Ella had her hands up at the sides of her mouth and was screaming something at him but he had no idea what it was. Everything looked too bright, too vivid. The edges of his vision seemed to *fizz* with a golden light, and he momentarily wondered if he might be having some kind of near-death experience. He could feel the thing at his back now. The Wolfan was almost upon him, and he knew that he would die here and now, in this place.

Something leaped over the roof of the car from the opposite side and charged.

The huge beast stood at least eight feet tall, and it was covered in a gray-and-white pelt. It ran—upright and on two legs—straight toward him at full speed, its features a contorted mask of fury. And even with his mind in the state that it was in, Trey could see that only one of the creature's eyes was capable of sight—the other inhabited by a dull, gray, misty orb. But the eye that could see was fixed on Trey's face, and it shone with such a dark malevolence that the teenager stopped in his tracks, unable to move any farther—certain death now rushed toward him from every direction.

The great snowy gray werewolf was almost upon him, its half-human, half-wolf hands set into vicious hooks that ended in great, barbed claws. Its mouth opened wider with each giant stride the creature took so that Trey looked into a face that seemed to be composed of nothing but teeth.

"Get down, Trey!" Ella bawled at him, and the sound of her voice finally forced its way into his head, wrenching him free of the fear-frozen state he'd been in. He let his legs buckle beneath him, his body folding to the ground as if some sniper hidden in the forest had shot him.

The two were-creatures met in the space above him, and Trey looked up to see flesh tearing beneath raking talons in the spot that he'd occupied fractions of a second before. The initial exchange was terrible. The black Wolfan's teeth found a purchase in the shoulder of the other, and it shook its head viciously, ripping open an ugly wound that fountained an arc of crimson into the air.

The giant black Wolfan's momentum drove its opponent back—its four legs generating more power than its upright, bipedal adversary—and the gray lycanthrope was sent crashing to the ground.

Trey had little doubt that the gray-white lyco was his uncle Frank, come here to rescue him from certain death at Jurgen's hands. He could see the amulet that he had so carelessly discarded, hanging around the creature's neck as it defended itself from the Wolfan's follow-up attack.

Ella's voice, loud and urgent, brought him back to his senses again. "Get up, Trey! Quickly!"

He was on his feet in an instant, up and running toward the car. At the sound of their cries, the Wolfan gave up its advantage over the other nether-creature, turning its back on it and setting off after the boy again. It had gone no more than three strides when the gray lyco flung itself at it, biting down hard into the Wolfan's back, and raking long wounds into the animal's flanks with its claws. The howl of pain that went up from the giant black Wolfan filled the air, and it turned to defend itself, rearing up on its back legs and throwing its body over to try and dislodge its assailant.

The nether-creatures sprang apart, circling each other and looking for an opportunity to attack. Both were bleeding from a number of wounds and their tongues lolled from their mouths as they sought to fuel their bodies with oxygen.

Trey reached the relative safety of the car and was bundled in through the back door by Marcus, who jumped in after him and slammed the door shut. Ella was already in the driver's seat. Reaching for the gear stick, she crashed the lever into reverse, at the same time twisting her body around to look out the rear window.

"Wait!" Trey shouted, leaning over the back of the passenger seat to get a look at the two nether-creatures through the windshield. "We can't leave him here like this."

"Frank told us to go," Ella shouted above the high-pitched sound of the engine in reverse. "He told us to get you into the car and to go. Not to wait for him. To get away from this place."

At the sound of the car moving away, the Wolfan's head swung in their direction. It turned its back on its adversary again and charged toward them.

"He's coming!" shouted Marcus from the back. "Move it, Ella. Get us out of here!"

Ella pressed her foot down hard on the accelerator, but the nether-creature was almost upon them, its lips pulled back in an evil grin that suggested it knew there would be

261

no escape for them. One more leap and it would be over the hood, and Trey doubted that the safety glass of the windshield would stop the powerful beast. He raised his arms in front of his face to try and avoid the worst of the glass that would shower in on them.

But the windshield never shattered.

The huge gray beast had pursued the Wolfan, and sweeping out an arm in a desperate last attempt to stop it, it had taken the creature's back legs out from underneath it just as it made that last terrible leap. Instead of crashing through the windshield, the Wolfan smashed into the wire grille that covered the front of the car, its huge paw becoming wedged in among the metal. It struggled to tear its trapped paw free, ignoring the deep cuts it inflicted upon itself as a result.

"Go, Ella!" Marcus shouted again. "He'll break free any moment. For God's sake, just drive over him."

But Ella did not respond to his urgent cries. Trey looked across at her and her eyes were fixed on the Alpha leader. A terrible realization had dawned on her. Her lips moved, but no words came. Trey understood what she was going through. She loved Jurgen; she had given up everything—even her humanity—to be here with him. But the thing outside now would never love her back—it was too filled with hate and anger.

"We can't go," she said in a small voice. She turned in her seat to face them both.

"Are you crazy?" Marcus said from the back of the

vehicle. "That thing out there isn't going to stop until we're all dead, and if you think this tin can that we're sitting in is going to hold it out, you've—"

"Ella's right," Trey said. He took Ella's hand in his own, holding the other out toward Marcus. Ella mirrored his movements as though they were sharing the same thought.

"Close the circle, Marcus," Ella said, nodding at their outstretched hands. "Open that back door and then join hands with Trey and me. We can stop this. If we work together, we can drive Jurgen away. We can force him away from here and away from Frank."

"And then what?"

"Leave that to me."

He stared at the two of them incredulously. There was a howl of pain from outside the car and Trey turned his head to see Jurgen rip his paw away from the car. The creature turned to look at his uncle. The gray werewolf's final effort had left him sprawled on the ground, his limbs flung out at his side. He appeared to be utterly exhausted—a waiting victim for the hate-fueled beast.

"Marcus!" Trey shouted, thrusting his hand in the other's face.

Marcus shook his head as if unable to believe his own foolishness. He kicked his foot at the handle that opened the back door, leaned forward, and took both the hands held out to him.

# 36

He was going to die. Frank Laporte tasted the blood in his mouth and did his best to block out the pain that spread like a forest fire through each and every part of him. He was too tired to fight anymore, too old and too tired. Looking up, he focused his one eye on the clouds rolling across the blue firmament, relishing the sight of them. It was so good to see again—to see the outside world and not just the inside of his cage—and it seemed to him that the sky above was the most beautiful thing in the world, bluer than any he could remember. He coughed and felt the tiny droplets of blood rain back down on his face.

He closed his eyes and sighed, feeling himself change back into a human once more, glad that the transformation was painless and swift, but sad to be descending back into the darkness behind his eyes again. He waited for death to come at the hands of the Wolfan, glad that he had been successful in thwarting its attempts to kill his nephew.

He couldn't hear the car engine anymore. He imagined Trey and the others driving off through the woods now, and hoped that his nephew would get as far away as possible from this place. He smiled to himself and waited for the end.

\* \* \*

The Alpha Wolfan sensed the other members of the pack even before they emerged from the back of the vehicle, feeling their presence as they transformed. Now that they were out in the open air he could smell their scent as it carried on the wind to him. He could smell Ella, and her scent excited him. He wanted her to share in the kill he was about to make. He wanted her to experience the killing and bury her muzzle alongside his in the blood of the freak-creature that had dared to fight him. He wanted her by his side again. But her scent was joined by the other Wolfan that accompanied her—Marcus and the boy that he'd come here to kill, and he remembered the threat that the young man still posed to him. He also knew that Ella and Marcus were responsible for bringing the *thing*—the half-man half-wolf abomination here to thwart him, and the hackles went up on the back of his neck as he turned to face them.

They came around the car and approached him cautiously, slowly separating and fanning out, Marcus and Ella going right and left of the newcomer as they moved toward him. At the sight of the young upstart, Jurgen felt the rage building inside him. He was bigger than all of them and he considered simply charging straight for the nether-creature in the middle, gambling that the other two would be too slow to react. But they were being cautious, their eyes tracking his every movement, their bodies low and tense, ready to respond to any threat. He was already injured and in a weakened state, and it occurred to him that if they chose to attack him together, they would easily be able to overpower and possibly kill him. He didn't think that Ella would ever hurt him, but—

He retreated, moving carefully backward and keeping them all in view. He looked at Ella, trying to read her intent from her body posture. Her eyes were locked on his, and he thought that he detected more than a hint of sadness and regret in them—as if she did not really want to be here with the other two. He knew then that she had been swayed by this newcomer, that this Trey Laporte had somehow poisoned her against him. He would not have had to try too hard to convince Marcus that the pack needed a new leader—perhaps even offering him the role if he would join him in deposing Jurgen. And the two of them must have worked on Ella—lying to her about him and forcing her along here with them. Ella loved him, Jurgen was certain of that. She'd always loved him. He needed to get her away from the other two; he needed to make her see how she'd been used—how this . . . boy had lied and connived and twisted her mind.

His eyes switched back to the creature in the center—the cause of all this. The Alpha wanted so much to kill him. Wanted to spring forward and tear and bite and rend. Wanted to taste the newcomer's blood in his mouth and feel the life ebb out of his dying body. But he could see no way of doing that with the other two there to protect him.

They'd backed him up past the edge of the lake now. He had little option but to retreat. He would let the newcomer have this small victory—for now at least. He would nurture the anger that he felt. Nurture and grow the hatred inside him so that he would be able to use it—use it to Change as he had earlier. He didn't need the pack. He would go out on his own, a lone wolf. And then, when they thought that he'd gone forever, he would come back and pick them off one by one. Kill them all for their treachery. All except Ella. He would keep her with him, and they would start a new pack of their own—not one made up of a ragtag bunch of misfits, but one filled with their own children—a pack of pure-bloods. That had always been his plan, and now this treachery made him realize how right he'd been. How right he was to have bitten Ella and turned her into one of them.

They'd pushed him far beyond the last cabin, and there was nowhere for him to go but into the forest behind. He stopped backing away and saw that they paused in response. He glared at them, a low growl deep in his chest warning them not to pursue him. They crouched low, their teeth bared and the hackles on their necks raised as if ready to spring forward and attack if he did not leave now.

Jurgen was about to turn and go when the door to Lawrence's cabin flew open and the ginger-haired boy came running out brandishing the shotgun.

"Jurgen!" the boy shouted at the top of his lungs, running toward them. "I'm coming, Jurgen."

The first shot sounded like a cannon going off and all four of the nether-creatures dropped to the ground as the lead shot flew over their heads. The stupid boy had fired while running and could have hit any one of them. He was still shouting madly, running in their direction, the sights of

267

the gun dancing over each and every member of the group. He stopped about twenty meters from them, planted his feet, and pulled the gun to his shoulder. The second report seemed even louder to their sensitive ears than the first. It was answered by a high-pitched yelp of pain from Trey's right. Marcus leaped into the air, twisting his body in writhing agony as the shotgun pellets tore through him, and landed on the ground with a howl.

Jurgen reacted first. The Wolfan knew that was Trey was weak—it had turned to see how badly Marcus had been hurt, taking its eyes off Jurgen and exposing its throat to him. The giant black nether-creature seized its opportunity and leaped forward, teeth bared and ready to kill.

He never expected the blur of white that he caught in his right eye to attack. And even as Ella's own teeth sank into his neck—biting down hard to bury her fangs in the soft flesh and crushing his windpipe—he could not believe that it was truly her that was doing it. In his mind she had been replaced by some other creature—a perfect facsimile of the white-furred beauty that he'd chosen to be his partner. He dropped to the floor, his eyes desperately seeking her out as his life ebbed from him. There was a dull, pulling sensation deep within him and he began to transform into a human again. He couldn't breathe. He was drowning. His lungs filled up with his own blood. His vision was already blurring and darkening at the edges as his brain began to shut down.

And then there she was, human again, kneeling over him with her long blond hair cascading down around his face.

He felt a lukewarm splash on his cheek as her first tear fell, and he managed a small smile at her. "I loved you," he managed before diving down into oblivion.

Trey was running across the field, his legs eating up the ground beneath him as he hurried to make it to his uncle's side. He threw himself down on the ground beside the prostrate figure, lifting the old man's head into his lap with one hand while the fingers of the other fluttered in the air over the terrible cuts and tears that covered his uncle's face and body.

"Uncle Frank?" he said.

The old man's forehead creased a little, and his head moved a fraction in Trey's lap.

"Trey?" the old man said in a barely audible whisper. "Run, boy. Get away from that madman. He'll kill you. He'll kill us all."

"Shh. Try not to move. Don't worry about Jurgen— he's . . . gone." He shook his head in despair at the terrible state that the old man was in. "I'm going to get you some help. I'm going to get an ambulance or a helicopter or . . . or *something* out here and then—"

The old man lifted his hand and waved away the boy's words. He reached up and touched his nephew's cheek, patting it gently with the tips of his fingers.

"No," he said. "Too late for that." He hooked his index finger in front of the boy's face, beckoning his nephew to come closer.

"Forgive me," he said, patting the boy's cheek again.

Trey fought back tears. "For what?"

"I lied to you." Frank coughed again, and Trey watched a fresh tendril of blood snake its way from the old man's mouth and run down the side of his face. "I lied to you about who you are and what you are. And I lied to you about your father."

"Please, Frank—"

"It was me that attacked your mother that day. I did that terrible thing to her and then I blamed it on your father."

Trey shook his head, unable to take in what his uncle was saying.

"Why? Why would you do that?"

"I wanted him gone. I thought he wanted to take over and I wanted him to leave. I wanted to blame him for it so that he'd have to leave." He coughed, struggling to get the words out. "I didn't mean to hurt your mother so badly, I just . . . lost control. I think your father knew it was me. I think that your friend Lucien Charron knew too, and that your father stopped him from taking revenge. I didn't deserve that—not after what I did to Elisabeth—I didn't deserve his compassion. Your father should have let the vampire kill me. Instead, Lucien took my sight. He said that I would never again see the precious pack that I loved so much." He shook his head a little. "I'm so sorry, Trey. Please forgive me."

"Hush now, Frank," were the only words that Trey could manage. He screwed his eyes shut to fight back the tears that threatened as a result of the jumbled mix of emotions that his uncle's confession had unleashed inside him.

Frank grabbed his hand, squeezing it with as much force as he could muster. "Take it back," he said.

Trey shook his head, frowning in confusion at the old man.

"The amulet. You must take it back. It's your destiny, Trey."

"Frank—"

"Please." The old man tried to pull himself up, but was simply too weak. "Take it back."

Trey extracted his hand from his uncle's and reached down to slip the silver chain up over the old man's head. He placed it over his own and took Frank's hand again. "OK?" he said.

The old man smiled and nodded. "You're a good boy, Trey. You are your father's son," he said, his hand slipping from Trey's as he spoke. "Good-bye, nephew."

Trey cradled his dead uncle in his lap as the last of the day slowly slipped away behind the ridge of trees to his right. He would have stayed like that, a tableau of grief and sadness had Ella not come and gently placed her hand on his shoulder. He looked up at her and she smiled sadly back at him. He stood on legs that struggled to support him and wrapped one of the blankets she'd brought him around himself, watching as she used the other to cover his uncle.

\* \* \*

271

They sat in Ella's cabin drinking hot tea and warming their bodies in front of the fire that she'd lit. They'd sent Lawrence back to Frank's house to fetch Trey some clothes. The boy had been a nervous wreck, repeating his apologies over and over again to Marcus, who Ella had patched up with bandages from the first-aid kit. Marcus had been more than gracious—shaking his head at the younger boy and telling him that he was going to be fine.

"At the speed we heal," he said, cutting off Lawrence's objections, "by the time tomorrow morning arrives I won't even know that I've been shot."

Lawrence had told them how he'd panicked when he'd looked out his window and seen the others facing down Jurgen in front of the woods. Because of the position of his cabin, he had seen none of the terrible things that the Alpha had done, and knew nothing about Luke's death until told of it by the others.

"I didn't know what was going on," he said, his hands still shaking as he held the steaming mug. "I thought you'd all lost your minds and were going to kill him. I only meant to fire over your heads. Scare you." He looked over at Trey and then lowered his eyes. "He was going to kill you too, wasn't he?"

Trey shrugged, and returned his gaze to the dancing flames in the fireplace. "I guess so."

"What happened to him?" Lawrence asked. "How did he get like that?"

"He got it into his head that everyone was against him," Marcus said. "None of us was safe from him anymore."

When they'd finished their drinks they'd given Lawrence the keys to the car, with instructions on what to bring back with him.

After he'd gone the other three had sat in silence, nobody wanting to be the first to try and piece together the events that had led to three deaths that day. But eventually they began to talk, going over everything that had happened and filling in the gaps for one another.

Trey got up and stood by the window, listening to Marcus as he unfurled the terrible story of how Jurgen had beaten and tortured his uncle, and how Frank had convinced Ella to find the amulet. The old man must have known that it would come down to a confrontation with Jurgen, despite his assertion to Ella and Marcus that he'd simply planned to give the chain back to Trey and convince him to leave. He stared out at the bodies lying next to one another outside Ella's cabin. They'd moved them there and covered them with blankets. In the light that spilled out from the cabin's interior they looked like strange mummified forms. There was a big clean-up job to do, and none of them relished the idea of burying their friends and loved ones. That was when Trey remembered Galroth and the demon's offer of help if it was needed. The stone that the demon had given him had been in the pocket of the jeans he'd been wearing before the three of them transformed and faced down Jurgen. He moved toward the door.

"Where are you going?" Ella said, getting up from her chair.

"I need to find something."

He left the cabin and moved off toward where the car had been. He easily spotted the torn remains of their clothing and bent down, tossing remnants to each side until he found what he was looking for. Thankfully, the pocket was still intact, and he fished around inside it, sighing with relief as his fingers met the smooth surface of the small red stone. He removed it and headed back to the cabin.

When he walked in, he sensed an atmosphere and could see from the irritated looks on Ella's and Marcus's faces that they'd been arguing about something. He closed the door and waited.

"I want to burn the cabins," Ella said. "I'm the sole pack Alpha now and my one wish before I disband it would be to remove any trace of the LG78—both past and present incarnations—from this place forever." She looked at Trey as if to suggest that he had the final say in this.

"Fine by me," he said. He paused a second. "I think my uncle's place should go too." He looked out the window for any sign of the Land Rover's return. "I'll have Galroth do it."

Ella frowned over at the teenager, unsure of what he'd meant and wondering who, or what, Galroth was. She was worried about Trey. When he spoke, his voice was flat and toneless, as if he was battling to control the emotions that were churning away inside him. She got up out of her seat and moved over to stand by his side. "None of this is your fault," she said, placing her hand on Trey's arm.

He toyed with the silver fist that hung beneath the blanket, his fingers tracing the shape of it as he thought of the things that his uncle had told him before dying.

"Maybe not," he said finally. "But I wonder if any of this would have happened if I hadn't come here."

# 37

Trey had changed into the clothes that Lawrence had fetched for him, and he now stood in front of the fireplace, taking in the three expectant faces staring back at him. Ella, Marcus, and Lawrence watched him hold the bright red stone in front of his eyes, fascinated by the swirling and eddying nature of the crystal's interior. He placed its smooth surface onto his forehead, holding it there with the tip of his index finger.

"Galroth," he said in a low voice, feeling more than a little foolish and closing his eyes so that he wouldn't have to look at the others.

At first nothing happened, and he was about to open his eyes and shrug when he felt his body go rigid, the muscles all locking, anchoring him to the spot. The sudden feeling of weightlessness that followed was unsettling, and if he hadn't been vaguely aware of the feeling of the floor through the soles of his feet, he would have sworn that he was floating. He had the odd sensation that some part of him *had* left his body, and that that part of him was now somewhere else altogether.

"Mr. Laporte?" Galroth's voice filled Trey. The sound wasn't received by his ears, but seemed to pulse through each and every cell of his body.

"Galroth, I need your help," he said, unsure if it was his

mouth that was making the sounds or if his thoughts were being unconsciously translated into the words.

"You are in danger. I will come."

"No, wait," Trey blurted. "I *was* in danger, but I'm not anymore. But I need you to help me with some things here—at the lake by my uncle's place. You don't need to get here using magic; I remember how exhausting you said that that would be for you. You can simply drive here. But you might need to bring some people with you—people who can help dig."

There was a pause. "I see."

The demon was silent again, and Trey thought that it had gone when its monotone drawl filled him once more.

"Your timing is impeccable, Mr. Laporte. I heard from Tom today. He told me that if I had not heard from you by this evening, I was to come by and check on you. Shall I contact him and tell him that you are safe?"

"Yes. Thank you."

"And you *are* safe?"

"Yes."

"I will be with you in about two hours, Mr. Laporte. Shall I bring excavation implements? Spades, pickaxes, shovels?"

"Yes, bring them. And bring some canisters of petrol— sorry, gasoline—too."

"Very good."

He felt the demon's presence disappear and he was left all alone in the void. "Galroth?" He was on his own.

"Galroth?" he repeated. Fear began to steal up on him as

he realized that he had no idea how to get back to his body. "How do I switch this thing off? How do I—"

He was standing back in the room. He blinked his eyes open and looked at the others. "He's on his way."

The demon came with two helpers. Unlike Galroth, the others had chosen human disguises that were unremarkable, and Trey wondered again why his Canadian escort had chosen such a strange mantle with which to camouflage himself in this realm.

The demons worked quickly, taking over the entire operation and asking the humans to stay in Ella's cabin until they were ready for them to come out. The way in which they went about the task suggested to Trey that this was not the first time that Galroth and his friends had been involved in a clean-up operation of this sort. When they finally called Trey and the others outside, the bodies were wrapped in sheets of tarpaulin that had been secured with rope. The unmistakable sight of the human bodies beneath the material caused Ella to issue a sharp cry, and Marcus pulled the girl to him, hushing and talking to her in a low, comforting voice.

Trey looked at a bag of white powder that Galroth had brought along. "What's that?" he asked.

"Quicklime," the demon responded in his slow monotone. "It helps with the decomposition. Are you ready?" he asked.

Trey nodded.

They buried Jurgen and Luke first. They'd dug their

278

graves by the lake, next to a willow tree that hung its branches out over the water. Nobody had any words to say as they lowered the bodies down into the holes and began to cover them, first with the lime and then with the excavated soil. When the demons had finished their task they moved back to the cabin to fetch the other body.

"Good-bye, Jurgen," Ella said in a small voice.

Trey reached out a hand and Ella held it in her own, squeezing tightly. He shook his head at the waste of these two young lives—young men who, like him, had become enslaved to the beast that lay dormant inside them, an inherited curse. They had not been given the chance that he had to control their powers and impulses, and eventually the beast had consumed them and destroyed their humanity forever.

Frank was buried a little farther away, under a small rise in the ground that commanded a view out over the surface of the water. Trey had sent Lawrence back to his uncle's house again, this time to fetch the body of Billy. He came back with the dog's body in one of the empty whiskey crates, and Ella berated him for his crassness.

"It's OK, Ella," Trey said, waving away Lawrence's apologies. "My uncle wouldn't have minded."

Ella found a purple blanket to wrap the little dog in, and they buried the creature with its owner.

Ella came over to Trey as he stood by the grave, mirroring his earlier action and taking his hand in hers. "He would have liked to be here at the end," she said. She nodded toward Jurgen's grave. "They both would."

279

Trey let the tears roll down his cheeks, struggling to pinpoint how he felt right now. He had lost his only living relative, a man who had admitted to terrible things before his death—things that Trey found impossible to forgive. And yet, Frank had saved him. Saved his nephew's life, knowing that it would almost certainly cost him his own.

He stood and watched the demons finish their work until the final grave had been filled. When the earth had all been packed down, Trey stepped forward and, at the head of the mound, placed the picture frame that he'd bought his uncle on that first day. He stood looking down at the people in the picture, realizing for the first time that the photograph must have been taken not far from here with the same lake in the background. His parents and his uncle all looked so happy.

"What will you do now?" Ella asked.

"Go home. There's nothing for me here." He glanced up and caught the hurt look on her face. "I'm sorry, Ella, I didn't mean . . ."

"It's OK. You're right. There's nothing here anymore."

"I came here to find someone that would understand me, understand what I am and how I feel. But my uncle wasn't like me. Neither were you or the other members of the pack." He shook his head, a short, humorless snort escaping him. "For a moment I thought that I could be happy here, that I could join you all and live with other creatures like me." He fingered the amulet beneath his T-shirt. "But now I realize that there are no creatures *like me*. I'm alone, like my father and his father were. I can't run from what I am and what I'm supposed to do."

"You're talking about this *destiny* that your uncle mentioned?"

Trey nodded.

"None of us have to do something because other people say it's so, Trey. You have choices. Free will. You mustn't think that you have no say in your own destiny."

He looked at her, a sad smile on his face. "Maybe."

Once Ella, Marcus, Lawrence, and Trey had packed all their belongings, Galroth and his helpers burned to the ground every building that stood on his uncle's land.

Ella, Trey, and Marcus had stood in front of Frank's burning house and said their good-byes. "What will you do now?" Trey had asked Ella.

"Go somewhere and make a fresh start. I have some money, so I think that I'd like to live somewhere hot. I'll have to take a leaf out of old Frank's book, and get used to being locked up once a month, but I guess it won't be that bad."

Trey looked at Marcus, who shrugged his broad shoulders. "Move back in with my dad, I guess."

They'd all hugged and then Trey climbed into the front seat next to Galroth. As the car pulled away, Trey leaned out of the window and waved good-bye to the three surviving members of the LG78, knowing that he would never see them again.

# 38

Lucien Charron turned off Charing Cross Road, which was still busy even at this time of night and walked past the now abandoned nightclub on the corner. The exterior of the building was festooned with peeling advertisements and notices pasted there by enthusiastic fly posters, but Lucien ignored all of these. He focused his attention on the entrance to the small, dark alleyway at the back of the former nightspot. Despite the fact that the club had been shut for some time now, the reek of stale urine still wafted out from the alley, no doubt used by the establishment's former late-night revelers as a place to relieve themselves at throwing-out time. He glanced behind him to check that he was not being observed, and then stepped into the blackness.

The buildings climbed steeply on either side of the alleyway, and the lack of any lighting would have made it difficult for anyone else to navigate their way through the space that was strewn with trash of every sort. Lucien had no problem seeing. A huge black rat paused its scavenging atop an open Dumpster, turning to regard the vampire with glassy eyes the color of coal. The creature issued a little warning squeak before continuing to rummage through its treasure.

There was a slight bend in the passageway and when Lucien rounded it he could see the demon up ahead. The huge creature was leaning against the wall looking around in a bored fashion but when it caught sight of the vampire, it stood up, raising itself to its full height and flexing its taloned hands in front of it. The Grell was huge, standing at least eight feet tall and made of great slabs of muscle that rippled and bulged with every movement that it made. Lucien walked right up to the nether-creature, nodding in greeting.

The Grell glared back, a less-than-friendly look on its face. It opened its mouth to reveal huge, ebony black teeth that it snapped together theatrically.

"You managed it then?" the vampire asked.

"Do you have any idea how difficult it was to locate her?" The creature's voice was a terrible sound—like rocks being ground against each other.

"If it was easy, I would have done it myself."

"And this is it?" the Grell said. "I am no longer in your service?"

"You have my word on it. You get me to the Netherworld tonight and put me in contact with the battle-angel and I will forget that I ever knew your true demon name. You'll be free."

"Free," the demon said, leering down at the vampire through bulbous red eyes.

Lucien held up his finger, halting the demon. "Free of any obligation to me," he said. "But if you should start to have any ideas about coming back to this realm and helping yourself to human flesh again, I'll enter your name into the Book of Halzog and he will come to claim you for his own."

The demon stared at him in wide-eyed fear.

"Think of it as a probation period, an *eternal* probation period," Lucien said with a wink.

The demon mumbled something under its breath and looked at its feet like a naughty schoolboy.

"I'm impressed," Lucien said, nodding toward the door behind the demon. "How long can you hold a portal like that open?"

The demon shrugged its massive shoulders, still sulking.

"Shall we go then?" Lucien said, stepping forward.

"How come you need me to do this?" the Grell said with a gesture of its head toward the door. "I hear that your halfling daughter is growing in power all the time. Why didn't you ask her to create a portal to the Netherworld for you?"

The vampire stared at the demon, his eyes unblinking in their ferocity.

The demon knew better than to antagonize the vampire—even a defanged one like Lucien Charron—and mumbling under its breath again, it reached forward and opened the door, holding it ajar. The space behind the door looked like nothing more than a shifting, swirling mass of gray, and Lucien calmly stepped into and through this, closely followed by the Grell. When the door slammed shut behind them, the entire thing simply disappeared, leaving nothing in the stonework of the wall to suggest it had ever been there.

# 39

Alexa came out of the kitchen carrying a croissant in one hand while thumbing a text message into the keypad of her cell phone with the other. Tom had just called to tell her that Trey was on a flight home and she was excited at the prospect of his return. She finished the message she'd written to Trey and hit the send button. She was about to call a florist to arrange for some flowers to be delivered when she felt that she was not alone. She looked up to see Philippa standing in the center of the lounge. Forgetting all about the flowers, she ran over to her friend, throwing her arms around her.

"Where's Lucien?" Philippa said with a frown, prying Alexa away from her.

"I'm so glad that you're back," Alexa said. "Trey's on his way home, you're here, and we can—"

"It's not Philippa, it's me," the Ashnon said, cutting her off and moving in the direction of the door that led to Lucien's office.

Alexa stepped back, frowning at her friend, unable to get her head around what she was saying.

The Ashnon paused with its fingers on the handle, turning to face her. "Philippa's gone."

Alexa shook her head, deep frown lines creasing her forehead.

"When I got back to the Netherworld I found out that she'd left the environment that I had placed her in to keep her safe. She ran out of the envelope of magic and was taken by something. Nobody knows what it was or where she's gone."

Alexa looked at the creature in horror. "But you said—"

"I said she was safe as long as she stayed within the confines of what she perceived as the hotel. I don't know how many times I, no, *we* explained that to her."

"Oh my God."

The Ashnon shook its head. "I don't think he's got her." It pushed at the door.

"My father's not here," Alexa said.

"Where is he?"

The girl was no longer listening. Her eyes had a slightly glazed look and she stared off into the distance, her mind still trying to come to terms with what the Ashnon had just told her.

"Alexa?"

Alexa looked up at the duplicate of the girl that she had become friends with—the girl who she had personally promised would be in no danger if she trusted them.

"Your father?" the Ashnon prompted again.

"He's gone to the Netherworld. He said that he has some personal problems that he needs to fix. He's seeking help from the Arel."

"The Arel?" The Ashnon made a whistling sound

through its teeth. "And he thinks that the battle-angels are going to help him? A vampire?"

"He said there was no one else," she said, and the words caused a pang of guilt and fear in Alexa. Philippa didn't have anyone else that she could rely on—Alexa and the Ashnon were her only hope.

She returned her attention to the Ashnon. "What are we going to do?" Alexa's voice had taken on a harder edge. "We *have* to find Philippa."

The demon shook its head as if it thought the task futile. "If there is any way that you can contact your father, you need to let him know what has happened."

"Do you think that she's still alive?"

The Ashnon looked back at her—Philippa's face set into an unreadable expression as it took in the other teenager. "Oh, she's alive all right. If she was dead the link between her and this body would have been broken, and I wouldn't be here like this."

"Thank goodness."

The demon shook its head. "Not necessarily. In the Nether-world there are any number of things a whole lot worse than death." The nether-creature sighed. "I have to go. I have to look for her."

Alexa heard a fizzing sound accompanied by the un-pleasant pulling sensation that she knew signaled the im-minent disappearance of the demon. She transferred her weight onto her heels, leaning her body back.

"Wait!" she shouted over the din. "You can't just go like

this. We need to discuss the best way to try and get her back. We need to—"

But the Ashnon had already gone. There was a sudden blast of air that blew Alexa's hair about her head and she was left staring at a blank space where Philippa's doppelganger had stood moments before.

She sank down on the sofa, placing the now-forgotten croissant and phone on either side of her, and stared down at the cream carpet, trying to come to terms with everything that she had just been told. The Ashnon was right— her father *would* know what to do, but he was not here and Alexa had no easy way to contact him right now.

The phone rang, the dial tone signaling that the call was coming from the offices downstairs. She picked up the receiver, holding it to her ear.

"Hello, can I speak to Lucien, please?" an agitated voice asked before she could speak.

"I'm afraid he's not here right now."

"Tom?"

"He's out too."

There was a pause on the other end of the line as if the caller were desperately trying to work out what to do next.

"Can I help at all?"

Another pause and then, "We've had a tip-off from one of our people in the Netherworld. It's a strange one, and we're not quite sure what to make of it."

"Look, why don't you just stop your fussing and—"

"It's regarding a demon lord that your father has asked us to keep tabs on. Its name is Molok, and it's a collector."

"A collector of what?"

"Of humans. Last year it was very active, making a number of sorties into the human realm and snatching people away. The thing is, since we've been keeping tabs on this particularly nasty piece of work, the demon has ceased its visits. That's why we can't quite figure out what our source is telling us."

Alexa was sitting bolt upright on the sofa, the receiver held in a viselike grip.

"Go on," was all she could manage.

"Well, it would seem that Molok has somehow acquired a new specimen for its collection. We know for a fact that he has not opened a portal into the human realm recently, so we can't quite fathom out if the intel is right or not. We just need to know if Lucien would like us to look into the matter, or if he thinks that it's probably some kind of hoax."

There was no answer.

"Hello? Hello?"

The caller was speaking to himself. The receiver was on the sofa cushion where Alexa had dropped it, and the girl was already racing her way downstairs to find out more.

# EPILOGUE

Tom and Trey stepped out of the elevator and into the apartment. The Irishman carried what little luggage Trey had brought back with him, allowing the youngster to bring in the shopping bag full of gifts that he'd bought at the airport.

Tom had filled Trey in on Lucien's departure and the successful elimination of the Necrotroph.

Tom had noted how quiet and withdrawn his young friend had been since he'd collected him at the airport, but he'd put this down to travel fatigue. Trey had not wanted to speak about his trip and answered the Irishman's questions with monosyllabic replies or long silences when he would stare out the window at nothing in particular.

It wasn't until Tom had spoken about Lucien's strange behavior and how worried he was about his vampire boss that Trey had taken an interest, asking questions about his guardian and grilling Tom for details.

"There's something wrong with him, Trey. He wouldn't tell Alexa or me what it was, but I'm guessing it has something to do with his vampiric history. He's been doing an awful lot of blood lately and when I asked him about it he turned on me in a way that was very unlike Lucien."

Trey shook his head in disbelief. Lucien was always in

control and he could not imagine him ever turning on his best friend in the way that Tom described.

"He said that he'll contact us to let us know he's safe. Don't ask me how he intends to do that from the Netherworld, some kind of magical mumbo jumbo no doubt. It's not like he can pick up a phone now, is it?"

The elevator from the garage finished its ascent. Trey looked around him at the familiar surroundings of the Docklands apartment. His heart had done a fluttery little skip as the doors of the elevator had slid open, and he realized that it was not just the apartment that he'd been looking forward to seeing again. He threw down the bags and walked toward the kitchen.

"Alexa?"

He turned to Tom, one eyebrow raised questioningly, and was answered by a shrug of the Irishman's broad shoulders.

"Alexa?"

He walked into the kitchen and saw the letter on the table.

"What do you mean she's gone?" Tom said in a loud voice, pulling the letter out of Trey's hand and scanning it himself.

Trey looked through the windows at the bright sunlit scene outside. A riverboat packed full of tourists was making its way up the river, everyone onboard enjoying the weather and sightseeing.

The letter explained how Alexa had taken it upon herself to go after the Ashnon to try and help it find the Tipsbury girl. She also told of the tip-off that she'd received from downstairs, and ended her note with a simple line:

*Philippa put her trust in me. I now have to repay that trust by going to find her.*

Tom crumpled the letter inside a fist that he slammed down into the table, making Trey jump and look around. He swore in a long string of expletives and started to pace the kitchen, talking loudly to himself and cursing anyone and everything that he could think of.

"I'm going to go after her," Trey said eventually.

"What?"

"Alexa. I'm going after her."

"Ah no. If you think that you too are disappearing off into that godforsaken place like every other injudicious, cavalier, reckless eejit, you've got another thing coming. I'll—"

"What, Tom? What will you do? Because if you set one foot in the Netherworld, you'll be dead in seconds. You might be the toughest bloke I know on earth but your guns and bombs are not going to help you there. You'll be killed. And what good will that do to me or Lucien or Alexa?"

The Irishman glared at the youngster and for a horrible second Trey thought that he was going to lash out at him.

"I'm sorry, Tom, but I'm going to have to go after her. I've lost too many people that I care about to simply stay put here and let someone else try and get her back. And the more time that you and I spend arguing about it, the more danger that Alexa might be in."

There was a pause, and then to Trey's surprise the

Irishman nodded, reaching over to grab Trey behind the head, pulling him toward him and ruffling his hair. When he finished he held Trey at arm's length, staring intently into the teenager's eyes.

"OK, lad. You're right. Let's go down and speak to some of our people about how to go about this. I'll help you with whatever I can at this end."

"Thank you."

"Just promise me one thing, eh?"

"What's that?"

"You bring them all back safe. You and Alexa and that poor lass Philippa. You all get back here safe and in one piece."

Trey nodded at his friend. "I promise, Tom."

*To be continued . . .*

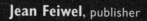